Consuming Fire

Consuming Fire

Thomas D. Davis

St. Martin's Press ❦ New York

Design by Ellen R. Sasahara

Library of Congress Cataloging-in-Publication Data

Davis, Thomas D.
    Consuming fire: a Dave Strickland mystery / by Thomas D. Davis.—1st ed.
      p.   cm.
    ISBN 0-312-14575-6
    1. Private Investigators—California—Fiction.   2. California—
Fiction.   I. Title.
PS3554.A937774C66   1996
813'.54—dc20   96-20243
                                                                          CIP

First Edition: September 1996

10 9 8 7 6 5 4 3 2 1

Consuming Fire

Prologue

A VIOLENT SOUND woke him. He bolted up, blinking hard, searching out the source of the noise. He saw, out in the darkness, a fierce surge of flame, some distance off, where there should have been nothing but trees.

He phoned for help, got a flashlight, and went outside. He took a shovel to fight the fire, then plunged into the woods. There was no moon, just glimpses of stars above the dark pines. The pale beam from the flashlight disappeared into the underbrush as he stumbled through the brambles and the poison oak. He saw that the fire, now diminished, was in a clearing. The thing burning was small, like a refuse pile, but he couldn't see it clearly through the intervening trees.

As he stepped into the clearing, he was slammed down onto one knee, his head snapped forward. For an instant he thought he'd been shoved, then realized the blow had come from himself. It was his body's compromise against fainting. Kneeling there, his head bent down, he was suddenly intensely aware of so much: the blast of heat against his scalp, and the wisp of coolness at the back of his neck, the stench from the flames, and the sweetness of the pine-scented air. He saw how the dark loam spilled over his spread fingers, saw how the firelight played off the silver numbers sitting on the ground near his hand.

Images of the fire flickered back into his consciousness. At once his

1

body began a violent trembling. Interior voices, full of panic, begged him not to look again. But he knew that he must. So he lifted his head and stared into the fire.

Into the burning face of a child.

So my mind recreated it, in the hypnotic half-light between sleeping and waking, from interviews I'd been reading the evening before. The burning child had been found two weeks earlier and had been the latest of three victims—children who'd been abducted, drugged unconscious (the police had taken pains to emphasize that point), then burned to death. The murders had occurred just fifteen minutes down the mountain from me in Santa Cruz County and so figured prominently in the local newspapers I'd been catching up on after having spent a few weeks out of town.

The images of the burning child had come after a night of bad dreams. I'd been having a lot of nightmares lately, perhaps as an aftereffect of my recent surgery, during which a plastic plate had been attached to my skull.

The plate had replaced a small piece of bone shattered five months earlier when I'd gotten in the way of a man trying to kill a young girl on a beach near Monterey. The girl, Becky, and her aunt, Janet, had taken me into their home for several weeks after my initial hospital stay: Weak, with my right side partially paralyzed, I'd needed help with everyday things. My visit had lengthened as I'd had to cope with further threats to Becky's life; I'd come to care deeply for Janet and Becky. I had stayed with them again after my recent surgery. Now, they were off in Montana for three weeks, and I was home. I missed them already.

My right-side paralysis was mostly gone, reduced to a slight limp, like residual stroke damage, with some muscles of the foot and ankle not getting the right signals from the brain. I was hoping that the limp would disappear eventually, but it was getting late for that kind of recovery and I might just have to live with the leg as it was.

I had one other "disability"—this one temporary and slightly comic—my newly reshaved head. There had never been any question of living "bald" for a time, not with all the scarring from my injury. I had chosen a longish wig because the shorter ones that matched my normal hair had seemed to lie unnaturally around the ears and so looked fake. Unfortunately the longer wig had made me look like an aging Prince Valiant. I'd grown a beard to change that image and now looked like an aging hippie. Actually, a drugged-out aging hippie, given my thirty-pound weight loss and what it had done to my face. Still, drugged-out hippie was better than death-camp survivor, which is what I'd looked like with a ski cap, no hair, and no beard.

The phone rang. I rolled onto my side on the bed and reached for the receiver, hoping the caller would be Janet. Instead it was my service: A Mrs. Bennett was trying to reach me, sounding very upset, talking about an emergency, claiming she knew me. I didn't recognize the name, but I got the number and dialed. A female voice came on the line, and I gave my name.

"Oh, Mr. Strickland, I'm so glad you called. This is Sylvia Bennett. I don't know if you remember me."

The voice was high-pitched and fast-paced.

"I'm not sure," I said.

"You put my husband in jail."

"I did?"

It was an idiotic response, but the woman had caught me off guard.

"You were working for Andrea Kaufmann at the time," she said.

"Oh, yes."

The Sylvia Bennett I now remembered had been a well-to-do fortyish widow remarried to a much younger man; the husband had been a self-proclaimed "financial planner," who had tried to bilk some of her friends. One of the friends had hired me. My vague visual memory of Sylvia Bennett was of someone dark-haired, slender, and always in motion. She'd been a take-charge woman, who'd let someone else take charge—the absolute wrong man.

4

"How are you?" I asked.

"I'm doing better now," she said. "Slowly recovering from my own stupidity."

"How's Mrs. Kaufmann?"

"I hear she's doing well. I don't see her much anymore. Or my other friends. They weren't much interested in being my friends after that."

There was something I caught then within the normal rush of her voice, a subtle sadness that laced it like a permanent scar. It hadn't been there in the voice that had first defended her husband against those "outrageous charges." But a lot had happened to her after that.

"I'm sorry," I said. "Are you still living in Milpitas?"

"No. I'm in Granite Valley now."

"Didn't one of those burned children get found in Granite Valley?"

"Yes. And another of the children was from here. What a horrible thing. All of us around here are just sick about it. And very scared."

"I can understand that."

"I hear you've had a bad time of it. An attorney I talked to said you'd been in some terrible accident. A skull fracture or something like that."

"Yeah. I got battered up pretty badly. What were you calling about, Mrs. Bennett? The service said something about an emergency."

"Yes. A good friend of mine has been receiving death threats. I'm sure you've heard of him: John Havens."

"Um . . . I don't think so."

"I'm surprised. He wrote a book on grief and healing that's received a lot of attention. John's been written up in most of the Bay Area newspapers. He lectures quite frequently, and he's even been on television."

"I might have seen his name," I said. "I don't remember. What kind of threats has he been getting?"

"There have been three letters. They say, 'You'll pay with your life,' that sort of thing."

"Pay for what?"

"The letters don't say."

"Have you talked to the police?"

"Yes. They came by and got the letters and took a statement. I was very disappointed with their performance. I kept asking them what they were planning to do about the threats, and they kept saying there wasn't much they could do at this stage. I suppose they don't have much time for anything these days with those children being murdered, but still . . . Anyway, that's why I'm calling you."

"Mrs. Bennett, I don't work as a bodyguard, if that's what you want. In any case, in my condition, I wouldn't do anybody much good."

"No, it's not that. John would never put up with a bodyguard. What I want you to do is try to find out who's sending those letters."

"Do you have any idea who that might be?"

"Yes. But I'd be much more comfortable discussing that in person. Would you please come talk to me."

I thought about it, trying to work up some enthusiasm for the idea. Instead the effort made me conscious of how really tired I felt.

"I don't know," I said. "I don't think I'm up to something like this yet. Why don't I give you the name—"

"No, Mr. Strickland, *please,*" she said. "I want you. John is inclined to ignore the threats and is barely tolerating my idea of hiring a detective; if he doesn't like the person I bring in, I'm not sure how cooperative he'll be. I know he'll like you. I think you'll like him, too. And I trust you."

"I appreciate that, but I won't do you any good if I don't have the energy for the job."

"It won't take that much energy," she said. "If it does, you can hire other people to assist you. Money isn't a problem. *Please.*"

The proposal seemed reasonable enough. Anyway, I wasn't sure how much of an issue stamina would be: with me exhaustion often had to do with mood and could disappear when there was something to engage me.

"All right," I said. "I'll come talk to you."

"That's wonderful. Shall we say ten o'clock tomorrow?"

"Day after—ten o'clock Wednesday. I've got commitments tomorrow."

"You couldn't . . . ?"

"No," I said, firmly.

"All right. To get to my house, you take the Granite Valley Drive exit, go straight up Kennedy to Meadowbrook, then take a right. I'm at two-nine-four."

"Okay."

"Thank you, Mr. Strickland," she said.

And she hung up.

THE FIRST GLIMPSE of Granite Valley comes as the highway drops down out of the Santa Cruz mountains going south toward Santa Cruz. The sight isn't impressive, though it has improved since the town cleared out its worst eyesore, the ruins of a long-defunct theme park located next to the highway. Gone, too, is the Happy Times Village sign that had continued to stand over the ruins, providing passing moralists with a cheap symbol of the vanity of human dreams.

The highway, as it runs its short stretch through town, offers views of office buildings and construction yards. The offices, occupied by high-tech firms, testify to the town's attempts to build up its business base. A few years ago, one of the firms tried to lure potential employees from among those commuting to San Jose by hanging a huge sign that read, If You Worked Here, You'd Be Home by Now. Then hard times came to California, and the sign came down. One laid-off employee suggested a new sign, reading, If You Worked Here, You'd Have Been Home All Day, but the company wasn't inclined to take the suggestion.

The "downtown" area of Granite Valley is shaped like a backward L that lies just to the west of the freeway, its base toward the south. The frontage road, Granite Valley Drive, forms the north-south spine; Vista View, formerly Big Rock Road, forms the east-west base. The latter leaves the highway as a string of gas stations, fast-food places, and shopping centers, winds through the hills past some ugly quarries that the Chamber of Commerce has never heard of, and ends at the small town of Bear Creek.

What's attractive about Granite Valley are the green hills that surround it and the houses that perch on those hills like nesting flocks of birds. Sylvia Bennett's house wasn't in the hills, but it was part of a small, expensive-looking group of homes set on a slope of meadow about a half mile up from the highway in the northeast section of town. The houses showed an interesting diversity, ranging from a renovated farmhouse to two new stone houses that looked vaguely medieval. One of the stone houses had a two-story pyramidal staircase, steep as a scaling ladder, rising to the second-story front door. All it needed was a moat, but then construction still wasn't complete. Less dramatic and more susceptible to invasion was Mrs. Bennett's house, a white split-level home with a large circular stained-glass window set into the second story.

As Mrs. Bennett opened the door, the visual image of her came overlaid with a sharpened memory so that I was seeing and remembering and comparing all at once. In the course of the investigation into her husband's financial dealings, I'd seen her drop maybe fifteen pounds off an already slim figure, while adding an apparent ten years to her face through weight loss and stress. In the three years since I'd seen her last, she'd gained back most of the weight and lost some of the years. She looked like a healthy, attractive woman of forty, several years shy of what I knew to be her actual age. She was, as she'd always been, even in despair, immaculately and elegantly dressed. She was wearing a tailored dark olive skirt and a silky beige blouse, along with tasteful gold jewelry. Her wavy medium-length dark hair had that near-perfect look that comes from constant professional and personal attention. Her hair was also touched up, now that I thought about it: there'd been a few touches of gray the last time I'd seen her.

I suddenly realized that while I'd been observing her, she'd been observing me. She was obviously taken aback. I'd warned her about the wig and the beard, but apparently it was taking her a moment to absorb the reality. At least I'd softened the hippie aspect of the look by wearing a jacket and tie.

"Can you see anything familiar under here?" I asked, smiling.

She looked embarrassed. "I'm sorry," she said. "I suppose I was staring. Yes, I recognize you now, but it took me a moment. You poor man. You must have gone through a terrible experience."

"It wasn't a lot of fun."

She shook her head sympathetically, but then her mind jumped to something else. "Did you get the message I left on your machine?" she asked.

"About the article? Yes. You sounded pretty upset."

"I still am. *Very* upset. I wish I could have talked to you yesterday."

"I was out all day. By the time I got your message, it was too late to call. What exactly does the article say?"

"Come in, and I'll show you."

Mrs. Bennett ushered me into a house of hardwood floors and Persian rugs, dark antique furniture and white-cushioned couches and chairs. She led me to the living room couch where I sat down and almost disappeared into the cushions; Mrs. Bennett, knowing better, perched on the very edge, her body turned as far toward me as the cushions against her knees would allow.

She picked up a section of newspaper that was lying on the glass coffee table and thrust it at me. "I can't believe they would print trash like this. It's totally irresponsible. And just plain mean. See for yourself."

The newspaper she'd handed me was the *Granite Valley Herald*. Mrs. Bennett's index finger tapped on the paper, directing my attention to the lower right portion of the front page.

Local Author Questioned in Child-Murder Investigation
By Edward Garza

Acting on an anonymous tip Thursday, police questioned local author, John Havens, and members of his therapy group in connection with the ongoing investigation into the murders by fire of three local children over the past eight months.

An anonymous caller suggested that Havens and his group might be involved in the murders. The caller claimed that parents of the dead children were members of Havens's group and that Havens's own son had burned to death a few years earlier.

Chief of Police Sam Parker told the *Herald* that the police routinely follow up all such tips. He emphasized that no charges have been brought against Havens or his group. The chief refused to comment further on that aspect of the investigation.

The *Herald,* conducting its own investigation, has learned that the parents of Jim Malander and Corinne Caldwell, the first two murder victims, are part of Havens's group. It has further learned that Havens's four-year-old son, Ricky, died in a mysterious fire in 1989.

Contacted by the *Herald,* Havens said that the charges were "completely false" and that the caller was a "coward engaged in malicious slander." Havens refused to comment further.

John Havens, a Granite Valley resident since 1991, is the author of

See **AUTHOR,** page 8

Small movements radiating through the couch pillows had been telegraphing Mrs. Bennett's impatience. Now, apparently, she'd had enough. As I began to turn the page, she put out a hand to restrain me.

"Isn't that the most irresponsible—the most malicious thing you've ever read?" she asked rhetorically, managing to lift the paper from my hands in a manner that suggested I'd asked her to take it. "All that insinuation. What the police got was a crank call, and the paper makes it sound like the police are about to put John and the rest of us in jail. 'Mysterious fire'—there was nothing mysterious about it—just some faulty wiring. And that 'investigation' of theirs . . . all they had to do to find out about Ricky was to read John's book. I can understand that little worm writing something like this, but Dan Scanlon—the publisher—I thought he was above this sort of thing."

"By 'that little worm,' you mean the writer?"

"Ed Garza, yes."

"Are you calling him that just because of the article, or did you know him before?"

"I've known him for a while. He's caused me some personal . . . unpleasantness."

"Have you talked to an attorney about this article?"

"Yes . . . I couldn't believe it . . . she says they're within their rights to do this. She says we can't touch them . . . it's not worth trying."

"What does she suggest you do?"

"She says we should ignore it, let it all die down . . . I don't know . . . I'm so frustrated . . . I don't know what I should do. Poor John . . . this is so stupid . . . the facts—what few facts there are—are all twisted. I mean, yes, two of the parents are in the group, but the article has the whole thing backwards. John writes about grief work, he's well known, and he volunteers time to help local people. It's natural the parents should want to talk to him. Instead the paper makes it sound like something sinister. And John's son: he did die in a fire, but it was an apartment fire—it's not as if he was kidnapped and intentionally burned. It's terrible, the things this person is doing to us—this call, those threats. . . ."

"You're assuming the letters came from the same person who made the call?"

"How could they not? These two things happening so close together."

"You intimated on the phone the other day that you had some idea of who that person is."

"I think it's Ruth, John's ex-wife. I don't know for sure it's her, but she hates him—she holds him responsible for the death of her son. I don't know who else it could be."

"Why does she hold him responsible? Was the fire somehow his fault?"

"No—it was no one's fault—unless maybe the apartment people. Some wiring in the apartment building caught fire. The whole thing was such a tragedy. John had gone to the basement for a few minutes to talk to the superintendent when the fire broke out. John tried to get to his son, but it all happened so fast—within a few minutes that whole section of the building was in flames."

"His wife blames him for leaving the boy alone?"

"I don't think so—at least, I don't see how she could. John had an intercom with him and was constantly checking on the boy—Ruth used to do the same thing when she had to run down to the laundry room."

"Then why does she blame him?"

"As John was trying to get to his apartment, he heard some children screaming; he stopped for a few minutes to help them. If he hadn't done that, he might have saved his son. That's what's Ruth thinks. She hates him for that. It's why she divorced him."

"Havens chose to save those other children instead of his own son?"

"Not deliberately. His son sounded all right. And those children—they were screaming—they were trapped behind some flaming debris, and a girl's dress was starting to burn. John saved their lives. He knew it was a chance, but he felt he had to take it."

"What a horrible choice to have to make."

"By the time he got close to his apartment, part of the hallway ceiling had collapsed in flames. He tried to get through—he almost died trying. But there was nothing he could do by then." Mrs. Bennett stopped and took a deep breath. "This is all in John's book, and he tells it much better than I could, though I think he's far too sympathetic where Ruth is concerned. And far too hard on himself. I'll lend you a copy of John's book before you leave."

"Thanks. So you think Mrs. Havens is behind both the threats and the call. Did the police give you any indication that the anonymous caller was a woman?"

"No. They wouldn't say. I asked them."

"Where does Mrs. Havens live?"

"She lives in Soquel. I can give you her address."

"The article says the boy died four years ago. You think Mrs. Havens is still angry enough at her husband to want to hurt him?"

Mrs. Bennett nodded vigorously, bringing forth a faint clinking sound from some small gold bells on her earrings. She said, "I was at a reception a couple of months ago when John and Ruth ran into each other by accident. Her eyes were blazing—she looked furious. John tried to say something conciliatory, but she wouldn't say a word to him."

"Has she threatened him before? Have there been any incidents she might have been responsible for?"

"No—not that I know of."

"But now, suddenly, she's sending these threats."

Mrs. Bennett hesitated. "Put like that it does seem odd. But John doesn't have any other enemies that either of us knows of. Who else might do it?"

"Why not some crank who knows his book—maybe connects it with the children?"

"I suppose that's possible."

"Or someone angry at someone else in the group. I'll need to talk to Havens as soon as possible."

"He suggested you come to his house tonight at seven. That will give you two time to talk before the group meets."

"They're meeting tonight?"

"Yes."

"Is Havens a psychotherapist?"

"No."

"Then how can he have a therapy group?"

"It's not a therapy group," she said. "It's a discussion group. John makes it clear to everyone who attends that he's not there to do therapy. He doesn't even charge people. The group is his way of accommodating some local people who want to talk to him about their grief experiences."

"Is Havens a full-time writer?"

"And lecturer. Most of his income, from what he tells me, comes from lecturing. Though that, of course, is a result of the book. And he's under contract for another book."

"What did he do before the book came out?"

"He was in advertising for a number of years. In New York. Then in San Francisco. The apartment where his son died was in San Francisco."

"How long has this talk group been going on?"

"Since last fall."

"How many people in the group?"

"Beside John, there are six, including myself. It's a small group."

"Why are you in the group?" I asked. "Did someone close to you die? Or is this somehow connected to that business with your husband?"

"In part it has to do with my husband—you can grieve for losses like that. But if that were all, this group wouldn't have been appropriate for me. Maybe you don't know that I miscarried. Not long after my husband was arrested."

"I'm sorry—I didn't know that."

Sylvia Bennett had put so much blind faith in that young husband of hers, believing in him even when believing should have been impossible. When her reason had finally broken through the thick clouds of romantic fantasy, the ugliness of the revelations had been awful—not so much her husband's coke habit as his woman habit, young things to whom he'd expressed open contempt for his wife. The ending must have been devastating for her.

"I read John's book, and loved it," she was saying. "I don't think I ever properly grieved for the child I lost and . . . for other things. John's book really struck a chord. Toward the end of last summer I went to hear him lecture. Afterwards I went up to talk to him. There were others who did the same thing, but finally it was just John, and myself, and a nice young couple, the Sullivans, who had lost a child to cancer. We all seemed to hit it off, and went out for coffee together, and arranged to get together again. John was being nice, but he also told us he was working on another book and it was good for him to get some other perspectives on his ideas. We got together a few more times, and the idea of the group came from that. The Sullivans eventually got transferred back to St. Louis—in March, I think—but by that time there were others."

"What others?"

"The Raleys—they joined last fall. She's a nurse, he's an accountant. Karen still comes regularly. Ken dropped out after a few months. He hasn't done very well, poor man—poor Karen, too, since she's had a lot of looking after him to do. Then came the Malanders, then the Caldwells. As you saw from the article, the Malanders and Caldwells had children killed by that madman."

"Those were the first two children killed?"

"Yes."

I shifted on the couch and sank down still farther into the pillows. I shifted forward, awkwardly, until I got to the firmer edging where Mrs. Bennett sat.

"Let's talk about our arrangements for a minute," I said. "Who, exactly, will be hiring me? You? Mr. Havens? Both of you?"

"I will."

"On his behalf?"

"Yes, mostly. But on mine, too, now that these accusations have been made against the group."

"Havens has no objections to your hiring me?"

"No. Especially now, with this accusation."

"Are you and Havens in a relationship together?"

"We're not 'in a relationship' in the way you mean," she said. "We're just friends."

The expression on her face indicated something more complicated than "just friends." A one-way attraction, perhaps? Maybe just a strong admiration. I supposed I'd find out along the way. I hoped, for her sake, she wasn't handing this guy her checkbook.

"The case has gotten more complicated since we first talked," I said. "We better get clear on what you expect me to do. I assume you still want me to look into those threats?"

"Yes. And that anonymous call."

"You know, it's possible that the threats and/or the call were made by some crank whose only connection with Havens is having read his book, who has no intention of actually doing anything, figuring that the police—or God, for that matter—will take care of it. If that's the case, it's very unlikely I'll ever identify such a person. My approach will be to work on the assumption that there's a real threat from someone—probably someone who knows Havens. If that approach turns up somebody, fine, we can figure out how to stop him or her. If it turns up nothing, it won't necessarily mean there's no danger to Havens—it could mean that I missed someone or that the person has only the most remote connection to Havens—maybe just as reader to writer. I'll do my best to resolve this for you, but there are no guarantees. I want you to know that before you hire me."

Mrs. Bennett thought a moment, then nodded. "I understand," she said. "I know you'll do your best. But there's something else I'd like you to do."

"What's that?"

"You must have some connections with the police. We can't get anything out of them. Would you try to talk to them? See how serious they are about that tip. Advise us of our situation."

"I'll try to get some information for you. But once I get it, I think you ought to get your advice from an attorney."

I LIVE ON A RIDGE top high up in the Santa Cruz mountains. The house itself is simple, looking like a railroad car that lost its way, then its wheels, then grew white wood siding and a red-shingle roof. But the view is spectacular, nearly a hundred and eighty degrees of mountains, sea, and sky. The back of the house looks out across a yard of grass and ground cover, jasmine and juniper, past a perimeter of red-and-green-leafed Photinia, toward a far ridge where the sunsets take place. The far ridge slants diagonally toward the south, merging with other ridges, all flowing like inverted riverbeds toward Monterey Bay. There are houses below me and to the far side of the property, but the arrangement of carport, trees, and hedges hides them all, giving the illusion of splendid isolation.

Some mornings, in summer, I wake inside a cloud, then watch it give way, receding down the mountain, breaking into wisps and curls around ridges and crags, gleaming in the sunlight. In the evening, as the sun disappears below the ridge, the light dissolves into pastel mists of gold and orange, pink and violet. The nights are quiet, the sky planetarium clear. Below, all around, the dark mountains loom, dotted with solitary lamps that look like fallen stars.

On the other side of the house, on land that slopes gradually downward toward the road, are a barn, a corral, and four of the most obnoxious geese on earth. I keep vowing to get rid of them—especially when I have to change the wading pools that they drink from, bathe in, then crap all over—but their effectiveness as "watch dogs" makes me hold back. Instead I content myself with an occasional cry of "goose pâté!" which heightens their frantic honking, at least in my lurid imagination. Needless to say, I'm not a would-be rancher or a universal animal lover. I bought the place for the view; the corral and the geese came with it. The geese are furniture, as far as I'm concerned, but I try to take good enough care of them.

As I arrived home, driving past the corral and up to the house, I was met by Bouffi, a male Great Pyrenees, who weighs about a hundred pounds. He looks like a polar bear, or a horizontal snowman, his thick coat bright white, his eyes and nose the color of coal. He has two facial expressions—happy and sort of idiotic when he opens his mouth, quizzical and slightly perturbed when he shuts it. Presumably those expressions have only a coincidental connection to whatever is going on in his head.

His father is a champion named Fluff. Bouffi, according to a female friend who speaks French and supplied the name, is a close French equivalent. I wasn't interested in the foreign touch; I agreed to the name because it sounded like Goofy. Anyway, he is rarely called Bouffi, at least by me: More often it's Bouffer, the Bouffer, or Bufford (pronounced Bee-*you*-ford), making it sound as if his lineage derives from the Ozarks rather than the French Pyrenees. There's some justice in that. He's a big, clomping kind of guy, nothing fancy about him. Recently the newspaper published a list of the most to least intelligent dogs, with one the best and seventy-nine the worst. Great Pyrenees were sixty-fourth, and in Bouffi's case, I'd say that's pushing it some. Maybe it's all that inbreeding.

I wasn't looking for a purebred dog, and I have no intention of ever showing him. Lured to my one and only dog show by a friend, I fell in love with a forty-pound furball with paws. I like to take walks in the mountains, and the Bouffer is good company, though I'd hoped he'd be a little more than that. The mountains are full of obnoxious dogs and my original image was of a hundred-pound tough guy at my side, snarling the other dogs back. On our first walk, when a dog that looked like a long-haired rat chased Bouffi into the bushes, I knew my fantasy was in trouble. But he has a good nature. He's great with the children we run across and with Becky, who's crazy about him. Sometimes Bouffi slips off the property when service people forget to close the gate, and usually I don't know where he goes. But not too long ago a neighbor, who raises sheep, told me that Bouffi had been spending hours at their place, watching over the lambs. I can forgive a lot in a dog like that.

Bouffer also has a good bark, though he isn't really much prevention against intruders. He'd never attack one; if anyone made a move at him, he'd go running away. His barking wouldn't alert anyone else: With my only neighbors out of eyesight of the house, either down a hill or behind a twenty-foot-high Photonia hedge, they wouldn't see anything, and, anyway, with so many dogs barking at so many things, from other dogs to Federal Express deliverymen, no one really pays much attention. I'd just have to hope that a would-be-intruder wouldn't know all that. We don't have much trouble in the mountains, and my place isn't one easily spotted from the road.

After playing with the Bouffer for a while, I went inside the house. I glanced through the bills and advertisements that passed for mail that day and then fixed myself some lunch. My idea of cooking is to throw a pork chop or a chicken breast into the oven at four hundred degrees, go do something else, and come back when I smell smoke. Put the result together with Minute Rice and a salad, and—*voilà!* This was lunch, and I wasn't after anything so fancy, so I made a sandwich with some deli turkey. Once the dishes were rinsed and stacked in the sink to be cleaned later when I ran out of things to cook with or eat off of, I grabbed Havens's book and went outside into the sunshine to read.

The front cover of the book showed a yellow-orange sunburst on a black background, overlaid with red lettering that formed the title and subtitle—*A Divine and Terrible Radiance: Living with Grief and Letting It Transform You.*

The black back cover had a color photo of the author above a series of red-lettered reviews: "An inspirational book in the best sense. Hard-won insights from someone who has faced suffering with his eyes open." *Los Angeles Times.* "In spite of the author's modest disclaimers, this is a profound book. I feel enriched for having read it." *San Francisco Chronicle.* "(A)n absorbing . . . book." *Publishers Weekly.*

In the photo Havens's face was shown in a three-quarters view that emphasized the left side of his face. He had a slender face, a trim salt-and-pepper beard, an aquiline nose, lots of forehead, and gray hair that was thinning in front. His eyes were slightly shaded and seemed to look out from beneath the prominent bone ridges of the brow like creatures from inside a cave. This effect was due to the fact that he was squinting into bright sunlight from which some camera lens had extracted faint red and yellow hues—perhaps hinting at the radiance of the book title.

The back jacket flap contained a brief about-the-author:

> *John Havens was raised in Scranton, Pennsylvania, and educated at the University of Pennsylvania, where he earned a degree in journalism. He worked for over ten years as a feature writer for several newspapers, including the* Philadelphia Inquirer, *before leaving journalism for a career in advertising, first in New York City, later in San Francisco. Mr. Havens is now a full-time writer and lecturer, living near Santa Cruz, California.*

I opened the book and flipped past the title page. The dedication was, "To Ricky, my son. I'm sorry." The following page gave the quotation from which the title was taken:

> *Great grief is a divine and terrible*
> *radiance that transfigures the wretched.*
> —Victor Hugo, *Les Miserables*

I turned to the next page:

PREFACE

I'm not a philosopher, I'm not a psychologist, and I'm nobody's guru. My child died horribly, and in a way I blame myself for. I thought his death would kill me, and it almost did. I survived because of an experience I had in the ward of a children's hospital more than a year after my son's death—an experience that led me to look at the world in a different way. What I saw wasn't something new, but it was new to me, one of those hard truths we'd all like to avoid because crashing into them hurts like hell.

I've never been big on hard truths. I didn't have to worry about them as a college student or newspaper writer in the late fifties and early sixties—those tame times. A lot of hard truths came with the war, but I was protected by fatherhood from soldiering and spent the war years happily writing advertising slogans for soap and beer. I disapproved of the protesters when that was fashionable, then disapproved of the war when the winds of opinion changed. I emerged from those times unscathed and moved on to California, more than ready for the Great Sellout that was to become the eighties.

It's been remarked often enough that we in advertising are selling more than products: we're selling the idea that happiness is achievable and suffering avoidable. This orientation went nicely with the comfortable truths of the New Age materialism that were spreading like the sushi fad through the lives of Californians. God, or at least the order of things, wanted you to be happy and successful. All you had to do was want it enough. In fact, if you didn't get it, it was your fault. For all failure was a choice. The poor chose their poverty. The sick chose their suffering. It wasn't your problem if they chose misfortune. It was your job to be healthy, happy, and self-absorbed (spiritually, of course), because that's what you were meant to be.

I not only sold these ideas, I bought them as well. Until that day when those clanging alarm bells took away my illusions and introduced me to horror.

CHAPTER ONE

Some things you think are safe, or at least safe enough—leaving your four-year-old son alone to play in his room in your eighth-floor apartment while you make a quick trip to the basement, monitoring the boy constantly via your hand-held intercom, knowing you're only a few minutes away from him, knowing he's a good boy, knowing that the room, the whole apartment, has been childproofed—except that you can't childproof the world—you can't childproof fortune.

As the deafening fire alarm sounds, I yell into the intercom at my son, Ricky, find out he's all right, just scared, tell him there's nothing to worry about, I'll be right there. I remember the warning about elevators and fire, so I open the stairwell door and start running up the empty stairs, except that soon they're not empty anymore, there's a flood of people moving against me. At first it's like a party, adults acting like kids at a fire drill, but by the fifth floor the mood has changed, people panicking, the smell of smoke in the air. I'm trying to push my way through them, screaming that my son is upstairs, and some try to help, but there are too many people, and it's too noisy, and there's too much confusion. I find my own fear rising as if on the swell of fear around me, but I've managed to talk to Ricky, twice, briefly and with difficulty, and there's no fire in his room and no smell of smoke.

By the sixth floor the crowds thin out, and I'm finally moving again. I can speak into the intercom without having to yell, can hold it up in front of me without fear that someone will inadvertently knock it out of my hand. I can tell Ricky's getting frightened, but there's still no fire or smoke, he's all right, and I tell him I'll be there in just a minute. As I speak, I picture him as he must be now, my slight, dark-haired son, staring toward that wall intercom as if toward an invisible adult, surrounded by the Ninja Turtles he was making war with when I left him maybe fifteen minutes before.

I open the door to the eighth floor, and there's a blast of heat and smoke, but then I see, with relief, that it's coming from the right, the opposite end of the hallway from my apartment. I start to the left, when I hear screaming behind me, and I look back, and see them, two boys and a girl, looking at me through three-foot flames from some ceiling debris that has them trapped just inside the open doorway of an apartment. I stand there for a moment, frozen, and then the girl, the smallest of the three, starts toward me, toward the flames, and suddenly her dress is on fire and I'm running toward her, leaping over the low flames of the debris, grabbing her, pulling her to the ground and smothering the flames with part of the rug that I roll around her, then getting up, grabbing coats from the closet to throw over the burning debris at the door, taking the children with me, then pushing them out into the stairwell—none of this is bravery, it's the eyes of the children and my own panic for them, and my panic for myself and for Ricky—my need to hurry this thing so I can get to my boy.

It all seems to have taken so little time—but I don't really know how much time, I just know it took too much. As I start running down the hallway, yelling into the intercom to Ricky that I'm coming, there's a huge crashing sound above me, and something falls on me hard, something burning, and I go tumbling, a fierce pain along my right side, and I'm dazed for a moment, and then I see that part of my clothing is on fire, and I roll over onto my right side to put out the flames and hear myself cry out—from the pain in my leg, I know it has to be broken. And then I hear the cries from the intercom, "Daddy, fire, help me," and I cry, "I'm coming, Ricky," but it's so hard to move. I try dragging myself, but there's so much smoke now, and burning things in my way, and I try not to breathe, but I can't help myself, and I start getting dizzy, and I keep trying to crawl faster, toward that voice, calling back to him that I'm coming, but everything starts getting darker, and I can still hear my son screaming as I sink down into darkness, sink down into hell. . . .

HAVENS'S HOUSE WAS one of a small group of rustic homes built at the end of a narrow valley that was nothing but meadow and trees. Havens's house was the smallest of the homes, a quaint, two-story angular wood structure stained a dark reddish brown. The house had an upscale counterculture flavor, accentuated by two stained-glass windows portraying nature scenes in bright, unnatural colors. The house was now run-down, as was the property as a whole, with its bare-dirt yard and its half-collapsed sheds.

The beauty of the place, as I saw when I got out of my car, was the view. Sitting a flood-safe fifty yards up a slope, the house looked down the entire length of valley between a steep, wooded hill to the left and a more modest, grassy incline to the right. In the foreground, just beyond the private road and the strand of trees that marked the end of the valley, a small herd of horses grazed. In the distance, past what looked like toy-sized office buildings and homes, the horizon was a series of low, gently undulating hills.

Havens emerged from the house as I came up the gravel path. The sight of him was pure sensory overload: I had too much secondhand knowledge of the man to get a coherent first impression. I found myself comparing him to the book-jacket photo, mentally checking off the oval shape of the face, the high forehead, the thinning hair, and the trim beard. His eyes, which had been shaded in the photograph, were bright, their irises the color of polished mahogany. There were surprises: I'd imagined him to be of average height and build; instead he was six two and lanky. As he reached out his right hand to shake mine, I saw something that hadn't been visible in the photograph, heavy burn scarring along the right side of his neck. There was more scarring on the back of the hand that emerged from the long-sleeved blue-and-beige sport shirt he wore with dark blue cotton slacks. It was impossible not to imagine the scarring running from neck to hand and along his side. I had a sudden, vivid image of this man in that burning hallway, struck down, trying to crawl through the smoke toward—

"Hi," he said. "I'm John Havens."

His words aborted my reverie, but the reverie didn't entirely die; it seemed to linger, ghostlike, somewhere behind him.

"I'm Dave Strickland," I said. "You've got a great view."

"Thanks."

"You been here long?"

"A couple of years."

"You own this place?"

"I'm just renting. I have an option to buy, but I don't know. . . ." Havens shrugged. "If I buy it, I'll feel like I should fix it up, and I'm not in the mood for that right now. As it is, it's kind of scroungy, but comfortable, and no trouble."

"I like it," I said. I glanced toward the house. "I understand your discussion group will be starting in an hour."

Havens looked at his watch. "Actually they'll start arriving in about forty-five minutes. If you have a lot of questions to ask me, maybe we should go inside."

"Good idea."

The interior of the house, like the exterior, was quaint, cabinlike, and in disrepair. The furnishings had a pieced-together, camped-out look. The place reminded me of a college rental minus the beer cans and strewn clothes. To the right was a small dining room that was used for writing, not dining. The tabletop was laden with a computer, a monitor, a laser printer, written-on note cards, blank legal pads, pens and pencils, and scattered stacks of books.

To the left was a small living room with a fireplace, two bookcases, a couch, an easy chair, a coffee table, two end tables, and a TV set on a metal stand. The tall bookcases seemed well made, but the aqua easy chair looked hard, the small couch was covered with a green floral sheet, and the tables looked like the kind you buy in pieces and screw together yourself. The end tables and one area of the floor contained stacks of magazines, newspapers, and books. Dining room chairs had been arranged in front of the couch and easy chair to form a circle for the discussion group.

Ahead of me I could see a small kitchen, a half-bath, and a steep staircase leading to the second story.

"I'll be making coffee for the group in a little while," said Havens. "If you don't mind waiting."

"No problem—I just had some."

I followed Havens into the living room. On my way to the couch I got distracted by the sight of books against the far wall and went to take a look. Three shelves of the bookcase held books that seemed quite old. Some were beautifully preserved leather-bound volumes, others were badly worn, with splitting spines and faded cloth covers.

"Are you a collector?" I asked.

"No," said Havens. "Not in the sense you mean. There's nothing systematic there, and I doubt if they're worth much. I just like picking up old books."

In front of the bookcase were two very large volumes sitting open on wooden stands, an Oxford English Dictionary and a leather-bound King James Bible with delicate, parchmentlike pages.

"It's a beautiful Bible," I said, turning away from the bookcase.

"Yes," said Havens. "It's not valuable, but it is beautiful. It was a present from the Sullivans. They were the first couple in the group; they've moved away."

"How are they doing?"

"Very well. Their pain was awful, but they used it to change their lives. That was wonderful to see."

Havens sat down in the easy chair, and I took a seat on one end of the couch. I was pleased to find the couch firm under the floral sheet: I'd half expected loose springs. As I positioned myself on the cushion, my elbow bumped into something. It was a corner of a book jutting out from the end table. I started to push it away, then noticed it was a copy of Havens's book. I picked it up and held it out in front of me.

" 'A Divine and Terrible Radiance,' " I read. "I like the title."

26

"It was my editor's idea," said Havens. "My second editor. My first one wanted to call the book 'Good Grief.' "

I laughed. "You're kidding."

"No. And neither was he. Believe it or not, that title was already taken. He was trying to think up something equally silly when he got promoted out of my life. He kept telling me he wanted a title that would emphasize the positive, upbeat aspects of the book."

"I didn't get the impression your book was real upbeat."

Havens smiled. "One reviewer said the book was about as upbeat as a crucifixion. But that it also had its redemptive aspects."

"Speaking of crucifixions, are you a Christian? It was hard to tell from the book jacket and the first couple of chapters where the book was heading in that respect. Are we supposed to find God at the end of this thing? Find out that Jesus is the only answer we need?"

I realized as I spoke that I was being tactless, that sarcasm was not the best strategy for establishing a good client, or semiclient, relationship. On the other hand, if we were going to butt heads on this point, I might as well know it now.

Havens didn't seem offended by what I'd said. If anything, he seemed amused. "You have a problem with God and Jesus?" he asked.

"I was a fundamentalist Christian for a long time. Now I'm not. I'm a little tired of religious messages."

"You won't get one in my book. I suppose I am a Christian, but only in the vaguest sort of way. I'd like to believe there's some Being up there who cares about us, and I value many of the principles of Christianity, as well as those of other religions. I sometimes use religious quotes in the book to illustrate a point. But the approach the book takes is philosophical and psychological, not religious. At the same time a lot of religious readers seem to have taken to the book. There are parallels. But no God at the end."

"Good," I said. "Now I'm looking forward to reading it."

"When you finish reading it, let me know what you think. I like discussing the ideas. That's part of what our group here is about."

"That, and consolation, I gather."

"Yes, that, too."

So far I liked Havens. He seemed gentle, good-natured, and at peace with himself. I found myself wondering how he'd gotten to this state from the horror of that hallway. I supposed his book would tell me.

"Mrs. Bennett tells me you're not worried about the threats you've been getting," I said.

"No. I figure anyone who's cowardly enough to send anonymous threats is too cowardly to act on them."

"That's not necessarily true."

"Maybe not, but it's that call I'm upset about." Havens grimaced. "I'm upset for myself, of course, but also for the people in the group. They trusted me. They came to what they thought was a quiet, private group. Now, suddenly, it's as if they're inside some episode of *Hard Copy.*"

"You couldn't have foreseen this."

"I know," he said. "I don't think anyone in the group is blaming me. But I still feel badly for them. It's awful for all of us, living under this kind of suspicion."

"Unfortunately, there's not much I can do about the suspicion. I can investigate the threats; I can act as liaison with the police. But the only thing that will lift the suspicion is having the police find the real killer."

"What if you learned the identity of the caller and showed the police he was a crank or someone obviously motivated to hurt me?"

"That wouldn't make much difference at this point. If the person were an out-and-out crank, that might take off a little of the heat. But as for someone wanting to hurt you, the police could take that as motive for their telling the truth."

"I suppose so."

"Speaking of the police, how did your talk with them go?"

"Okay," said Havens, with a slight shrug. "They acted serious and official, but nice enough. Once thing, though: They asked if I would agree to let them search the house and car. I was going to let them, but Sylvia was here, and she said we should call her attorney. Her attorney said, absolutely not. What do you think?"

"The same thing: Absolutely not. The police wouldn't have asked for a voluntary search if they hadn't tried to get a search warrant first: Obviously a vague anonymous call wasn't enough for the judge. In a way, I'm surprised they asked. There's the danger that all you manage to do is alert the suspect: He refuses the search, then cleans out all the evidence before you ever get enough for a warrant. It's always a judgment call."

"Yes, but the point is, I've got nothing to hide, and I don't want them to think I'm cleaning up evidence. I still think it would have been better to let them search and get them off my back."

"It wouldn't necessarily have gotten them off your back: They could just figure that you'd already cleaned up well or had the stuff related to the crime somewhere else. I'm sure the attorney told you that once you let the police into your home, they can take anything related to any sort of crime into evidence."

"But there isn't any evidence of crimes here because I haven't committed any," said Havens, in a tone of exasperation.

"What if you let the police in and they planted some."

Havens blinked at me. "I hadn't thought of that." After a moment, he said: "But that's ridiculous. Why would they do that?"

"They probably wouldn't, but why take the chance? The laws on search and seizure are there for your protection: Let the police earn their warrants. If it makes you feel any better, I can guarantee you that not one of those cops asking nicely and casually for permission to search would have given that permission in your place. I asked for voluntary searches when I was a cop, and I figured it was in a good cause. But I also knew I was sort of taking advantage of people who didn't know any better."

Havens nodded. "I'll pass it along to the others. Thanks."

"That's what I'm here for."

"You were saying before that finding the anonymous caller might not do me any good with the police. But I'd still like to know who that caller is."

"I may be able to find out. It's possibly the same person who's behind the threats. But whether it's one person or two won't make much difference in terms of my immediate approach—looking for people who hate you."

Havens gave a small grunt, as if he'd just been hit with something. He sat blinking at me for a moment. "It's a little startling to hear it put like that," he said. "Especially for someone who never knew he had any enemies."

"You've obviously got at least one," I said. "What about your ex-wife? Could she be behind all this? Mrs. Bennett seems to think so."

"I know. I can understand why Sylvia thinks that, but she's wrong." Havens hesitated. "I assume Sylvia gave you some background on Ruth and me—the divorce, why Ruth was so angry at me."

"Yes."

"Sylvia's reasoning might have made sense two or three years ago—though I really don't think Ruth was ever the kind of person to do something like this. But it doesn't make any sense now. Why would Ruth all of a sudden be trying to hurt me? I guess she's still angry at me, but she can't be *that* angry—not after all this time. At least, I hope not—for her sake. Living with that kind of anger is like living in hell. I know."

"How long's it been since your son died?"

"About four years."

"Is it possible that your book—and the publicity that's gone with it—could have stirred up your ex-wife's anger? Brought back old memories, or made her resent your doing well?"

"Anything's possible. But I just don't believe it's her."

"Given the fact that you and your ex have such a strained relationship, why are you both living in the same area? Especially this area. Weren't the two of you living in San Francisco when your son died?"

"Yes, but we've spent time here, too," said Havens. "Ruth's sister lived in Soquel for some years, and we used to visit her there. I spent a year working for a San Jose advertising firm when Ricky was two. We lived in Santa Cruz that year. After Ruth left me, she went to live with her sister in Soquel. Her sister has since remarried and moved away, but Ruth stayed on. As for me, I've always loved this side of the mountains. I assumed Granite Valley would be far enough away from Soquel to give Ruth all the room she needed. I hope I wasn't wrong."

"Was it a first marriage for both of you?"

"For Ruth. Not for me. I have a daughter, who graduated from Sonoma State last year. She works in Boston—that's where her mother lives."

"Any conflicts between you and her mother?"

"No," he said. "She was the one who left me. She's been remarried for quite some time—happily, by all appearances. We haven't interacted much over the last few years, but what interactions we've had have been pleasant."

"You and your daughter?"

"We get along great. Anyway, she and her mother have been in Europe for the past month. There's no way they could have been mailing notes from California."

"If it's not them, or Ruth, then who? Can you think of anyone else it might be—someone who might want to hurt you?"

"No. I've always gotten on pretty well with people."

"No business deals or affairs gone bad—anything of that sort."

Havens smiled. "No, nothing like that."

"You must deal with some pretty distraught people during your lectures, book signings, whatever. Do you remember running into anyone who seemed particularly odd? Maybe someone who was angry at something you said."

"No . . ." Havens drew out the word as if he were unwilling to let go of it until he was sure of its truth. "No. And I think I'd remember."

"What about the people in your discussion group? Could it be one of them."

"No," said Havens firmly. "That's not possible."

"Why not?"

"It just isn't."

"Because you like them? Because you feel responsible for them?"

"Because they're nice people." Havens looked at me and then gave a small nod of concession. "Okay, so maybe I'm judging this emotionally. But look at it logically. The people in the group asked to talk to me. If they don't like what's going on here, they can always leave. I'm not charging them any sort of fee, so it can't be a matter of money. And why would they make accusations against the group when they'd just be accusing themselves?"

"Good point, though I should try to find out exactly how the accusation was worded. By the way, I'll need to know the exact wording of the threats you received. Do you still have the letters?"

"The police took the originals, but I have copies. They're right over there on the table." Havens glanced at his watch. "I need to start the coffee. Why don't you come into the kitchen with me. We'll continue this in there."

I followed Havens, stopping alongside him at the dining room table while he pulled a sheaf of papers out of a file folder and handed them to me. In the kitchen I sat at the small dinette table, a cream-colored metal thing mismatched with three white-painted wooden chairs.

I glanced at the photocopies. There were six sheets of paper, copies of the three notes alternating with copies of the envelopes. The words in the notes had been formed from large cutout letters. The three messages were "You won't get away with it," "You deserve to die," and "You'll pay with your life." The addresses on the envelopes were done with very small, very neatly put-together cutout letters. The envelopes were addressed to Havens's home. One was postmarked Granite Valley, another, Santa Cruz, and the third, San Jose. I noticed that the photocopies showed single tape lines above and below each envelope address.

I looked up at Havens, who was inserting a plastic tray of coffee into the automatic coffeemaker. He had placed two unopened boxes of cookies on the counter next to the coffeemaker.

"How were the envelope addresses done?" I asked.

"Apparently the person cut out the letters, taped them together to form the address, photocopied the address, and then taped it onto the envelope."

"Self-styled address labels." I glanced down at the pages in my hand. "When you read the words, 'You'll pay,' what was the first thing you thought of? Pay for what?"

"For Ricky," said Havens without hesitation. I must have looked surprised because he said, "There's nothing odd about that. Ricky's death is the one thing in my life I feel really guilty about. Oh, I've worked through a lot of it. I realize his death wasn't my fault. The fault, if you can speak of it like that, lay in the situation. I'd have felt guilty either way. Even if I'd left those other children to die, I'm not sure I could have saved Ricky. But that's all on a rational level. At a deeper level I still feel the guilt. Maybe I always will."

"I know how that goes," I said.

"How do you know?" asked Havens.

"I've lost some people close to me, including one to suicide. There's always that primitive feeling of guilt—the feeling that it was somehow your fault. You can try to wash away the guilt with therapy, rationality, common sense, whatever. But it always leaves stains."

"Well put," said Havens. His eyes seemed to study my face. "You've thought about this some."

"Yeah, some."

"I really would like your reaction to my book when you finish."

"Sure," I said.

Havens glanced up at the kitchen clock. "It's getting late," he said. "I've got to get this stuff ready."

"Let me help."

He gave me some assignments—placing the cookies on plates, getting out the milk and sugar. When it looked as if everything was set, I said, "You said your first thought was that 'you'll pay' meant for Ricky. Did you have a first thought about who was saying you'd pay?"

"Ruth," said Havens, "but don't get excited about that. It was a perfectly natural reflex. It's not just that she's been angry with me about Ricky. It's also that in my mind she's become the embodiment of my own judgments against myself. As soon as I started thinking rationally, I realized it couldn't be Ruth. For the reasons I gave you."

"Did any other name come to mind?"

"No."

"Does your ex-wife have any relatives who might hold a grudge against you for Ricky's death?"

"No. Her father's dead, and her mother's in a nursing home in southern California. Her sister's her only sibling, and she's too fun-loving and self-involved to get passionate about something like this."

"Mrs. Bennett gave me the impression there was some sort of animosity between her and the man who did that newspaper article. What's that about?"

"Garza had a thing for Sylvia at one point and got pretty obnoxious about it," said Havens. "He's kind of a crude guy, not Sylvia's type at all, and she wasn't remotely interested. At one party he got drunk and acted pretty rude toward her. I . . . uh . . . had to remove him from the room."

"What do you mean?"

Havens shrugged. "I just got him in a hold and dragged him out of the house. I didn't hurt him, but I think I embarrassed him a lot." Havens gave a small shake of the head. "Maybe there was a better way I could have handled it. But he was being pretty bad, and he wouldn't leave Sylvia alone."

"So now this guy you removed is the one deciding what to report about you two and the group."

"I'm afraid so."

"Are you and Sylvia in a relationship together?"

"Not of the kind you mean. We're just good friends. But she has been a sort of voluntary assistant, helping me with things connected to the group or my lectures." He smiled, his face affectionate. "Sometimes she tries to be a little too helpful. She keeps trying to turn me into some sort of institute. I tell her to save her money. I'm fine just the way I am." The smile disappeared. "Or, at least, I was."

5

THERE WAS A KNOCK, and Havens went to answer the door. The couple he ushered into the hallway were a surprise—more offbeat than I would have expected. The man, who was large and well muscled, wore his dark hair in a ponytail and sported an earring; he was dressed in a white T-shirt, dark jeans, and boots. At first glance he looked like a biker, but that impression was dispelled almost at once. His movements were too passive, even shy, his voice too soft. The woman with him had a counterculture look—long hair, no makeup, peasant blouse, and a full, bright-colored skirt.

I heard Havens greet the couple and compliment the woman on her skirt. As the three of them moved toward the kitchen where I was standing, the woman began telling Havens about how she'd had the skirt made by an African woman she'd met at a Santa Cruz street fair. When they got to me, we went through one of those awkward moments where people are face-to-face and waiting for introductions that can't yet take place because someone is still saying something. The moment was made more awkward by the fact that the woman seemed oblivious to it, going on in great detail about the process of getting the skirt. Finally Havens deftly interrupted her and made the introductions.

The man, Jack Malander, was in his late thirties. He had a dramatic face—brown skinned, with high cheekbones and a jutting bone structure. There was something vaguely defiant in his eyes, but it was half-hearted, or maybe just overwhelmed by the even stronger sense of defeat he conveyed. I wondered if that look of defeat was simply the result of his grief; somehow I doubted it.

His wife, Susan, was in her early thirties, fairskinned, with straight dark hair that fanned out over her shoulders. The African material of her skirt had an orange, beige, and brown pattern that was mostly squares and squiggles. Over her white blouse she wore a large necklace of bronze-colored metal squares. Given the counterculture look of her, I would have expected someone mellow. Instead she was as chatty as a cheerleader.

But not bubbly, and not happy. Her talky manner seemed to have an undercurrent of desperation about it, a compulsive element that made it seem as if she were the instrument, not the instigator, of the words that came out of her. She didn't look well. Her skin was blotchy, her shoulders hunched, and her gestures nervous, creating the illusion of elderliness superimposed on her obvious youth.

Susan was going on now about something minor that had happened to a friend of hers whom Havens didn't seem to know. Havens gently cut her off—perhaps he'd had practice as the group leader—and told me the Malanders were artists.

"Jack's a sculptor," said Havens. "Susan makes decorative baskets and wreaths. They sell to local shops in the area. They do terrific work. I've got a few of their things."

"My stuff's crap," said Malander sullenly, his words directed toward me. "It's just house and garden decoration. It puts food on the table, is all."

"Jack . . ." said Susan in a tone of weary reproof.

"The things you do are very nice," said Havens firmly, "even if they're not what you want to be doing eventually. They give people pleasure."

"That's what I tell him," said Susan. "A friend of mine has his art pieces all over her house, and she'll, like, stop and look at them—she says they bring so much beauty into her life. But that doesn't matter to him. No, with Jack it's got to be something they'll want to sell in some rich people's gallery. It's so elitist."

"Let me show you their things," said Havens to me.

I followed Havens into the living room, with the Malanders trailing behind. Havens pointed out two of Malander's pieces, both done in a reddish claylike material. One was the bust of a woman, perhaps eight inches tall, flattened at the back to allow hanging. Havens had put the piece in a large clay pot of flowers, which he had resting on the sill of the small picture window. I got the impression that the piece had been made to allow this as well, since it narrowed into a dull spike at midtorso and since the woman's elbows jutted out in a way that provided extra support against the dirt. The face had classical features, but there was a suggestion of wild curls piling up on the shoulders. The eyes were done vaguely. They were either closed or looking dreamily into some distance.

The other piece was a standing figure, maybe fourteen inches tall, a monk with a California-mission look. He was portrayed as if he'd stopped in the middle of digging, whether for a garden or a grave, to pray or contemplate or simply notice. There was a suggestion of a shovel carved as if part of the robe, and a protruding bare foot sitting on the top of the blade; the monk's hands were resting together on the shovel handle. The figure had long matted hair, and a full, rough beard.

Both figures were sentimental, upscale-gift-shop art, but they were beautiful in their way, and there was a soft sadness to the figures I found touching.

"I like them very much," I said to Malander, "but since you don't, tell me what you'd like to be doing."

"I'm already doing it," said Malander. "I just can't sell it."

"That's changing, though," said Havens, putting a hand on Malander's arm. "Jack's been doing some incredible stuff the last few months. One of his sculptures has just been accepted by an important Santa Cruz gallery."

Malander shrugged, but I could see a faint spark of pleasure in his gloomy eyes.

Havens led us back to the hallway where he pointed out a wreath of Susan's that hung on the dining room wall. It was attractive, a Christmas-size wreath of interwoven sticks that had been shellacked, then done up with artificial leaves and flowers.

I was just starting to ask Susan some polite how-to questions, when the front door opened and a woman peeked her head inside.

"I thought I heard voices," she said.

"Hi, Karen," said the others.

The woman came into the house and was introduced to me as Karen

Raley. She was tall and thin, with pale skin and short dark hair. She didn't look well. She had heavy dark circles under eyes so red they looked stained. She moved and spoke with an air of permanent weariness. Her tailored clothing hung loosely on her frame, lacking ten to fifteen pounds for a fit.

"How are you doing?" asked Susan.

"Hanging in there."

"How's Ken?" asked Havens. He glanced at me. "Ken is Karen's husband. He's been having a really rough time of it."

"He's pretty much the same," said Karen to Havens. "Sometimes he's so depressed he can barely move. Other times he's so agitated he can't sit still. I feel so sorry for him."

"Is he still resisting the idea of getting help?" asked Havens.

"Oh, yes. I can't even discuss the subject with him anymore. It's really frustrating."

"Can't you, like, force him to go into the hospital?" asked Susan.

"If it goes on much longer, I guess I'll try," said Karen. "But it would be difficult legally. He's not a danger to himself or others; he does take care of himself in the evenings when I'm at work."

"You still working in the emergency room?" asked Jack Malander.

"Yes."

"Isn't it awfully difficult to be around people who are so badly hurt when you're still . . . you know ? . . ."

"I'm used to it," said Karen. "At work, I mean. It gets me out of myself. It feels good to do something for other people."

The front door opened and a good-looking young blond couple entered. They were introduced to me as Craig and Lisa Caldwell. Both were nicely groomed and were neatly dressed in khaki and cotton plaids. At first glance their obvious health and the care they had taken with their appearance seemed at odds with their being parents who had recently lost a child. But closer inspection showed their pain, eyes moist and bright as if with fever, blinking at everything with a look of cosmic confusion. They had their grief, all right; it just hadn't had time to wear them out.

Sylvia entered just after the Caldwells. She gave each of us a quick greeting, and then stopped in front of Havens, touching his arm as she asked him how he was, looking into his face with affectionate concern. Havens seemed both pleased and a little embarrassed by her attention. When he ended the encounter by drawing back, Sylvia glanced around at the others and proceeded to take charge of the gathering. She ushered those needing coffee into the kitchen, standing over us as we filled our cups. That done, she ushered us into the living room, seating me in a straight chair directly across the circle from Havens's easy chair.

In the straight chairs to my left were Craig and Lisa Caldwell, with Sylvia at the end of the row, next to Havens. On the couch to my right were Karen Raley, then Susan and Jack Malander. Havens cleared his throat.

"You've all met Mr. Strickland," he said. He glanced at me. "Is it all right if we call you Dave?" I nodded, and he continued. "As you know, Sylvia originally called in Dave to investigate the threats I've been getting. Now, with what's happened the last couple of days, we also want him to find out who's accusing us. And to act as a kind of liaison with the police. I asked him here today so you could meet him, and he could meet you, and we could take care of any general questions you or he might have. I assume he'll also want to talk to you individually."

Havens looked at me for confirmation, and I nodded.

"Are you going to try to find the person who killed my daughter?" asked Lisa Caldwell.

She fixed those eyes, with their semblance of fever, on my face. The expression in them made shaking my head harder than it should have been.

"No," I said. "There wouldn't be any point. The police have all sorts of people on it already. They've got whatever evidence has been collected, the lab facilities to analyze it, and access to whatever expert consultants they need. They have the authority to compel cooperation. I have none of that, and anything I tried to do would be a joke in comparison. Plus, if the police got any inkling that I was trying to involve myself in their case, they'd be furious; they'd make it difficult, if not impossible, to do the things I've been hired to do."

"Lisa," said Havens, "we've been over all that before. I told you Dave wouldn't be looking for the killer. He's been hired to do other things."

"Nothing else is important," she said.

Havens looked at her with pain in his eyes. He seemed to formulate, then discard, some response. Finally he said simply, "I know."

Then he turned to the others. "Maybe I could get things started by telling Dave a little more about us," he said. When no one objected, Havens said, "Dave, you've met Karen. She and her husband, Kenneth, lost their little girl, Terri, last summer. Terri drowned in their pool."

"While we were away," said Karen quickly, a clarification I imagined she'd made often during the last few months. "That stupid babysitter . . ." She cut herself off and closed her eyes. "Don't let me get started on that again."

"Karen's a nurse," said Havens. "Her husband, Ken, is an accountant. Ken was in the group for a while, but this whole thing has kind of overwhelmed him."

Havens gave Karen a sympathetic look, but her eyes were closed and she couldn't see it. He turned toward the Malanders.

"I know you had a chance to get acquainted with Jack and Susan. They lost their son, Jimmy, back in February."

"To that murderer," said Jack in a low growl.

"He must have gotten Jimmy in the woods just behind our house," said Susan, her voice rising with emotion. "He was six, almost seven, certainly old enough to play outside by himself. I did check on him all the time, I really did, but I should have checked on him more, I shouldn't have—"

"Susan, don't," said her husband softly, putting a big hand on her arm.

Havens gestured at the Caldwells, sitting just to my left. "Craig and Lisa lost their daughter, Corinne, back in April," he said. "She was murdered, too."

I glanced at Lisa Caldwell. She had squeezed her eyelids shut with such force that deep lines were radiating along her cheekbones and up into her forehead. Her hands were clenched in her lap. Her husband, Craig, had a hand over hers, not saying anything, waiting patiently, just lending his presence, in what I imagined must be a familiar ritual. He looked at me.

"I want that murderer caught, just like Lisa does," he said. "But I understand that's not your job, Mr. Strickland, and I don't agree that nothing else is important. I think it's horrible having people think that maybe we killed our own children." His voice caught, and he swallowed hard. "I don't understand how someone could accuse us of something like that. I want to know who it is." His jaw clenched for a moment, then released. "And it worries me to think that someone might want to hurt John. I want that person found. I'll do everything I can to help you. I know Lisa will, too, when she's feeling better."

"Thanks, Craig," I said. "I appreciate that."

I looked around at the others. "Probably the person behind the threats and the call is simply out to hurt John," I said. "If that's the case, the rest of you are just bystanders suffering the fallout from the attack on him. But there are other possibilities that might involve you more directly. It's possible that someone you know is attacking John and the group because of some animosity toward you."

"That seems pretty far-fetched," said Jack Malander. "If the caller were after someone other than John, why involve him and the group at all?"

"You may be right that it's unlikely," I said, "but I can give you some possible scenarios. Suppose someone were jealous of someone in the group, misinterpreting the relation between that person and John, or that person and someone else here. That might be reason to lash out."

"How would jealousy fit in?" asked Malander. "I mean . . ." His eyes shifted quickly to Karen, then Sylvia, and he seemed to lose confidence. "I mean . . ."

"There are other possibilities," I said. "Maybe someone blames you for the death of your child, thinks you should be punished rather than comforted, and so resents the group. Maybe someone—let's say someone paranoid—believes you actually did kill your child, and assumes the others in the group did the same with their children. Maybe—"

"Stop!" said Lisa Caldwell fiercely. "Why are you saying such things? Why are you even thinking them? You have a sick mind, do you know that? You—"

"Lisa," said her husband gently, "that's enough."

"It's true," she said. "He—"

"Lisa, stop," said Havens, more forcefully. "You're not making any sense. Dave is a private investigator. He's been a police detective. He

41

knows about such things firsthand. It's his job to think about them. If he didn't, he couldn't help us."

"I can't stand this," said Lisa in a soft, teary, almost childlike voice.

She bent over, put a fist against her mouth, and squeezed her eyelids shut. Tears leaked out from beneath her lids. Her husband put an arm around her shoulders, and with his free hand took a handkerchief and dabbed at her eyes. He whispered something to her, his face solicitous; she shook her head. She sat there rigidly, her eyes still closed, her body all clenched up.

"I'm sorry, Lisa," I said, glancing from her to Craig, who gave me an apologetic look. "I didn't mean to upset you." I looked around the room. "I'm just trying to emphasize that we could, in theory, be dealing with someone whose primary animosity is toward one of you, not toward John. What I need you to do is think over who you know and see if you can think of any possibilities. Then we can talk about it when I meet with you individually. Will you do that for me?"

No one answered me, but there seemed to be positive responses conveyed by the slight head nods and shoulder shrugs. After a moment of silence, I decided to change the subject.

"What do you do in this group?" I asked.

When no one answered right away, Havens said, "Jack?"

"Sometimes we discuss some of John's ideas," said Malander. "Sometimes we share other things we've read. But mostly we talk . . . and listen."

"And just be there for each other," said Susan. "I can't tell you how much it means to come here, with John, Karen, Sylvia, everyone— to be able to be myself, and let down and share whatever I'm feeling. Sometimes it seems like this is the only place, other than with Jack, where I can be myself. I have this friend, Elise, and we've always been really close, and she's sweet, really she is, she works at a day-care center, and I thought she'd understand, but I don't know, it just doesn't seem like we can communicate on this. And there's this other friend—"

"It's hard to talk to people who haven't been through it," said Karen. "They just don't get it."

"They don't really want to listen," said Sylvia. "They just want to tell you what to do—pull yourself together, think positive, get on with

42

your life. And all the time you're feeling so lost, so paralyzed—all you really want is someone there with you, someone who'll listen."

"A lot of times people mean well," said Havens. "They just have no idea what to do."

"They're scared, too," said Karen. "Your grief reminds them that they're going to die, and they don't want to face the fact of their death. Even the health professionals I work with, you'd think they'd be better. They know the dos and don'ts all right, but when you really want them to be there for you, forget it. Being around sickness and death all the time, they've built up so many defenses that they're terrified to let them down."

"You know what I hate most about that anonymous call?" asked Susan.

"What?" answered a couple of voices.

"It's that deep down I feel like he's right." There were some murmurs of protest, and she said, "I'm talking about me, not you, and I'm just talking feelings. I know that madman killed my son, but I still feel responsible for Jimmy's death. I was his mother, I was the one who was supposed to protect him, my little guy—and I should have, I should have kept him safe . . . oh, damn."

Susan brushed her fingers awkwardly at her moistened eyes, then looked down and started fumbling through her purse looking for tissues.

"That kind of guilt is so very tough to deal with," said Havens. "You all know what a struggle I had with it—am still having with it. It just doesn't want to go away."

"The worst of it is," said Karen, "no matter how hard you work on the guilt and tell yourself that it's just an irrational feeling, it seems there's always some small piece of reality it can hang on to. I feel guilty for being gone that day. I know that's stupid, and maybe, just maybe, if I keep telling myself that long enough, I'll finally believe it. But what about picking that baby-sitter? How am I going to convince myself that I was right to settle for that irresponsible idiot with her incessant phone calls? Why didn't I care enough about my daughter to find someone really responsible?"

"Corinne was taken right out of our backyard," said Craig. "She was just sleeping there on her blanket on the back lawn, playing with her toys. We only left her alone for a minute to answer the phone. . . ."

"*I* left her alone," said Lisa tearfully in a soft explosion of words. "I was the one, not you."

"No, Lisa," said Craig.

"I didn't think there was any danger," she said, her words a kind of extended sob. "I didn't . . . oh, Corinne, I'm so sorry."

Lisa bent over, sobbing. I looked at her, feeling sorry for her, but also feeling distinctly uncomfortable. The emotional atmosphere in the room had become heated and oppressive. I'd been trying to listen with a sympathetic detachment, but now I was beginning to lose my detachment. All this emotion was setting off too many vibrations in me. I'd suffered anxiety attacks in the past—bad ones after my wife's suicide, worse ones after my recent head injury. The anxiety attacks had diminished over the last few months, both in frequency and intensity, but I was still susceptible to them. I could feel some warning signs now, the revving up of the nervous system, the pressure on my chest, the impression of light-headedness. I had done what I had come to do; it was time to get out of here.

"This is obscene," I heard Karen saying over the sounds of Lisa's now-soft sobbing.

"What do you mean?" asked Havens, sharply.

"I mean, what are we doing here, putting on some kind of freak show for your detective? I hope he's enjoying himself."

"Karen!" said Havens. "That's rude and unfair."

"Maybe so," she said, "but he's got no business being here for this. This is our private place. It's not for strangers."

"I agree," I said, "I'm not feeling too comfortable myself. I had no intention of being here for the really personal stuff. It just sort of snuck up on me. We were talking business, and then suddenly we were . . . into this."

Karen's face relaxed a little. "I'm sorry if I sounded like I was attacking you," she said. "It's not really your fault. But I think you should leave now."

"So do I," said Jack Malander.

"No problem," I said. I stood up and looked around the room. "It was nice meeting all of you. I'll be calling each of you later."

I felt grateful for the ejection since it was getting me out of there

44

faster than I could have politely managed on my own. I knew that just being away from this place would subdue whatever anxiety I was feeling.

"Maybe Dave has been through a grief experience," said Susan.

"That's not relevant," said Karen. "This is our group—and he's not here as a participant anyway."

"I know that," said Susan, "but he's going to be spending some time with us, and I'd like to know if he's been through any of the things that we're going through."

"You don't want to listen to my problems," I said, not at all liking this latest development.

"I'd be interested in what you have to say," said Craig.

"So would I," said Havens.

"Another time," I said.

I took a step back, and my leg bumped against the chair. I had a momentary flash of panic, an irrational sense of being trapped here. I took a step to the side and got free of the chair.

"Dave, wait," said Havens. "You told me you'd lost some people close to you. If you'd feel like talking about it some, it's always helpful to us to hear about other people's experiences."

Everyone was looking at me, and, unlike earlier, it felt painful. With anxiety, it's as if some protective coating has been stripped away from you: the gaze of others seems to run through you like an electrical charge; the presence of others, voices, even light, can feel like a physical assault. All this was at a bearable level now, but there was no guarantee it wasn't going to get worse. I wanted to get out of there.

But I also knew I'd stay. When I'd first started having panic attacks after my wife's suicide, "I don't run" had become my private anthem against retreat, my incantation against insanity, the emblem of my hope that by standing up to these things, I would finally defeat them. I had come through. If I started running now in the face of these aftershocks, the whole awful process might start all over again.

There was also a more calculating motive—the thought that talking about my experiences might insinuate myself into these people's confidence, whereas leaving would simply reinforce the them-versus-me theme voiced by Karen Raley.

None of this meant that I had to give myself up to the emotionality of the group. I'd give them a few basics, prove what I had to prove to myself by staying a bit longer, and then leave.

I moved back to my chair, limping slightly, my bad leg seizing up a bit as it often did when I was anxious. As I sat down, I could feel a nervous electricity running through my body, with occasional small jolts that made me want to jump up out of my chair.

"My wife and daughter died a few years ago," I said. I tried to keep my voice sounding matter-of-fact, though I did have to clear my throat to get all the words out.

"How did they die?" asked Malander.

"My daughter died of crib death. My wife killed herself a year later."

Several people in the group made sympathetic sounds.

"Are you comfortable talking about it?" asked Susan.

"Comfortable enough, I guess."

"How'd your wife kill herself?" asked Karen.

There seemed to be some sort of challenge in her eyes. Maybe she wanted to make me pay for having stayed against her wishes. Maybe she wanted to make me expose my grief the way the others had exposed theirs. It wasn't going to happen, partly because I wasn't going to let it, partly because my grief was much older than theirs. But I wanted to give her enough so she'd feel there'd been some openness on my part, some parity.

"She slit her wrists," I said. "Sitting in a warm bath. It happened on a Sunday afternoon a year after our daughter died. While I was gone for the afternoon."

"And you found her?" asked Karen.

"Yes."

"It must have been terrible," said Craig.

"Yeah," I said. "As a cop, I was used to seeing much worse. But that didn't count for anything that day. I remember I couldn't stop vomiting."

I hadn't meant to say that last thing. As I said it, I felt a faint touch of nausea, which, in turn, heightened the memory. Katie's skin had been so pale against all that blood. I could remember walking into the house, calling her name, walking back to the bedroom, knocking on the bathroom door, then reaching for the door handle. My next memory, darkly tinted, was of my knees slamming down against the tile floor, my chin cracking against the rim of the tub, the vision of blood filling my eyes. I think I cried out, I'm not sure.

"Did you know she was suicidal?" asked Karen.

My plan to stay unemotional wasn't working. Constricted feelings filled my chest, making it difficult to breathe. I felt as if I were trembling, though I detected no motion in my hands.

"Yes and no," I said, trying to keep my voice level. "She threatened it from time to time. She even made one halfhearted attempt. But she was seeing a therapist, and I thought the worst of the danger had passed. In fact, she seemed almost happy the last couple of weeks of her life. I know now that can happen when people have finally made up their minds. I didn't know it at the time."

"Did you—do you—feel guilty for not having been with her that day?" asked Karen.

I just looked at her, not answering, suddenly annoyed. I felt as if she were pushing me, though it also occurred to me that she might be simply running through some list of symptoms these people tended to discuss.

Did I feel guilty about not being there that day? Of course. How could I not?

It's awful living with, and trying to save, people who are trying to destroy themselves. You hurt for them, and you're afraid for them, and you're weighted down with responsibility so heavy you think it's going to crush you. And all the time they're drawing you into their pain. Deep down within their suffering, they're playing with your life, just as they're playing with their own. And sometimes, when you feel as though you can't take anymore, you think, *Please, just go, and let me finally rest,* knowing you don't mean it, even while knowing you do, and feeling guilty as hell for having thought it at all.

Yes, I feel guilty for not having been there. I should have always been there. And yet, still, she would have found a way. That's what I believe. That's what I have to believe.

"Do you feel guilty?" Karen persisted.

My annoyance flashed suddenly into anger, though part of me knew perfectly well that whatever I was feeling had much more to do with my own vulnerabilities than anything this woman was doing.

47

"Why don't you give it a rest?" I said, leaning toward her, watching her pull back.

The anger had set off alarm bells in my head, but it had also given me some relief, drawing energy from the anxiety and into itself. That happened sometimes if the anxiety attack was mild enough.

"What got you through it, Mr. Strickland?" asked Craig, with some urgency in his voice, from the other side of the circle. I had the feeling he was trying to distract me away from Karen. "I mean, if you don't mind discussing it," he added cautiously.

I looked at Craig. "I'm not sure I'm through it," I said. "I'm not sure I'll ever be. But what got me through the worst of it was anger. And stubbornness—not wanting to get beaten by it. The normal things that help people survive."

"I hope you did more than survive," said Havens.

I shrugged.

"Did you have a good support network?" asked Susan. "I mean, friends, family, maybe a group like this one."

"No," I said. "I didn't have any friends or family I felt I could talk to. Maybe it wasn't my nature to talk about it anyway."

"Very male," said Havens. "I got myself in the same corner."

"When things got really bad, I did go see a therapist," I said. "That helped some."

"You didn't join a group?" asked Susan.

"No."

"Do you feel you've come to terms with your wife's suicide?" asked Malander.

"I suppose I have," I said. "If there's really any way to come to terms with something like that. It happened. Nothing's going to change that no matter who comes to terms with what. I've tried to understand it from her standpoint, but I'm not sure I can. I can understand her suicide, yes, but not the way she did it, without seeming to try to fight her grief for my sake, or let me in to help. I've tried to go on with my life. And forget."

"Has your view of the world changed as a result of losing your wife and daughter?" asked Havens.

"Yes," I said. "I like the world a lot less than I used to."

"Did anything good come out of the tragedy for you?" he asked.

"Something positive that worked itself out in your life?"

"No," I said. "Nothing."

"That would make what happened doubly awful," said Havens. "But I have a hard time believing that. There must have been some good thing that came out of it. Isn't there some way in which you are better because of your loss?"

I might have come up with something, but I wasn't in the mood. "One good thing," I said sarcastically. "I'm a better hater."

I WAS SITTING AT my kitchen counter, wearing old cords and a sweater, working on my second cup of coffee. The fog in my head was beginning to clear, as was the fog outside, which had slipped past the edge of the ridge and was working its way down the slope.

Havens's book was sitting on the counter in front of me. I opened it, blinked at the page, and decided I was awake enough to read the print. I flipped past the prologue and the first-chapter account of Ricky's death. The second chapter, I saw, flashed back to Havens's earliest years. I began skimming.

Havens had grown up in rural Pennsylvania. His father was a salesman of farm implements, his mother a housewife with chronic health problems. John was an only child. When he was ten, his mother was diagnosed with advanced uterine cancer. She survived for three years, but complications of surgery and other treatments made her an invalid for the last two years of her life. The care of her fell heavily on the boy. John's father began traveling more, claiming the pressure of medical expenses, though he seemed uncomfortable with his wife's illness and, when home, often slipped off on errands that would last most of the day. John took his mother's death hard. He had thought, guiltily, that there would be some sense of liberation in her death for him, but he felt none. Instead he suffered nightmares and depression. He'd become something of a loner during his mother's illness, and he remained one for a couple of years after her death, with "brooding filling the hours that nursing her had filled."

Then his father remarried, and the remarriage pushed John back out into life. His stepmother didn't like John, though he knew it wasn't personal: she didn't like children. For that matter, she didn't seem to like his father much either, and the two adults fell into a pattern of nagging and arguing that made home a place the boy wanted to avoid. Throwing himself into school activities, like basketball and the school paper, gave him an excuse to stay away from home, and the activities themselves drew him back into social relationships. By the time he left for the University of Pennsylvania, he was considered outgoing and popular, and he felt pretty good about himself and his life.

He met his first wife, Margaret, during their junior year of college. They got married senior year and had a daughter, Sharon, a few months after graduation. According to Havens's account, the marriage was good during his eleven years in journalism, then became troubled after the move to New York and advertising. At first the troubles stemmed from the pressures of his job and his wife's initial dislike of the city. But the destruction of the marriage came from the eventual changes in themselves. His wife got involved in the political movements of the period; these energized her and, for the first time, gave her her own circle of friends and associates. The more involved she became, the more she viewed Havens and his life as superficial and even criminal. Havens just wanted their lives to go on as before, but in defending himself against his wife's attacks and needing a position from which to attack back, he found himself becoming increasingly conservative. The marriage began to degenerate, and one day, bolstered by her women's group, Margaret walked out.

Hurt, but with his beliefs intact, Havens took an advertising job in San Francisco to get away from New York and to be closer to his daughter, who was at Sonoma State. Soon the challenges and successes of his new job, along with the attractions of California and the single life, made Havens forget all about his divorce, and he began to feel happy again.

Havens came into a client's office one day to find a "bright and attractive" new receptionist, named Ruth. They got into a relationship and then decided to get married. Havens would have preferred to put off marriage, but Ruth wanted a child. Her first marriage had been childless, she was now forty-one, and time was running out. Havens was nervous about starting another family, but decided he loved Ruth enough to try it. When Ruth got pregnant, Havens found himself getting excited at the prospect of a child; when Ricky was born, Havens was delighted. Ruth was ecstatic. Havens couldn't remember ever having seen her looking that happy, or that beautiful.

Six months after the child was born, the marriage developed problems. Havens began to resent his wife's almost total concentration on the baby. He knew from his first marriage how intense the mother-infant relationship could be, but with Ruth it went far beyond that. She was obsessed by the child. She never seemed to get tired, never seemed to want a break, didn't want to talk about much else. The things she didn't have time for were things related to her husband. Havens tried to understand, then tried to talk to his wife, then started quarreling with her. The only thing she seemed to hear when he talked was that he didn't love their child as much as she did.

Then one day, when Havens was close to giving up on the marriage, he fell in love with his twelve-month-old son. It was one of the rare times he'd been alone with his son for several hours at a stretch, his wife having been forced out of the house for root-canal work on an infected tooth. Havens took his son to the park with a blanket and a small picnic, and the two of them spent the afternoon together. His son seemed happy being there with him—Havens had been afraid the boy might spend the time screaming for his mother. In fact, the child seemed to find Havens endlessly fascinating. Havens became fascinated in turn, warming to this cute, smily, helpless thing. He began to realize how much his perception of his son had been distorted by his wife's behavior: how he had resented the child for his wife's preoccupation with him; how his enthusiasm had been dimmed by what had seemed to him his wife's excessive feelings; how her intense approach to mothering had turned what might have been his natural affectionate responses into magnified obligations, and so made them seem unpleasant.

From that day forward Havens insisted on his own time with his son, insisted on doing certain things his way. Amazingly, the marriage suddenly changed for the better. It was as if his actions had dissolved that fantasy world of mother-and-child that his wife had been living in since the child's birth; or maybe it was that Havens had simply managed to break his way into it. Ruth became a more attentive and affectionate wife. Though still devoted to her son, she seemed to relax, step back a pace, and involve herself with other things. For the next couple of years, his family life seemed to Havens perfect, and he couldn't remember being happier.

Then Ricky died, and Havens and Ruth faced the funeral arrangements in a state of shock. Finally, they were alone, just the two of them, with their grief.

The awful paradox of being part of a couple who have lost a child is that the person you've always looked to for comfort has none to give you and, in turn, is looking to you for comfort you can't give. The one whose presence was once associated with so many good things now only makes you think of death. It would have made a great difference if we could have reached out to other people, but neither Ruth nor I had family we were close to, and our only "friends" were business associates we couldn't have shared our grief with. So we were locked into our own little world of pain.

At least I had my work. I felt no joy in it, but it got me out of the house, got me into something outside myself. Ruth had nothing but her memories, and she became obsessed with those memories as she had once been obsessed with our infant son. She resisted most of my efforts to get her out of the house, to get her involved with people. Instead she stayed at home, sleeping, weeping, and spending hours in Ricky's room.

I became the caretaker. I'd like to think that I did it out of love, and I guess, in part, I did. But I didn't feel loving. Such feelings had been numbed by my grief. The feeling I was most conscious of was panic, feeling that if I didn't hold up, our marriage, our lives, and our world would simply collapse. I suppose I was running on anger as well, at Ricky for having died, at Ruth for giving in so completely to her grief, at myself for having failed them both. As the caretaker, I tried to hold my feelings in, but my pain wasn't to be denied. It came out in episodes of fierce headaches, bent-over stomach pains, and difficulty getting my breath: when I slept, there were nightmares.

About four months after Ricky's death, Ruth came out of this period of depressed solitude. She began working more around the house and relating more energetically to me. Her mood now was angry and anxious. I assumed that this was a natural step toward healing and was relieved to see it for her sake. But nothing in our relationship was any better, we had simply moved from one kind of unhappiness to another. With the exception, perhaps, of some household chores, Ruth still wasn't interested in anything but Ricky. She became obsessed with the reasons for Ricky's death, trying to find in it some meaning that would give her comfort. She continued to spend time in Ricky's room, though more actively now. She cleaned it until it shined, keeping everything just as it had been, turning it into a kind of shrine. Ruth couldn't bear to be touched, even though touching was what I craved more than anything. I suppose her attitude must have been a function of her depression and maybe her anger toward me. But I think, too, she thought that she wasn't entitled to pleasure or comfort now that her son could have neither. Whenever I'd try to get her focused on us and our relationship, she'd just get angry, accusing me of not having loved Ricky enough, of not caring enough that he was dead. The only companionship she had to offer me was the companionship of misery.

I know I must come across as selfish and petty. That's how I come across to myself. I know Ruth was hurting far beyond my capacity to understand. She must have been totally lost, out of control in the midst of a flood of frightening feelings. I can see now how impossible it would have been for me to give her what she needed. I was hurting too much myself, and Ruth didn't want to be helped. But for all that, I wish I could have somehow made a difference.

Ruth continued her search for reasons, wanting, I suppose, to find some cosmic purpose in it all. When she couldn't find her cosmic reasons, she turned to, or rather turned against, me. I was the reason Ricky was dead: I hadn't loved him enough. I had, in fact, chosen to save strangers rather than my own sweet child. I suppose that hating me was what she needed to get her through, and there was a semblance of truth in what she said. Her hatred was the final push I needed, if, indeed, I needed any, to hate myself.

After too many days and nights of accusation and recrimination, Ruth left me, going to stay with her sister who lived in one of the beach towns south of San Francisco. I hoped it was just a matter of time before Ruth changed her mind, moved to the next stage of the grief process, and came to see me in a more forgiving light. But it was not to be. Now I began to collapse. Holding her up, it turned out, had been the only thing holding me up. Now that I was alone, all the grief that I had been fighting to keep inside came out with a sick fury, as if it had become infected by the repression of it. Tears came and wouldn't stop. Thoughts came and wouldn't stop either, obsessive thoughts about Ricky and the fire and my own guilt. Moods came so black and so heavy it was as if I had been buried alive in some bog, cut off from the world, cut off from everything but my own dark pain.

DRIVING SOUTH ON Highway 1, I took the Soquel exit, turned
left under the highway, drove past a Spanish-style elementary school,
and stopped for a red light. Here, on Soquel Drive, was the main part
of town, two blocks of low buildings containing a bank and local shops.
On the wall to my left was a bright mural, a piece of Americana, rural
folks gathering flowers on a hill above a village of white buildings. The
setting in the mural was charming and clean, everyone's fantasy of
small-town life. It made the real town look a little shoddy by comparison.

I turned right. Up ahead, past some stores, was a quaint, tall-towered
Congregational church, the only part of town that looked like anything in the mural. The road curved up a small incline past a store selling statues and fountains with lots of cherubs and nymphs, sitting next
to a store selling Western boots and buckles—one-stop shopping, I assumed, for the mentally deranged.

At the top of the incline I saw that the numbers were getting close
to the one I wanted. Since no parking was allowed along this section
of Soquel Drive, I parked on a side street, and walked back to the main
road.

Ruth Havens's place was just across the street, a rectangular cot-
tage, with one end toward the road. Its wood-shingled roof, with lots
of jutting angles, seemed too big for the house, making it look like
someone trying on the wrong-sized hat. The house was run-down,
roof shingles loose, yellow paint faded, the small roof over the front
steps cocked at an odd angle.

What had obviously gotten attention was the yard, which ran along the front and right side of the house. I could only see a small part of the yard because it was hidden behind a tall hedge, but the hedge was healthy and trimmed, and there were flowering rosebushes and a bed of pink and white flowers outside the hedge at the left side of the house. The yard was quite a contrast to the house, and to the yard of the house next door, which had a swing set, wagon, play car, plastic toys, and a couple of old pieces of machinery, all sitting on brown grass.

A young woman wearing a backpack came bicycling across my vision, perhaps heading for summer classes at the community college just down the road. I looked for cars, and, seeing none, crossed the four-lane street.

The entrance to Ruth Havens's front yard seemed to be off a dirt path at the front-left of the house. Once on the path I found a small gate, part of an old and now superfluous three-foot picket fence that ran outside the thick, six-foot hedge. The yard inside was beautiful, all garden, mounded beds of flowers outlined in stone and separated by bark and ground cover; beyond the beds were jasmine and sunflowers and more rosebushes. The enclosed yard was its own little world, having all the beauty and orderliness that the plain and cluttered neighborhood did not.

Two cats, one golden, one speckled gray, were sunning themselves on the thick cement front steps. On the ground at the opposite end of the yard was a small radio softly playing classical music. There seemed to be no one in the yard. I was about to step through the gate when a woman emerged from behind the far side of the house, pushing an empty blue wheelbarrow. She came to a stop next to a small metal stepladder. It was obvious from a glance at the tops of the bushes that she'd been doing some trimming. The woman was thin, with a mop of short brown hair. The clothes she wore for gardening were old and loose, faded slacks that might once had been light green, a white blouse, and a blue cardigan worn against the coastal morning chill.

I said hello and, when she didn't hear me, said it again. This time the woman turned abruptly, giving me a hostile look.

"Mrs. Havens?" I asked.

"Yes."

"I'm Dave Strickland, a private investigator."

"Investigating what?"

"Someone has been making threats against your ex-husband."

Her look mellowed into something ironic. "And you think I might be responsible," she said.

She made it a statement, not a question.

"I don't know," I said. "Do you think it's an unreasonable idea?"

"No. I don't think it's unreasonable at all."

She was obviously having fun with me. Or better, playing with me, since she didn't look like someone who had much fun. Her eyes were hard, and there were deep lines in her face that seemed to have been etched by frowning. She looked like what mothers used to warn their children they'd look like if they made too many faces.

I said, "An anonymous caller made an accusation against your ex-husband and some local people he's helping. The accusation was reported in the *Granite Valley Herald*. Did you see the article, or hear about it?"

"Yes."

"Do you have any idea who might have made that call and sent those threats?"

She shrugged.

"Is there any possibility it's you?" I asked.

"Anything's possible," she said.

"Are you telling me you did?"

"I'm not telling you anything. You're the private detective. I don't want to spoil the fun for you."

"This isn't a game, Mrs. Havens."

"Oh, I know that," she said. "Anyway, it doesn't really matter who's doing it. The point is, someone is."

"As in, 'It's a dirty job, but someone has to do it'?"

"Someone has to do it. But it's not so dirty. It's well deserved."

"Do you really think your husband killed those children?"

She shrugged again. "I know he killed mine."

"And you still hate him for it?"

"Yes," she said matter-of-factly. She looked at me for a moment. "And now I think I've had enough of this conversation. Good-bye."

She turned her back on me, grabbed a garden rake that had been

58

leaning against some bushes, and started raking clipped leaves and twigs into a pile. As I stood there, watching her, I felt something brush against my leg. It was the golden cat. It looked perky and playful. I picked it up, and began petting it.

"Those are nice gladiolas," I said, referring to the flowers in a bed next to where Mrs. Havens was working.

I waited to see if she would respond. When I was just about sure she wouldn't, she said, without turning, "Are you a gardener?"

"No. I did plant a bunch of fruit trees and bushes at my place. But no flowers. They're too complicated and take too much time."

"They do take a lot of time," she said, pinching a bunch of leaves between one hand and the rake and depositing the leaves into the wheelbarrow. "You know about flowers, though."

"Not really," I said. "I know about gladiolas because my wife loved them. I know the star jasmine because I put some in at a friend's recommendation. I know the sunflowers from paintings. And, of course, I know those flowers to the right of the gladiolas are daisies."

"They're marguerites," she said.

"See how complicated this stuff is. What are those flowers over there—those pink and purple ones?"

She glanced at me, then along the line of my outstretched arm.

"They're petunias," she said.

"And those yellow, kind of spiky ones?"

"Dahlias."

"They're all very nice."

Mrs. Havens began walking back toward me, her eyes on the cat in my arms. She stopped just in front of me, reached out, and petted the cat.

"You're being pretty obvious, Mr. . . . uh . . ."

"Strickland," I said. "What do you mean?"

"I mean, you're here to get me to answer some questions, and you just happen to be fascinated by flowers and fond of cats. That's a little hard to swallow, don't you think?"

"Actually I don't like cats much," I said. "I like kittens and any cat that seems kittenish. This guy seems playful."

As if to illustrate the point, the cat began squirming in my arms. I

59

handed the cat over to Mrs. Havens, who stroked it twice and then put it down. She said, "They say men dislike cats because cats remind them of women and men basically dislike women."

"They say women all wish they had penises so they could be like men," I said. "There're a lot of those theories going around."

She gave a dry laugh. "I supposed that's true." She glanced around. "I suppose they'd also say that flowers and cats would be the natural consolations of a childless old woman."

"They probably would. But who cares. Anyway, you're a long way from being old."

"Not inside, I'm not." She looked at me. "You said your wife loved gladiolas—past tense. That means either your wife changed her taste in flowers or you are divorced. I'd guess the latter."

"My wife's dead."

She made no gesture of sympathy or apology. But her eyes widened with interest. "You have any children?" she asked.

"No," I said, not wanting to get into that.

But the woman seemed to read something in my face. "You had a child, though," she said.

"I don't think that's relevant to what we're talking about."

"You want me to talk to you, you've got to talk to me," she said. "You had a child who died?"

"Yes."

She made a small purring sound. Her eyes were bright and watchful, like those of a predator who's just seen something small and edible. "How did he die?"

"*She* died of crib death."

"How much later did your wife die?" she asked.

"A year."

Her eyes grew brighter. She was feeding off this. "And their deaths were connected?"

She was projecting her pain onto my life, and it just happened to fit. I didn't confirm the point, but she wasn't interested in my confirmation. She had her own fantasy now, and I was irrelevant. Her eyes shifted away, became dreamy.

"How she must have loved that child," she said. "She makes me feel shabby for still being alive. I guess you choose either sadness or hate. If you choose hate, like I did, it just won't let you go."

She drifted off into reverie. Her brow was furrowed, her eyes intent on things I couldn't see. After a few moments, she said, "I thought of killing myself. I still do. I suppose I don't because of cowardice. But there's something else, too. I feel that as long as I'm alive, my son is not quite dead—his memory is alive in me. If I go, he disappears with me. That seems wrong somehow. Someone ought to mark his life a little while longer."

"I know you loved your son very much," I said.

"Yes."

Her face softened as her eyes filled with memories. "Ricky was such a beautiful boy," she said. "I know every mother says that, but he was special. He was never a problem." She laughed. "Of course, I don't know what he could have done that I'd have considered a problem. I enjoyed everything about him. He was my treasure. My dream come true."

She was, at most, half talking to me. The rest was reverie, a kind of dreamy litany.

"You waited a long time to have him," I said.

"I never meant to wait so long," she said. "I mean, I did wait until I was almost thirty to marry, but then I wanted children right away. Frank, my first husband, said he wanted children as well, but he thought we should wait a year or two to give us some time as a couple first. I agreed, but the 'year or two' kept stretching into more. One day, when I finally insisted, Frank told me he'd decided he didn't want children after all. I was so hurt and furious I could have killed him. I moved out, thinking he'd change his mind and come after me. He did come after me, but he didn't change his mind. When it became obvious he was willing to give me up rather than start a family, I divorced him.

"I had an unhappy, weepy year recovering from all that. And then I went husband hunting. It's an old-fashioned, derogatory phrase, but that's what I was doing. Or maybe, potential-father hunting, because getting married and having children was my real goal. I'd thought about becoming a single mother: I'd also thought of just marrying anyone I found reasonably likable in order to have children. But I decided I couldn't do either.

"I wasn't having much luck with my hunt. The men I dated just weren't right, and that included John. He was attractive and seemed like a nice enough guy, but he was superficial and too full of himself. I would have moved on to someone else, but then I found out I was pregnant. I knew if I kept the child, I would be raising it on my own or with a man I liked but didn't love. But I no longer cared about those other things. Now that I was pregnant, there was no way I wasn't going to have that baby. John had a fit. He kept after me to have an abortion, and finally I got so angry I told him to get out of my life."

None of this had been in Havens's book, but that was understandable. This episode would have been an embarrassment to both of them and without much point in term of the book's theme.

"But he came back," I said.

"Yes. About a month later. I didn't know if he was doing it just out of guilt or from some other motives, too, but I liked him for that. Just as I came to hate him for what he did later."

"I understand he was badly hurt trying to save your son."

My words seemed to dissolve her reverie. Her face hardened, and she glared at me.

"He should have died trying," she said. "He had no right to stop trying while Ricky was still alive. But the worst of it was, he let his son die so he could save other children."

"Have you read this book?" I asked.

"Of course. Have you?"

"I've read the first few chapters. You don't accept your husband's explanation for why he went to help those children?"

"I don't accept much of anything my husband says, Mr. Strickland. He's always got his reasons; I don't care what they are. Your first duty is to your own child. You brought that child into the world, and that child depends on you and trusts you, and you have no right to put anything ahead of that child's life."

Her gaze seemed to dare me to disagree. I said nothing.

"And now he's making money off the child he let die," she said bitterly. "Parading out his own suffering—making himself out to be an expert on it. My husband doesn't know what real suffering is."

"Have you done anything to try to ease your own suffering?" I asked.

For a moment she looked at me as if she didn't understand the question. Then she shrugged. "I saw a therapist for a while. It didn't work out well. In the end she wanted me to give up my bitterness. But how could I give it up when it was all I had? She sent me to do volunteer work with children, hoping it would get me outside myself, maybe resurrect some maternal feeling. But all it did was make me more depressed. I didn't see why those children should be happy when my son was dead. And so I retreated to this." She gestured vaguely toward her garden.

"Your husband seems to have come to terms with what happened," I said.

She gave a hard laugh. "That makes him all the more contemptible," she said. "He has it all figured out, why his son's death was okay. But it's all just rationalization—empty men's logic. It means nothing next to a dead child. He has no right to explain away the death of my son."

She looked at me intently. "How about it, Mr. Strickland? Do you have some nice pat philosophy that helps you explain away the death of your wife and child?"

"No," I said. "I don't want one either."

"Good for you."

She gave me a crooked smile, conveying the sense that we were accomplices in something. In a way we were, both of us refusing to accept the world as it was. But I didn't like hearing my own words coming out of the mouth of this woman in whom bitterness lived like a metastasized cancer. I thought, by contrast, of the sense of peace that John Havens conveyed. And I realized, not for the first time, how tired I was of being angry.

I APPROACHED GRANITE Valley from the south, the more attractive approach since it gave a fuller view of the hills and the houses
set against them. I took the last exit and crossed over the highway,
keeping my eye on the tall sign for Denny's. I was supposed to meet
someone at Denny's at half past three, a Granite Valley police detective named Joe Witmer.

I didn't know Witmer; in fact, I hadn't talked to him yet. The appointment had been arranged by an old cop friend, Frank Ramirez. I
didn't know anyone at GVPD and had asked Frank to put in a word
for me. He'd gotten this Witmer to agree to meet me during his coffee break. I'd owe Frank one, though he'd already extracted some pay-
ment: Frank was an incessant talker and an inveterate joker, and the
two phone conversations I'd had with him had been marathons. Some
of the gossip had been good, though.

When I came off the exit, it was only three, and I decided I had
time to get gas. I pulled into one of the stations at the first intersection and began pumping regular unleaded into the Taurus I use when
I'm working. I glanced idly toward the full-service pumps, admiring
a red Toyota Supra and the attractive woman at the wheel. Then my
eye fell on the attendant pumping gas, and I nearly dropped the noz-
zle. This was like the worst sort of dark humor. Here I was in a town
where children were being burned to death, and the attendant at the
first gas station I pulled into was a convicted arsonist.

Earl Ritchie—Jesus.

I watched him, still in a state of shock. Ritchie, who was wearing a blue cotton work shirt with a pair of jeans, was dark haired, five ten, and wiry. He was thinner than I remembered him, and stronger looking, too; maybe he'd done his time pumping iron. He was now sporting stubble and a small earring.

Ritchie had torched a restaurant for a Korean family who'd decided to ditch their Asian work ethic for a little Yankee ingenuity. I'd been hired by the company that insured the restaurant, and it had been my investigative work that had led to Ritchie's arrest and conviction. If I remembered correctly, Ritchie had drawn an eight-year sentence, tough for an arsonist with no prior felonies.

Ritchie had been something of a character. His dream had been to become a country singer. His voice was okay, though nothing special, and his guitar playing consisted of good rhythm and a few chords, but there were plenty of singers who'd made it with those same qualifications. Ritchie was constantly begging bands to let him sit in and would appear for any bar's talent night he was eligible for. Consequently, a fair amount of my investigation had been spent in local country bars— something I didn't mind because I like country music. In fact, it had been in one of those bars where I'd found the man who'd actually hired Ritchie. I'd learned later from the police that Ritchie had had a habit of humming during pauses in their interrogation. There was one line he'd hummed so often that the police detectives got so they could hum it, too. I heard about this from one detective who claimed he was going crazy trying to figure what song it was. I was able to save the cop's sanity and give him a good story to boot: The line was from an old George Strait love song, "A Fire I Can't Put Out."

When my tank was full, I walked over to the full-service area where Ritchie was filling out the credit card charge for the driver of the Supra. I waited until he'd handed the credit card and receipt back to the woman, then thrust a twenty at him.

"Ritchie," I said. "It's been a long time."

He glanced at my face with guarded interest and gave no sign of recognition. He opened the cash drawer and began collecting my change. "Do I know you?" he asked.

"I was the insurance investigator." As his head shot up, I said, "I'm wearing a little extra hair till some head injuries heal," I said.

He stared hard at my face, as if trying to strip away the wig and the

65

beard in his mind's eye. Maybe he was stripping away the years as well. His eyes became more intense, and his face seemed to darken.

"Strickland," he said quietly, as if to himself. Then his eyes met mine staring back. He started, his manner suddenly flustered. "What're you doing here?" he asked.

"Just getting some gas. The real question is, what are you doing here? A town where kids are burning, and they've got an arsonist pumping gas? How come the cops haven't put you in jail or run you out of town?"

Ritchie was wincing as I spoke. He was moving his body slightly, and I realized that he was positioning himself between me and the office window, as if he were worried about someone reading my lips. He had his palms out in a placating gesture.

"Keep your voice down, will you, man? I'm clean—the cops checked me out. But I can't afford any hassles. Mike—the manager— he's been fair with me, but with everything going on, it wouldn't take much for them to dump my ass out of here."

"I'm not here to hassle you," I said, lowering my voice. "You say the cops checked you out?"

"You kidding? After that first kid died, they came down on me like whores in heat. And after the second one, too. They checked me out every which way. I'm clean. Hell, I torched that place for money. That don't mean I'd do something sick like what's going on around here."

"How long you been in Granite Valley?"

"About a year and a half. You know, new start and all that kind of stuff. My PO said I'd be better off getting away from my old friends. He was right. And this isn't too bad a place, really."

"Your family here with you?"

Pain stirred within his dark eyes. "Naw," he said. "There's no way that girl was going to wait all that time for me to get out. She took off with the kid about a year after I went in. I still don't know where they are."

"I'm sorry," I said.

"That's the breaks," he said in a voice that had lost its tone. He looked over his shoulder at a Dodge pickup pulling up to one of the pumps. "Look," he said, "I got to go."

"Me, too," I said, realizing, with a quick glance at my watch, that

I was close to being late. "Maybe I'll see you again."

I hadn't meant anything by that remark, but it stopped him in his tracks.

"Don't come back here again, man. Please. You'll just get me into trouble. You got to talk to me about something, I'm in the book." His expression changed into something lighter. "Or, you want to catch some good music, I'm singing at a bar over in Bear Creek every Sunday."

"You finally made it, huh?"

He shrugged and grinned at the same time. "I just sub for the regular singer sometimes. He's taking Sundays off this summer so he and his new old lady can get away some. It's a kick for me, man."

"You're off parole, I take it."

"Yeah. As of four-five months ago. You gotta excuse me now."

I got into my car and drove up the street to Denny's. I yielded to a bus pulling out, then parked in the nearly empty lot. I glanced at my watch and saw that it was 3:33 P.M. I got out of the car and hurried inside.

The stools at the counter were all empty. I glanced over the booths with their green fabric backs and pinkish brown vinyl seats; the booths were mostly empty. At a booth near the front a brown-haired woman in her thirties was sitting over a cup of coffee doing paperwork. It struck me that she resembled someone I knew, but I couldn't figure out whom. Three booths farther on two nearly identical high school girls with long dirt-blond hair were chatting over hamburgers. In a couple of booths toward the back was a middle-aged couple in summer wear and two men in suits. I stood there for a moment, waiting to see if anyone seemed to be waiting for me. No one did. Perhaps he was late.

To be safe, I asked the waitress who approached me with a menu if she knew a police detective named Witmer.

"Sure," she said brightly. "She's right over there." She pointed at the woman doing paperwork.

"That's Joe Witmer?" I asked.

"Yes," she said. "JoAnn Witmer."

"Oh," I said.

I looked at the woman again. She was maybe middle thirties, short brown hair, a bit stocky; she had a round face, nice features, healthy-looking skin. Over a white collarless blouse she wore a blue seersucker jacket with the sleeves rolled back. She glanced up once in my direction, without expression, and went back to her paperwork. Once again it struck me that she looked like someone I knew; it would come to me eventually if there was anything to it.

I was still thrown off a bit by the fact that this detective was a woman. My assuming Witmer was a man was understandable, since female police detectives were still a rarity. But why hadn't I been told by Ramirez? Had this been one of his jokes or hadn't he known himself?

I walked over to the woman's booth. "Excuse me," I said. "Are you Detective Witmer?"

She nodded, her expression both polite and a little wary.

"I'm Dave Strickland," I said. "The investigator you agreed to meet."

Her expression turned into a glare. "Is this some kind of joke?"

"What do you mean?" I asked, puzzled.

"I mean, I know Dave Strickland."

"You know me?"

"I know Strickland, and you're not him." She slid out of the booth and stood, taking a step back from me. "What's going on?"

My brain was totally muddled now. This male detective, who was actually a female, claimed to know me, even though I didn't know her, and was telling me I wasn't me. Because I was trying to answer too many questions at once, it took me a couple of seconds longer than it should have to provide her with an obvious piece of the puzzle. I said, "The reason I don't look like me is because of this wig and this beard. I got my head banged up pretty badly, and I had surgery, and they had to shave my head."

Witmer's blue eyes narrowed as she studied me. After a moment, she nodded, and I could see the muscles in her face relax.

"Yeah, it's you," she said without visible enthusiasm. "What happened?"

"I was chasing someone and got blind-sided—shoved over a small cliff onto some rocks."

"Must have hurt," she said without visible sympathy.

"Yeah."

She sat down, and I sat across from her. The waitress, an older woman with her hair back in a bun, poured me some coffee. The waitress refilled Witmer's cup, and asked me if I wanted anything to eat. I told her, maybe later.

"You don't remember me, huh?" asked Witmer after the waitress had gone.

"Well . . . I guess I do, sort of," I said. "You look familiar. Where would we have met?"

"Oh, around," she said. "It's not important."

Important or not, she didn't look too happy with me. I was about to ask her where she'd worked before when she said, "What do you want?"

That threw me off. If Ramirez had set this up right, she should have known.

"I thought Sergeant Ramirez would have told you all that. Or maybe you didn't talk to him personally."

"Oh, I talked to him," she said.

So the SOB had known Witmer was a woman. If he'd told me, maybe my mind would have come up with a memory before I'd gotten here, and I wouldn't be making such an ass out of myself.

"He said you wanted to talk to me about John Havens," she said. "What I don't understand is, why I'm not talking to his attorney."

"I suggested they have their attorney handle this, but since they'd already hired me on another matter, they—"

"What other matter?"

"To look into those threatening letters that Havens has been getting. You familiar with them?"

"Yes."

"I'd also like to find out who made that anonymous call."

"Why do you care who the caller was?"

"Because it might be the same person who's sending those threats."

"You're assuming the accusation is a fabrication."

"That or a delusion. How seriously are you taking it?"

"We're investigating it."

"Yeah, but, I mean, do you really think there's anything there?"

"We're investigating, Strickland. That's all I can tell you."

"Can't you help me out a little bit here?"

"Sorry."

"Do you know who made the call?"

"No. But if I did, I wouldn't tell you."

"Will you tell me if it's a man or a woman?"

"No."

I decided to try a different tack. "Can we talk a little bit about the murders? I've been sort of out of things the last few months with this head injury."

"The only stuff I can talk about is the stuff that's public knowledge, and it's all in the back issues of the *Herald* and the *Santa Cruz Sentinel*," she said. "Try the library."

"I guess I will," I said.

In different circumstances I would have assumed Witmer was a cop too full of herself or maybe just unsure of herself, who was trying to hide her insecurity behind a phony toughness. But I sensed that there was more going on here, a real hostility toward me. Had we met on some sort of case before? Had I stepped on her toes in some way? I kept hoping memory would help me out, but so far, nothing.

"I can't talk about the homicide investigation, but I can talk about the threats," she said. Maybe she'd decided she'd been overdoing it a bit and wanted to send me away with something. "Not that we've got all that much. We did dust the letters. The only clear prints we got belonged to Havens."

"You doing anything on it?" I asked.

"Nothing much we can do. Nothing to go on."

All of a sudden her face broke into a beautiful smile, though not for me. She was looking to the side and behind me, waving at someone. The smile stirred something in my memory, but nothing specific came to me.

"Hey, Carol," Witmer called.

"Hi, Jo," said a thin voice.

There was movement behind me, and a woman came into view, a slender, gray-haired woman with a nice face. She was wearing jeans and a white cotton top, and she was carrying a Louise Erdrich novel.

"What you up to?" asked Witmer.

"Just killing a little time," said the woman, gesturing with her novel. "I'm supposed to meet Leslie in forty-five minutes."

"How is she?"

"Much better," said the woman. "I think she's just about over the worst of it."

"I'm really glad to hear that."

The woman glanced at me, and I nodded to her. I expected Witmer to introduce us, but Witmer just said, "I saw Bill the other day," and went right on talking. I was going to introduce myself anyway, but the woman was turned away from me now toward Witmer, and I decided, what the hell. Since I didn't want to sit there looking like a dummy, and craning my neck to boot, I turned toward the windows. There were a couple of advertising cards set in plastic, one for hologram baseball cards, and another for desserts. Some of the desserts looked pretty good, and I realized that I was hungry. Somehow ordering dessert while sitting here with Witmer seemed like a ludicrous idea. I tried to imagine myself stuffing down a piece of chocolate cream pie under the eyes of this grim, maybe diet-conscious, guardian of the peace.

I laughed to myself at the thought. At that same moment, Witmer laughed at something her friend had said. It was a really nice laugh, unguarded, young, laced with a kind of giggle. Another surprise from my grim cop. I glanced at Witmer and got some flash of memory. I turned away from the women and looked inward, trying to catch it.

The memory was bathed in darkness. I thought at first I simply wasn't remembering well, but as I concentrated I realized that this was a memory of a dark place, a memory laced with alcohol. I was in a cop bar, sitting around bullshitting with some guys I'd worked with before I'd gone out on my own. This was some months after Katie's death, and I hadn't wanted to be alone—or sober for that matter. There were two—no, three—other guys, and a couple of female cops who'd just joined us. One of the male cops was bragging me up to the women, partly to boost me up, partly to brag himself up as well, since the two of us had worked together for a while. I danced later with one of the women—a blond—not Witmer's color, but then colors could change. The face, from what I could see of it through memory, had been similar. We'd talked and danced some more, then left for . . .

Oh, shit.

I turned quickly toward Witmer, who was looking back over her right shoulder, saying some last thing to her friend, who was moving on. I looked hard at Witmer's face. *Please,* I thought, *tell me I didn't sleep with this woman, and then forget. This woman I'm supposed to use my connections to get information from.*

I did.

Strickland, you turkey.

Witmer was turning back to me now, all the brightness draining from her face. As her eyes met mine, I said, "JoAnn, I'm sorry I didn't remember you."

"Don't call me JoAnn. You call me Detective."

"I'm really sorry I didn't remember you."

"Came to you in a flash, did it?"

"More like a muddle," I said.

"Hard to keep track of us all, I guess."

There was a slight smile on her lips, but there was absolutely no humor in it. And no mercy in her eyes. Of all the people I had to run into.

"It's not that," I said. "Normally I'm not this much of a jerk. My wife had killed herself that year. I wasn't functioning very well. And I was drinking way too much."

"Do you remember that we went to bed together twice?" she asked.

"Yes," I said, lying.

"I doubt it," she said.

"Weren't you? . . ." I made some sort of gesture toward my head. "Your hair . . ."

"I was blond then," she said in a tone of grudging concession.

"Well, there . . . you go . . . and maybe you were . . ."

"I'm a little heavier now, if that's what you're trying to say."

It wasn't, but I'd take anything I could get. Witmer glared at me as if the weight gain were somehow my fault.

"Well, see," I said, "maybe that's . . ."

"Strickland, you prick."

There wasn't much to say to that, and I didn't. We looked at each other for a moment, then Witmer began gathering up the paperwork spread out in front of her.

"Wait a minute," I said. "Can't we talk a minute? I don't want to leave it like this."

Her hands stopped their gathering, but otherwise she made no response.

"Look, I really am sorry," I said. "I can understand why you're pissed off. I would be, too. But I wish you'd try to understand what kind of shape I was in."

"Strickland," she said, "don't waste your time trying to soften me up. It's not going to work, and I'm not giving you a goddamn thing on this case."

I leaned toward her, putting my forearms on the table. "Let's forget about the case," I said. "I'll tell them to have their lawyer talk to you. Better yet, I'll recommend they get some other investigator. I'm not going to do them any good if I can't work with the local police. And resigning is really okay with me. I was reluctant to take the case in the first place."

"Why?"

"Nothing about the case. I thought it was a little too early after my surgery to be doing this kind of stuff. I was probably right."

Witmer nodded, not saying anything.

"So the case isn't an issue," I said. "How have you been?"

"Okay," she said, her voice flat.

"How long you been in Granite Valley?"

"Couple of years."

"You like it here?"

"Yeah."

"Why'd you leave San Jose?"

"Different reasons. Pay's better, for one."

Witmer's eyes were working hard, perhaps appraising me, perhaps trying to decide if she wanted to have this conversation. Her laconic answers seemed to be a temporary compromise between giving in and walking out.

"Congratulations on making detective," I said. "You sure got promoted fast."

Her eyes narrowed. "What are you implying?"

"Jesus—I wasn't *implying* anything," I said. "I was just trying to make conversation. I could use a little help."

Witmer's face seemed to soften just a touch. "Making detective isn't such a big deal," she said. "It's a revolving position here, like it is in a lot of small departments."

"Yeah, but not everybody revolves into it, and some guys wait years. How many patrol officers they got here?"

"Sixteen."

"How many women?"

"I'm it."

"You get a lot of resentment from the guys when you got promoted?"

"Some, but it helped the way it happened. There was a series of rapes here. One of the victims refused to talk to any of the men. I talked to her and followed up and got the guy. It happened a second time, and the chief decided it was important to have a 'woman's touch,' so he made me detective. Some guys didn't want anything to do with sexual assault. And a lot of the guys here like being in the field—they're not much interested in all the desk time and paperwork. But like I said, some guys were pissed."

"How many detectives in the department?"

"There are supposed to be two, but the other guy's on disability leave."

"So you're on this thing all by yourself?"

"Two of the bodies were found on county land, so the sheriff's in on it, too."

"They cooperating with you?"

"Yeah. There's a mandatory task-force approach here in Santa Cruz County that's really good—sheriff's people, local people, and an assistant DA. So I'm not getting cut out of any information. Of course, cooperating with someone and taking them seriously are two different things."

Witmer's eyes turned reflective for a moment, and then she looked back at me. Her face closed up. I wondered if she regretted talking as much as she had. She glanced down at her watch. "I've got to get out of here."

"Me, too," I said.

I got a dollar out of my wallet, fished a couple of quarters out of my pocket, and put the money on the table.

"That should cover my coffee, and my part of the tip," I said as I slid out of the booth and stood up. "I'm glad things worked out for you. And I'm sorry about that other thing."

I turned and took a couple of steps toward the door.

"Strickland, wait," Witmer called out behind me.

I turned around.

"Come back here a second."

I returned to the booth, and Witmer gestured at me to sit down. When I was seated, she said, "I'm not going to give you anything on the case that isn't public knowledge, but I'm not going to do any better for a lawyer or any other investigator Havens and his group might send around. Whatever my personal feelings toward you, I know you were a good, honest cop. That's better than I'm likely to get if they send in someone else. What I'm saying is, there's no reason you can't continue working for Havens. I won't let my personal feelings affect my behavior professionally."

"Thanks," I said. "I appreciate it."

"You should read those newspapers, but what's public knowledge is basically this: three children murdered, between the ages of two and eight. The first was taken from woods behind his house, the second from her backyard, and the third from a deserted road. The children were given an inhalant we're not naming to knock them out, then taken to the woods and burned to death. We managed to get the man who discovered the second body not to talk to the media, but those who discovered the first and third bodies said there was a fuel can next to each victim, a trail of burned rope that looked like a kind of fuse, and remnants of rope and tape apparently used to bind and gag each victim. They also saw numbers lying next to the bodies."

"What do you mean, numbers?"

"In one case, the witness said the numbers looked like the kind you buy to put on front doors or mailboxes. There were six of them lying next to the body of that victim."

"Some kind of ritual killing?"

Witmer shrugged.

"I'm surprised that business about the inhalant is public knowledge," I said. "There was no way witnesses could have known about that."

"We didn't want people thinking that the kids were conscious when they were set on fire."

"Yeah, I can see that. Are you willing to tell me if you've eliminated any of Havens's group as suspects?"

Witmer thought about it for a moment. "I suppose it wouldn't hurt," she said. "You'll be getting the stories from them anyhow. Havens is not eliminated. Mrs. Bennett is eliminated—in the sense that she has an alibi for at least one killing. What's the name of that night nurse?"

"Raley. Karen Raley."

"We've eliminated her."

"What about her husband? Ken, I think his name is."

"The one that sits around staring into space all day? No, He's not eliminated. Neither are that sculptor and his wife—the Malanders."

"What about the Caldwells?"

"They're that young couple?"

"Yes."

"They're okay."

"I assume you know you've got a convicted arsonist pumping gas down at the intersection."

"Yes. How do you know him?"

"I did the investigation for the insurance company. I was the one who turned him over to the cops."

"Answer a question for me. Looking over his file, I couldn't believe the sentence he got for a first felony conviction. What was the story there?"

"I was trying to remember myself. It seems to me he got some judge who was on an election year tough-on-crime kick."

"Tough for Ritchie, not too bad for the rest of us," said Witmer.

"I suppose. Ritchie told me you guys had looked at him and he had alibis."

"A couple of solid ones." Once again, a glance at the watch. "I really have to go." Witmer pushed her papers together and slipped them into the briefcase.

"Would you be willing to tell me whether that anonymous call was made by a man or a woman?" I asked. "It might really help me in investigating the threats."

"You didn't hear it from me," she said. "It's a man."

"Damn," I said. "Thanks."

She looked up. "Why the 'damn'?"

"It eliminates my best suspect. At least, it eliminates her from being both the caller and the person making the threats."

"Who?"

"The wife."

"What's her story?"

"You haven't read Havens's book?"

"No."

"She blames him for their son's death. He left the boy alone in the apartment while he went down to the basement, though he did have an intercom. That's not the main thing, though; she did that, too. The main thing is that in trying to get to his son, he stopped for a few minutes to save some children who were about to burn. He thought it was safe—thought his son was all right—but by the time he got finished saving the other kids, his own apartment was an inferno. The delay might not have made a difference, but there's no way to know."

"She's still angry at him?"

"Very."

"Interesting."

We both stood up, Witmer leaving my dollar on the table and picking up the two quarters along with the check. Our waitress met us at the cash register and rang up the two coffees.

"How's that cute little girl of yours?" asked the waitress.

Witmer grinned. "Great."

"Marissa, right?"

"Right."

"I haven't seen her in a couple of weeks. You bring her back now."

"Thanks," said Witmer, "I will."

As we walked to the door, I said, "You have a daughter?"

"My partner does."

I didn't know if I should hold the door for Witmer, so I compromised by letting her go first.

"Your partner—is he a cop?" I asked as we were passing between the inner and outer doors.

Witmer said something that I knew I couldn't have heard right.

"You say he isn't?"

"I said, no *she* isn't."

We were outside now, walking almost side by side, with Witmer just slightly ahead. This was one of those surprise situations where your brain ceases to function, leaving you twisting in the wind, feeling like a jerk. What do you say? "My God, you mean you're a lesbian!" wouldn't exactly be the height of sophistication. "That's cool" would sound pretty lame. My mind finally settled for "Oh."

Witmer glanced back and gave me a sarcastic smile.

"Don't look now, Strickland, but your mouth is hanging open."

"I'm sorry," I said. "You kind of caught me by surprise. I mean, I didn't think . . . you know, because we . . ."

"You were the last, Strickland. After you, I knew I'd had enough of men."

Witmer marched off toward her car without another look back. I stared after her.

I assume my mouth was still hanging open.

9

I'D SPENT THE last two hours in the small Granite Valley library going through old copies of the *Santa Cruz Sentinel* and the *Granite Valley Herald*. I'd been reading the accounts of the murders of the three children, seeing what I could add to the quick summary Witmer had given me and what I had gotten from the Malanders and Caldwells.

The first victim, Jimmy Malander, age six, had been killed back in February. The boy had disappeared while playing in the woods behind his house in Bear Creek and his burned body had been found in an old quarry on county land the next day by some sixteen-year-old kids who'd gone off looking for a place to picnic and drink. The teenagers had been interviewed by the press and a number of things had emerged of the sort Witmer had mentioned: There'd been tape over the victim's mouth and remnants of tape around his ankles and wrist; there'd been a gas can next to the body and a trail of burned rope that looked like "a kind of fuse." The kids agreed that there had been some gold-colored numbers next to the body, but they couldn't agree on what the numbers had been except that there'd been some twos.

The Santa Cruz Sheriff's Department had handled the case. The department had been a lot less talkative than the teenagers, simply giving the basic information and promising an intensive investigation. After the appropriate tests results were in, they announced at a press conference that the dead boy had been drugged into unconsciousness before being burned and wouldn't have suffered in the fire. It had been the one comforting factor in an otherwise shocking murder.

The second victim, Corinne Caldwell, age fourteen months, had been taken from her backyard in April. Her burned body had been found in a ravine the next day; since the ravine was in Granite Valley, that had brought the GVPD into the investigation. The hiker who'd found the body had refused to be interviewed by the media, saying that the police had asked him not to talk about what he'd observed at the scene. Once again it was reported that the child had been drugged before being burned.

The newspaper articles between the second and third killings talked about the formation of a task force involving both county and city officers, gave optimistic forecasts and rumors of arrest, and finally settled down to reporting lack of progress.

The third killing had been a month ago, in June. The victim had been eight-year-old Peter Kiedrich, his parents, Arthur and Greta; the father's occupation was given as Unitarian minister. The boy had apparently been abducted while riding his bicycle alone on a deserted road against his parents's orders; the bike, slightly damaged and showing a small smear of the boy's blood, had been in the woods just off the road. As I already knew from my earlier reading, this boy's burning corpse had been found by a man who had a cabin nearby; the police had speculated that the murderer hadn't known about the cabin, which was out of the way and surrounded by lots of vegetation. Obviously the police hadn't had any luck keeping the man, Fred Patton, from talking: Patton had given a number of interviews.

In addition to talking about his shock in finding a burning (by then already dead) child, Patton mentioned that the boy had been gagged with tape and bound with ropes and that there'd been a gas can next to the body. He said he'd seen some silver-colored numbers lying on the ground next to the body, but said he'd been too shocked to notice what the specific numbers had been.

I glanced at my watch and saw it was time to go. I had appointments in Bear Creek with Ed Garza, the newspaper man, and a little later, with the Malanders.

The road from Granite Valley to Bear Creek started out among condos and shopping centers, moved north past a deserted quarry and a solitary bar, then ascended into sandy hills pierced with old quarry cuts. High up in the hills was a working quarry, with cranes and metal sheds and a huge pit ribbed with tracks for the trucks to drive.

The road made some long, graceful curves, the quarries disappeared, and the hills became a thicker, richer green. Farther on, the road began to descend toward treetops and glimpses of town. The road ended in a T, with a shopping center left and a field of horses right; straight ahead was a park with an old covered bridge.

I took a right, then a left, and there was the town—a stretch of low wooden and stucco buildings set against a pine-covered ridge. I passed a hamburger stand, then a seedy-looking bar called Beer Creek, with two Harleys parked in front and a sign advertising Live Country Music; that had to be the bar where Ritchie sometimes played. Farther down, across the street, was a market with a quaint side-wall mural of a horse and wagon and a covered bridge; the market sign advertised Organic Produce and Natural Meats. Just beyond the market, I came to a stop behind an old gray Dodge waiting to make a left turn toward an office offering Acupuncture, Nutrition, and Herbology. A Chevy pickup, going too fast, squeezed by us on the right, showing a bumper sticker that read, "Gun control means using both hands." I shook my head at the contrasts, intrigued as always by the odd combination of hippies and hillbillies found in so many of these small northern California towns.

There were more businesses farther on: an espresso shop, a vegetarian restaurant, a gourmet pizza parlor, and several gift shops displaying wooden ducks and mounds of sachet. In the midst of this variety, as immune from fashion as a fossil, sat the Christian Science Reading Room.

I drove past a bank and a bowling alley, saw that the downtown was behind me, and decided I'd missed what I was looking for. I was about to turn around when I saw a sign that said News/Herald, and pulled off the road.

The isolated gray building looked like a lean-to with windows. It housed, in addition to the newspaper, a pet-food store and a beauty shop. The far side of Bear Creek seemed an odd location for the *Granite Valley Herald,* but apparently the publisher had begun with the more generic *Inland News* and added the *Herald* later when a suddenly prosperous Granite Valley had seemed to warrant its own paper.

I parked on a small gravel strip just in front of the building. From what I could see through the windows, the newspaper office was mostly one large room, with a single cubicle at the front left corner. A squat, swarthy man sat at a desk in the cubicle. He looked my way briefly as I got out of my car. I assumed the man was Garza, who was the editor of the *Herald* as well as the writer who'd done the article on Havens. I'd called earlier to request a meeting, and Garza had readily agreed, though he'd tried to get more over the phone than I'd been willing to give him.

I walked across the gravel strip and into the office. Beyond a small reception counter were several desks, all empty; there were only two people in the room, a man and woman at the back standing in front of an artist's board, doing some sort of layout work. The woman waved and said she'd be right with me.

Copies of the *Inland News* and the *Granite Valley Herald* sat on the counter in front of me. The papers were fairly substantial, and even given the fact that they shared some articles, putting these papers out daily would have to be a sizable job; I wondered how it was managed out of this near-empty office. I supposed that with the reporters having computers and faxes and with the printing being done elsewhere, this office would be used only for editing and ad work.

When the woman came to the front, I told her I was there to see Garza, and she disappeared behind a partition off to my left. I glanced over the front page of the *Herald*. Today's article on the investigation carried Garza's byline. The article, a catalog of nonresults, included references to the investigation of Havens and his group. Whether from animus or editorial desperation, Garza wasn't letting up on that one.

The woman came back and led me to the corner office. The man I'd seen through the front window stood up as I entered, introducing himself as Ed Garza. He was short, brown, and heavyset, wearing rumpled gray slacks and a white dress shirt with a crew-neck T-shirt showing at the open collar. On a coat rack just inside the door hung a blue seersucker jacket and a tie, tied but loosened, that could be put on by putting one's head through the loop. Dress for the active newsman, I supposed.

The small office was a total mess. Part of the problem was the lack of space, but it wasn't only that. On Garza's desk, surrounding the

Macintosh that sat in the center of it, was a clutter of papers and files, knickknacks and snacks, with no attempt at order. On the bookshelves above the desk, books lay flat or tilted against one another, as if someone had just borrowed the bookends. On a table on the other side of the desk were spilled piles of newspapers and files. On the thick window dividers that protruded into the room like thin shelves were a Dr. Pepper can, a plastic Slurpy cup, a candy bar, and a roll of paper towels. Maybe Garza was cultivating the image of the frantic or eccentric editor. Or maybe the guy was just a slob.

I took a seat on a straight chair next to Garza's desk and handed him my business card.

" 'Dave Strickland, Private Investigations,' " he read. He looked up. "You say you've been hired by John Havens?"

"On his behalf, yes."

"He didn't hire you himself?"

"No."

"His attorney?"

"No."

"Then who? . . ."

Before he finished the question, he answered it himself. "Sylvia Bennett," he said with a look of disgust.

It wasn't a question, and Garza didn't even look at me for confirmation. He thought about it for a moment, not getting any happier, then refocused on me.

"So what does Havens need an investigator for?" he asked.

"He's been getting threats."

"What kind of threats?"

"Death threats," I said. "Anonymous letters."

I hadn't been sure if Garza knew about the threats. Since he didn't, I was happy to tell him. His knowing might get him thinking about Havens in a different light. Anything that helped take the heat off Havens could be considered part of my job.

A fact that didn't escape him. He said, "So it turns out this guy who's been accused of murder has been getting death threats. Convenient. How do I know you're not just making this up to divert attention?"

"You could check with the police."

"The police are investigating these threats?"

"I'm not sure how much investigating they're doing," I said. "But they came out to Havens's house, did a report, and took the letters."

"When was this?"

"A couple of weeks ago—before the anonymous call was made. I don't know the exact date, but it'll be on the report."

Garza picked up a pencil and started scribbling something. As he wrote, he said, "So this is why you came here—to tell me about the threats?"

"I wanted to ask you if you had any idea who might have made the anonymous call."

"No," he said, still writing. "I don't."

"Would you like to know?"

"Of course." Garza put aside his pencil and looked up. "I can understand you and Havens wanting to know the accuser's name, but I'm not sure knowing it would do you much good. It won't stop the police from investigating Havens."

"You're right, but I'm coming at this from a different direction: I'm thinking the caller may be the one who's sending the threats."

Garza seemed taken aback. He frowned, considering the idea. After a moment, he shook his head. "I don't see how that would make sense. It seems to me you'd do one thing or the other—go after Havens yourself or try to get the police to do it. You'd be working against yourself if you tried to do both at once."

"Unless it's all just harassment."

"You're assuming, of course, that the accusation is false," said Garza. "That's what you're paid to do. But it could be that the caller is making the accusation because he has good reasons to believe Havens is guilty."

"If he had good reasons, he'd have given them to the police instead of backing up his accusation with that absurd pair of statements about the children's parents being part of Havens's group and Havens's son having died in a fire."

"What's so absurd about those statements? Both are true, and they could be relevant to the murders."

"What's absurd is that if you put the statements together as support for the accusation, the implication is that Havens and his group are a diabolical cult devoted to murdering children. That's a little tough to swallow, isn't it? You know Sylvia Bennett, don't you? Does she strike you as a good candidate for a murder cult?"

"Yes."

I did a double-take before I realized this grim-looking man was kidding me.

"Gotcha," said Garza, a small smile creeping into his face. "Yeah, I'm joking. But if either of them needs a character reference, don't bother coming to me. The three of us aren't the best of friends, as I'm sure they told you."

"That's hardly reason enough to accuse Mrs. Bennett of murder."

"Whoa, now, wait a minute," said Garza, holding up his hands in a mock defensive posture. "I didn't make up the story. I just reported it. As soon as the police lay off, I lay off, too."

"Why don't you try something more useful?"

"Like what?"

"Like trying to figure out who's threatening Havens. Like trying to find out who made that phone call."

"In other words, you want me to do your job."

"Do a little investigative reporting. You find something, share it with me, and I'll share with you, and you might get a pretty good story out of it."

"I'll think about it," said Garza.

"Good."

"Let's get back to the accusation," he said. "You're trying to dismiss the whole thing, but I'm not sure it's just a coincidence that Havens's son died in a fire and now someone's going around burning children to death."

"I'm not sure it's coincidence either," I said. "But I think if there is a connection, it's with the description of the boy's death in Havens's book. To me the fact of the book points away from Havens, not toward him. Why advertise the episode if you're going to go around duplicating it? On the other hand, it's not so hard to imagine some psycho reading the book and getting excited by the idea of children burning to death. Since there must be thousands of people who know about the incident through reading Havens's book or seeing him on TV or hearing him lecture, that makes for a hell of a lot of suspects."

"What about the fact that the parents of two of the children are in Havens's group?"

"I don't see how that could relate to the identity of the murderer, apart from that absurd murder-cult scenario. The accuser seems to have cause and effect backwards. The parents joined the group after their children were killed, not before, and that was perfectly natural given that Havens, as a result of his own grief, works with grief-stricken parents."

"So you're assuming that the caller is just someone who jumped to the wrong conclusion?" asked Garza.

"It's a possibility. It's also possible that the caller is someone who knows Havens isn't guilty, but hates him for some reason and wants to cause him pain."

"You have any ideas on that?"

"No," I said, having no intention of discussing Ruth Havens with Garza. "Another possibility is that the caller's animosity is primarily toward someone in Havens's group and only toward Havens indirectly. It's even possible that the caller is the killer trying to focus suspicion on Havens—which would make some sense if the killer had read Havens's book. Though in that case I don't know how the death threats would fit in."

"Maybe they're not supposed to fit in," said Garza. "Maybe the caller and the letter-writer are two different people."

"Maybe."

"In fact—and this is just off the top of my head—I don't think I'd focus on the caller if I were you. I think it's more likely that the caller is just someone who believes, rightly or wrongly, that Havens is guilty."

"Why do you think that?"

"Partly it's just a feeling. Partly it's what I said before. I don't see someone going both the police route and the death-threat route. If you focus too much on the caller, and there are two people, you're going to miss the one that's a real danger to Havens."

"That's true."

"There's not much you can do about the accusation anyway, except wait for the police to find the killer." Garza smiled. "And, of course, hope it isn't Havens."

"The police may never find the killer. His type often doesn't get caught."

Garza's smile disappeared. "Don't say that," he said. "Don't even think it. We've got to get this nightmare over with."

10

WHEN I LEFT THE newspaper office, I drove away from town, toward the Malander place, which was just down the road. I'd talked to Susan Malander earlier in the day, telling her I'd try to stop by before my appointment with Garza; she'd said they'd probably be around afterward, if I didn't make it before. I thought of calling them now, but they were only five minutes away, and a pay phone might be as many minutes in the opposite direction. If they weren't home, at least I'd know where their house was for the next time.

A sign for a local state park was just ahead on the left. I turned right, away from the park, though it seemed as if the park spilled over onto this side of the road. There were huge redwoods, a crush of other trees, and thick underbrush. The homes here, mostly modest ranch-style structures, seemed dwarfed and out of place.

Very little sunlight reached the ground. On a warm July day like this one, the shade was wonderful. But come winter and rain, the houses here would be miserably cold and damp, with mold growing on everything.

After several twists and turns, I found the Malander house in the middle of a redwood grove. Except for some faded blue trim, the small house was the same red-brown color as the trees. In the yard, which was nothing but shade and dirt, there was an old redwood stump the size of a picnic table.

I parked on the street. A packed-earth driveway, pierced by a pipe, crossed a dry creek bed that lay between the house and the road. Set back from the house was a small garage, which obviously served as Malander's shop, since pieces of his work were arranged just outside it, either hung from a trestle or laid out on the ground. I heard rock music coming from the garage so I headed there first.

Inside the garage was a partition dividing front from back. The front area seemed to be for storage and display, the back for work. Through an opening at one end of the partition, I could see Malander wrapping black plastic around a head-sized object sitting on a table in front of him. I called to Malander twice over the now loud music before he heard me. He yelled back that he'd be right there.

As I waited outside, I was struck by something I'd noticed only subliminally a moment before. Most of the maybe forty pieces of art on display had the same woman's face I'd seen on the piece at Havens's house, the face with the classical features and the wild hair. Here it was on masks and busts, pots and plant stands. My first thought was that I'd stumbled onto the Colonel Sanders of sculptors, a guy who could do only one thing right. But there were other works, mostly masks, some styled on the primitive, others on the classical. Obviously all these pieces were being made from molds, then reproduced in whatever numbers Havens thought would sell. I supposed I could hardly expect the guy to rant and rave and tear at his hair for a month like some nineteenth-century romantic to produce a single work of art that would sell for fifty bucks and be put in someone's flower pot.

The music stopped, and I looked up to see Malander coming out of the garage. He was dressed in jeans and a work shirt, his clothing marked with what looked like bits of clay and smears of plaster dust. He gave me a small smile that did little to alter that same gloomy look I had seen in his face the other day.

"Hi," he said.

As he spoke, I caught a heavy smell of alcohol on his breath. He held his hands out, palms up. They were strong hands, marked with calluses and coated with clay. "I won't shake," he said. "My hands are a mess."

"This looks like a good place to work," I said. "This is your shop as well as your studio?"

"It's not a shop. We're not zoned for commercial here. I sell most of my stuff through stores."

"Then why display things?"

89

"Sometimes shop owners stop by to see what I've been up to." The small smile reappeared. "And maybe a few customers. But quietly. The neighbors are pretty cool about it. Each Christmas I give them something I've done."

"What are these pieces made of?" I asked. "Some kind of clay?"

"Cement, mostly. I do the original in clay, make a mold from that, and do the copies in cement."

"Why the reddish color?"

"I add a dye."

"Could I take a look at your work area?"

"Come on."

I followed Malander to the back of the garage. As I passed the partition, I blinked, hardly believing my eyes. It was as if a different artist had been at work back here in the dimmer light, an artist with taste and power. There were no duplicates here, only individualized pieces in a dark material, some ambiguous, some tragic, some grotesque. It was as if in moving from the front of the garage to the back, I had moved from heaven to hell, though not in the sense of good to bad, and not only in the sense of light to dark. During my one summer in Europe, while standing in a Renaissance church in Tuscany, a guide I'd overheard discussing frescoes had impressed me with an observation I'd later learned was commonplace, that the depictions of hell were usually more interesting and artistic than the depictions of heaven. I'd verified that observation for myself, later, in other churches. The figures in paradise often wore the same bland face, were locked in virtue and inactivity, and, in spite of the theological doctrines of heavenly ecstasy, looked bored as hell. In contrast, the damned were full of life, their faces etched with character, if bad character; the damned were denied looks of triumph or joy, but in their anger, their meanness, their loneliness, and their pain, they were much more accessible and human than those abstract figures that sat in judgment on them. It was as if suffering was the natural habitat of human beings, and while we might long for its absence, we couldn't seriously imagine a world without it.

"I'm impressed," I said. "These are great."

"A little better than the shit outside, huh?"

"No comparison."

I moved in to take a closer look. Several of the figures were bulbous and intentionally crude, full of unsmoothed ridges and depressions that suggested wounds or decay. The barely formed faces were menacingly skeletal or crudely militaristic or, in one case, half animal-like, suggesting creatures which had devolved, retaining only the worst aspects of human beings.

One piece in particular caught my attention. At first glance it seemed to portray a parent and a child in a domestic pose. The parent figure was sitting on the ground with his right knee raised, holding a child who sat in his lap. But the parent's face was skeletal and cruel, the child's face contorted in agony, as if the embrace were the embrace of death.

Next to that piece was another, the only one in this section of the garage that seemed to me awkwardly done, though I found it intriguing. On a base, a small figure lay in front of an upright piece of stone carved with a face both eerie and ambiguous. The figure looked like a bare-fisted fighter who'd simply toppled over sideways while maintaining his stance, so that even on the ground, his body was slightly bent and his fists were still extended. I was wondering if it was some sort of antiboxing thing, or something more symbolic about man being defeated by larger forces, when I remembered that the pugilistic stance is one automatically formed by very badly burned bodies. It was then I noticed how childlike the small figure seemed. Suddenly the piece took on the appearance of human sacrifice, a child being burned to death at the altar of some dark god. It occurred to me how perfectly the rough surface of the piece conveyed disfigurement by fire, though that must have been coincidental since the other pieces were rough-surfaced, too.

"How long have you been doing this kind of work?" I asked.

"I've always tried to do serious work, as well as the commercial crap. Until recently, though, it wasn't very good."

"Has the serious stuff always been this . . . grim?"

"It's always had a dark mood, though the mood's gotten darker in the last few months—for obvious reasons. But my work's gotten better, too."

"I assume these pieces are headed for that art gallery you mentioned."

"If the gallery can sell the piece it has."

"Good luck." I glanced toward the front of the garage. "Is there some place we can sit and talk?"

"Susan's not here. She had to deliver some things. I'm not sure when she'll be back."

"Why don't you and I talk," I said. "If Susan doesn't get back before I leave, I'll catch her another time."

"Okay. Come on."

I followed Malander to the backyard where two old rusted lawn chairs sat on a pseudolawn of mown weeds. Here a gap in the trees allowed a sizable patch of sunlight to reach the ground. We sat down facing a wall of woods. If there was another house back there, I couldn't see it.

"Have you had a chance to think about what we discussed the other night?" I asked. "About any possible enemies you might have."

"We didn't have to think about it. We don't have any enemies that we know of."

"Was there anyone in your family, or out of it, who acted strangely about your son's death?"

"No."

"Have you ever heard anyone express angry feelings against Havens?"

"No."

"Do you have any idea who might be sending those threats?"

"No," he said, but there had been a slight hesitation this time.

"Come on," I said. "You never know what might help."

"It's nothing big. It's just that I'm not sure I'm allowed to talk about it."

"Why not?"

"It sort of relates to the group and the stuff we talk about there."

"You're talking about confidentiality? I thought it wasn't a formal therapy group."

"It isn't," he said. "But we still agreed we wouldn't talk about what was said there."

"There's someone threatening John's life and accusing you all of murder. Isn't finding that person more important than not passing on a few remarks?"

"I suppose so," he said, but not with much conviction.

"If you feel uncomfortable about telling me everything, at least point me in the right direction. Give me some kind of hint."

Malander looked embarrassed. "This is getting blown up out of proportion," he said. "It's not that big a deal. In fact, I never even met the man."

"Who?"

"Karen's husband. Ken Raley."

"You never met him?"

"No. He left the group before Susan and I started coming."

"You think he might be sending the threats."

"It's not that definite. All I think is, if I were you, I'd want to check him out."

"Why?" When Malander didn't respond right away, I added, "Because you know he has emotional problems?"

"Yeah. And because I got the impression he had a big argument with John before he left the group."

"What was the argument about?"

"I don't know. Maybe some of John's ideas. John says it was just a grief reaction. That's probably all it was."

"Does Karen talk about her husband's emotional problems in the group?"

"Yeah, but I wouldn't feel comfortable passing that along. Anyway, it's not like she's describing any deep, dark secrets. It's just that her husband's had a real tough time of it."

"Okay," I said. "Thanks for letting me know. Tell me, how did you first hear about Havens? And how did you come to be in the group?"

"We heard about John through one of the store owners who carries our things—his name's Morris, a real nice guy, has a shop over in Granite Valley. Morris knows John and told us about his book. In fact, Morris lent us his own copy. It took Susan a couple of weeks to get around to it, but once she did, she read it straight through. Then she made me read it. We were both impressed. The next time we talked to Morris, he said he'd mentioned us to John, and John mentioned the group. So we called John and started going."

"Do you feel the group has helped you?"

"Definitely," said Malander. "Though not in some kind of

Pollyanna way. John isn't offering any magic solutions or easy answers. No one's saying we're necessarily going to see our children again in some magic kingdom in the sky. The children are really gone, and the pain of it really hurts. But you can let the pain crush you, or you can try to make something out of it. That's basically John's message, and there's nothing easy there. But it gives you a place to start. Plus it helps to be around someone like John who's been through it—and others who are going through it. And sometimes you feel like you can help someone else, and that helps some, you know?"

"Yeah."

"And just talking it out—maybe that's the best thing of all."

For a few moments we sat in silence, looking out at the woods.

"Was your boy taken from back there in the woods?" I asked. "I seem to remember Susan saying something about that."

Malander nodded. His eyes glowed with incipient tears. "Yes," he said. "He was taken from back there. He was seven and he loved those woods. He played back there a lot with some other boys from the neighborhood."

"I take it he wasn't with his friends that day."

Malander shook his head. "Danny—that's one of his friends—said Jimmy went over to his house that day—cutting through the woods— to see if he could play. He couldn't. Danny said Jimmy went back into the woods—maybe coming back home, maybe going to look for another friend. That was the last anyone saw of him until they discovered the body."

"When and where was that?"

"The next day. Near one of the quarries."

Malander's voice had grown lower and huskier.

"I assume the police talked to all the neighbors?"

"Yeah. The sheriff's department has jurisdiction here, and they had people all over this place, talking to everyone."

"Did they figure out how and where your boy was grabbed?"

"They know the guy used some kind of inhalant to knock him out, but they aren't saying what kind. There are some roads back there, some paved, some gravel, some dirt. There are some houses, but also stretches without houses. The cops figure whoever took Jimmy might have seen him on or close to one of the roads. I don't think they pinned it down or found anything useful back there."

"Your son was the first child killed by that guy?"

"Yeah. I've thought sometimes, if only one of the others had come first, we would have been warned, we could have kept a better eye on him. Maybe we should have anyway."

"I grew up in a house with miles of woods in the back," I said. "I spent half my boyhood in those woods—until I started playing sports. I had great adventures there—alone or with my friends. What are you going to do—lock a kid in the basement and make him scared of everything? Not when there isn't some specific danger. And there wasn't—not before your boy was taken."

"Thanks," said Malander. "That's what I try to keep telling myself. Anyway, maybe knowing wouldn't have been enough, maybe the guy would have found another way. Knowing didn't help those other kids, did it?"

11

AFTER LEAVING MALANDER, I explored the area behind his house, driving my car along narrow roads that crisscrossed a quarter mile of woods. I had no thought of trying to discover something new about the kidnapping—that would have been absurd at this late stage. I just wanted a chance to reflect.

There were stretches of road with and without homes, and long driveways heading off into the trees to single lots that might be built on or empty. There were plenty of places where you could grab a child and not be visible from any house. Still, doing so would be tricky. The roads all seemed to be in regular use, either leading from one stretch of houses to another or out to the main road. You'd need luck, not only that a car not come by during that minute or minute and a half that it would take to subdue the child and get him into the trunk, but also that no one notice you and your car in the area before or after the snatch. Then again, all crimes took luck, and people got away with them all the time.

When I got tired of driving the small web of roads, I pulled off onto a narrow shoulder and parked. Looking down a stretch of asphalt road not much wider than a driveway, I began to run over in my mind how one would go about abducting a child.

If you were smart, you'd make a pass or two through an area looking for an opportune victim in an opportune spot. If the right opportunity didn't arise, you'd move on to someplace else, always trying to minimize the possibility that someone would notice and remember you. If you were patient enough, the chance would come. You'd lure the child over or simply pull up next to him, grab him, slap the cloth with the inhalant over his nose, and, as soon as he stopped struggling, get him into the trunk. You'd tape his mouth, bind his wrists and ankles, shut the trunk, and get the hell out of there.

In order to keep your car clean of any traces of the child, you'd have plastic sheeting laid down in your trunk. You could wrap the child in it when you maneuvered him from the car to the murder scene, but you'd need gloves because plastic picks up fingerprints easily. You'd have to make sure the gloves weren't torn because a hole in a glove finger could result in a partial print. You could leave the plastic at the scene to avoid driving away with something obvious in your car that could connect you to the victim. But besides avoiding having traces of the victim in your car, you'd also need to avoid having traces of your car on the plastic left with the victim. Thus you'd need a second layer of plastic in your trunk lying underneath the layer that touched the body, but not the same kind of plastic—that could be too suggestive if you were stopped: You'd need something else—garbage bags, perhaps, an easy item to explain. Another matter: Even if you'd managed to move the body from the trunk to the scene without touching the plastic to your clothing, there'd still be the chance that you got fibers from your clothing on the victim when you grabbed him, so you'd need to get rid of your clothes fast—changing somewhere, or simply slipping off a layer of clothes you'd worn over other clothes—stuffing the clothing, the inhalant, the gloves, and whatever else you wanted to get rid of into those garbage bags and throwing them in some Dumpster out of the immediate area. Now you'd be home free, unless, of course, you'd made some other kind of mistake. With the sophistication of forensics these days, being careful enough seems like an impossible infinite regress, no leaving evidence on the thing that touched the victim, or the thing that touched the thing that touched the victim, or the thing that touched the thing that touched the thing. . . . Or so it seems in theory. In reality, there's contamination of evidence and other police screwups, inconclusive test results, and smart defense attorneys who work on finding legal loopholes, prosecutor errors, and juror quirks. In the end, even the accused who's bungled everything might walk.

And, of course, mistakes would never matter if you were never a suspect.

I looked around at the woods. It was a beautiful day, the sunlight creating a radiant display out of what looked like hundreds of different shades of green. The beauty of the day seemed at odds with thoughts of death. But a boy had been taken from this place and murdered, and, awful as it was to think about, the same thing was likely to happen to other children before this maniac was caught.

One might have thought it tricky to the point of impossibility for the murderer to find a vulnerable child now that his three murders had sounded an unignorable alarm. But it was hard for people to be on guard every minute of every day. And it was amazing how blithe some people could be in the face of something that should have terrified them. A series of rape/murders had taken place during the early seventies on or near the campus of the University of California at Santa Cruz. It became apparent at a certain point that the victims were being grabbed while hitchhiking, but when the university administration tried to discourage hitchhiking, a huge outcry went up that the university was trying to repress student liberty. The administration compromised by suggesting that the students only accept rides in cars displaying university stickers. The murders continued. It turned out that the murderer's mother worked at UCSC, and the murderer, Ed Kemper, had the appropriate sticker.

I started my car and made my way back to the main road. In Bear Creek, I stopped for coffee and a roll, then went to the small park, where I walked around for a while to exercise my bad leg.

Back in Granite Valley, I saw a Safeway store on my right and remembered I needed something for dinner. I pulled into the lot, parked, and got out of the car. As I walked through the parking lot, I saw Witmer emerge from the store. She was wearing beige slacks and a white blouse, and she was carrying a bag of groceries. With her was a slender dark-haired woman holding the hand of a little girl who clutched a toy bear. The dark-haired woman was apparently Witmer's partner. Intrigued, I moved toward them.

I saw Witmer notice me, then immediately look away, focusing more intently on her companion, hiding like an ostrich in plain view. I surprised myself with what I did next. Part of it was seeing Witmer vulnerable and wanting a little good-natured payback after the hard time she'd given me the other day. The other part of it was seeing what a pleasant face her partner had and how cute the little girl looked swinging her bear and singing something to herself.

"Hi, JoAnn!" I cried as I veered into their path with my arms thrown out. "Nice to see you."

This time it was Witmer's mouth hanging open. I kept coming at them with the bonhomie of a salesman.

"This must be Marissa," I said, pointing down at the girl. I looked up at the woman. "And you must be . . ."

"Sarah," she said.

"It's nice to meet you," I said.

In fact, I meant it. There was something instantly appealing about Sarah. It had nothing to do with good looks. She could have been attractive enough if she'd wanted to make the effort, but she wasn't making it, and had, I suspected, a philosophical objection against making it. She was wearing nondescript slacks and blouse, had longish dark hair she obviously didn't do much with, and wore no makeup on a complexion that was naturally pale.

But she had what seemed to be a genuine sweetness about her. I always find this appealing, but the appeal takes on a certain nostalgia when it's combined with simplicity, evoking for me childhood images of Biblical females, not to mention my pubescent fundamentalist fantasy of the woman who, I thought, would one day toil by my side in the fields of the Lord.

I doubted, however, that Sarah was simple inside. There was a soft irony in her eyes as she appraised me.

"You're? . . ." she asked.

"Oh, sorry, David Strickland." I almost added, "I'm sure JoAnn must have mentioned me," but that seemed to be laying it on a bit thick. Anyway, it was enough to see Witmer looking glum and uncomfortable.

"You and JoAnn are old friends?" asked Sarah.

"Oh, yeah, we go back a long way, don't we, Jo? Fellow cops and all that."

"Are you still a peace officer, Mr. Strickland?"

"Call me Dave, please. No, I'm a private investigator now."

I noticed Marissa looking up at us, unselfconscious because ignored.

The girl was cute as could be, with a round face, light brown skin, big dark eyes, and curly black hair.

"Hi," I said to the girl.

The greeting broke the spell of unselfconsciousness and sent the girl scurrying behind Sarah's leg.

"She's a doll," I said. "How old is she?"

"She's four," said Sarah, smiling proudly.

I squatted down to be eye level with the girl. Marissa was standing behind her mother's left leg. An eye was visible on one side of the leg, a dangling bear on the other.

"Hi, Marissa, I'm Dave."

The eye disappeared.

"You don't want to talk, huh? Well, I'll just talk to your little bear friend here. Hi, Mr. Bear, it's nice to meet you. *Well, hi, Dave, it's nice to meet you, too.*"

I'd lowered and hoarsened my voice, trying to imitate what I dimly remembered to be the voice of Yogi the Bear. The attempt was pathetic, but good enough, I hoped, for the four-year-old set.

"Is Marissa a good girl?" I asked the bear.

I noticed the girl's eye had reappeared.

"Oh yeah, she's real good." My bear imitation was taking on a drawl, so that I was sounding like one of those crusty sidekicks in the old Westerns. *"She's a little shy, is all. But we have lots of fun. She likes to sing and shake me around."*

A giggle came from behind the leg. Above me, I heard Witmer clear her throat.

"I think we'd better be going," she said.

"I'll walk you to the car," I said as I stood up.

As we moved down the row of cars, with Witmer walking ahead, I asked Sarah what kind of work she did.

"I'm doing clerical work at UC while I work on my degree," she said.

"Degree in what?"

"Women's studies and religion."

"The goddess—that sort of thing?"

Sarah gave me a look of surprise and amusement.

"Don't tell me you're into feminist theology."

"The sister of a friend of mine is," I said. "I'm an ex-fundamentalist Christian, so we have some pretty lively discussions."

We had stopped by a dark green Honda Accord. Witmer had opened the trunk and was putting the grocery bag inside.

"It was nice to meet you," I said to Sarah. I looked down at the girl. "Good-bye, Marissa."

"Make him talk," said the girl, holding up the bear. Her shyness had disappeared.

"Good-bye, Dave," I said on behalf of the bear. I looked up into Witmer's face and gave her a big smile. "Good-bye, Jo. I hope we get a chance to visit soon."

"Why don't you join us for dinner?" said Sarah. "Unless you have other plans."

I was watching Witmer's face fall.

"Well, I don't know . . ." I said.

"It's going to be pretty simple," said Sarah. "Barbecued fish and salad."

"I'm sure *Dave* has other plans," said Witmer.

"Well . . ."

"Make him talk more," said the girl.

"Marissa, not now," said Witmer.

The joke had gone far enough. But I liked Sarah and Marissa, and the idea of company at dinner was appealing, especially after my earlier depressing reflections on murdering a child. Of course, a grumpy Witmer could spoil the evening, even retaliate by withdrawing the grudging cooperation she'd granted me. But I had hopes that some dinner conversation, even under duress, might loosen Witmer up and get us on friendlier footing. I felt bad about not having remembered her and didn't want to leave things the way we'd left them the other day. The evening could turn out to be a disaster, but . . .

"Sure," I said, "I'd love to come."

WITMER, SARAH, AND I were sitting around a wooden dinette table in a wallpapered alcove just off the small kitchen. We were sipping Pinot Grigio, the remnants of salmon and salad spread out in front of us. Marissa was in bed, having been fed earlier.

101

"He doesn't see Marissa all that often," Sarah was saying to me, speaking of her ex-husband, a Spanish-language professor who had once taught at UCSC but was now teaching somewhere in upstate New York.

"Which is fine with me," said Witmer.

"But not with me," said Sarah.

"I think we're better off without him around," said Witmer.

"Maybe we are, but Marissa isn't," said Sarah. "It's important for her to see her father and know he cares about her."

It was the usual stepfamily stuff.

As the two women went back and forth on the subject of Marissa's father, I sat back in my chair and sipped at my wine. Overall I was pleased with the way the evening had gone. During the dinner preparations and the meal itself I'd asked whatever questions and made whatever comments had been necessary to keep all of us talking—figuring that constant conversation was the best way to defuse the tensions between Witmer and me. Sarah had been easy to talk to; Witmer had been work. I'd throw questions Witmer's way and not get much back, but then Sarah would add something, and Witmer would respond to that, and eventually Witmer would talk. She hadn't exactly gotten friendly, but she had livened up a bit. I would have liked to see the conversation get a bit more personal, but I could hardly expect Witmer to share confidences with someone she was half ready to strangle.

"Did you get enough to eat?" asked Sarah, and I realized she was directing the question to me.

"Yes—thanks," I said. "The salmon was great."

Sarah got up to clear the table, and Witmer and I got up to help her. After we transferred the dishes to the sink, Sarah said she'd forgotten to get the whipped cream she needed for dessert and asked Witmer if she'd mind running to the store for some. Witmer hesitated for a moment, then gave me a big fake smile.

"Dave, why don't you keep me company?" she said. "We haven't had a chance to visit—just the two of us."

"I shouldn't leave Sarah with the dishes," I said.

"You two run along and have fun," said Sarah. "I'll finish up."

"Come on, *Dave,*" said Witmer.

I wiped my hands on some paper towel and followed Witmer outside. We got into the Accord, Witmer putting her shoulder bag on the floor beneath her legs and placing a cellular phone in the space between the seats. Neither of us said anything while she started the car and pulled out of the drive. As we started down the street, she turned her head toward me for a moment. I could see from the light of the street lamp that she was glaring.

"Strickland, before I tell you to go get fucked, tell me what the hell the point of that whole charade was."

"It wasn't really a charade," I said. "The meeting in the parking lot started out as a joke—a little payback for your having made me feel so uncomfortable yesterday. But accepting the invitation wasn't a joke. I like your family a lot, and I was in the mood for company. Mostly I was hoping that after spending an evening with me—even a forced evening—you might become a little friendlier. Obviously, I was wrong."

Witmer didn't respond. After a moment, I said, "Come on, JoA—I mean, Witmer—aren't you taking this a little too far? I've already said I was sorry for not having remembered you. I wish you'd consider the circumstances."

There were a few seconds of silence, and then Witmer said, "Ah, hell." I waited to see exactly what that meant.

"I don't even know why it got me so pissed off," she said. "Maybe it just seemed so typically male."

We'd been climbing uphill from Witmer's place along residential streets. Now we intersected a larger street that ran along the top of a ridge. Witmer took a right, then stopped in front of a small local store. The unlighted store had apparently closed early, the explanation having been printed on a cardboard sign that neither of us could read from the car. Witmer uttered a mild curse and drove on.

I said, "I don't think I'm usually as much of a jerk as I apparently was with you."

"Actually, you were sweet," she said. "Drunk, but sweet. I was in just as bad a shape as you were—drinking too much, screwing around, trying real hard to convince myself I wasn't gay. I liked you. The thing wouldn't have gone anywhere—except maybe as friends—but I didn't know that at the time. It hurt when you didn't call after that second time. Then when you didn't even remember me the other day . . ."

"I really am sorry. But we still could be friends."

"Things have changed, Strickland. Besides, I'd find it hard to believe the motives of someone I knew wanted informa—"

Witmer was interrupted by the sound of the cellular phone. She picked it up.

"Yeah? . . . Yeah . . . Oh, shit. Where? . . . A quarter mile from . . . then left? . . . Okay, I'm on my way."

Witmer hit the brake, made a quick U-turn, then accelerated along the ridgetop road.

"What is it?" I asked.

"Another child—goddamn it!" Witmer jerked her head toward me. "I'm going to have to take you with me, Strickland. When we get there, you stay in the damn car, and I'll find some way to get you back when I can."

Witmer punched numbers into the phone with her thumb and told Sarah quickly what had happened. We drove on in silence, first on a level road, then ascending again through streets lined with houses on shaded lots. After a few minutes the houses became sparse and trees turned to woods and street lamps disappeared. The only light came from our high beams trying to cut through the thick darkness.

Witmer was craning her head toward the windshield, looking for something. She made a small sound as an old graffiti-scarred water tank appeared along the side of the road. A quarter mile farther on, we could see the emergency lights of a patrol car some hundred yards off to our left in the woods. Witmer slowed, found a small road covered with rotting leaves, and drove toward the lights. Reaching the patrol car, she came to a stop, told me to stay the hell put, and jumped out.

I waited a moment, then followed.

There were actually three other cars at the scene, two patrol cars and a Buick sedan sitting between them. Next to the sedan two officers were interviewing what I judged to be a middle-aged couple. At least the officers were interviewing the man. The woman was off to the side, quietly sobbing. I could catch enough about what the man was saying to know he was recounting how the couple had seen the fire and discovered the body.

I slipped around the outside of one of the patrol cars to get a look at the headlight-illuminated murder scene where Witmer was now talking to two other patrol officers.

The child, who looked to be a boy about six or seven, was lying in a small clearing on a bed of burned leaves. There was the smell of some kind of fuel oil in the air. The body hadn't formed the automatic pugilist position, that would have taken a lot more heat than would have been generated by fuel oil out in the open. Instead the small body was simply sprawled out on the ground. I could see remnants of tape around the mouth and strands of rope at the ankles. The clothing was pretty well burned, but it was still possible to make out what the child had been wearing—multicolored high-tops, jeans, and a red shirt. There was some blackening of the skin, but mostly it was reddened and blistered—third-degree burns. The features of the face were still recognizable.

The mercy of it was, if the child had been given enough of whatever inhalant was used, he needn't have felt a thing—and he would have died fairly quickly from asphyxiation. I hoped that was so. That there were no obvious signs of thrashing about indicated that it probably was so.

I was startled to see a sheet of plastic off to the side of the body, as if my earlier imaginings had somehow conjured it up. A fuel can lay near the body. The fire had obliterated any labeling on its visible surfaces, though what forensics called "the dependent side"—the side toward the ground—would probably be readable. No doubt the can and the tape and the rope and the clear plastic drop cloth would be traceable, if at all, to a uselessly large array of retailers. Near the body were a grouping of shiny, gold-colored numbers reading 323219.

A patrol officer tapped me on my shoulder, had me explain who I was, and then ordered me back to Witmer's car. Before obeying, I glanced at the body one more time. I was reminded suddenly of that sculpture of Malander's, the one with the small, burned-up figure lying like a sacrifice before that eerie face. There was no such face visible in the woods. But it was out there somewhere in the darkness, if we could only see it.

105

12

THE WORLD WAS dark and empty, the ground hard and cold, as if it were night in an asphalt desert. In the distance, a fire appeared, what seemed to be a pile of burning rags. I moved to the fire, seeking warmth. The rags began to move, and a small head appeared—my God, there was a child in there. Its face was turned toward me, full of pain, its eyes fixed on mine, its mouth working soundlessly, mouthing *Help me.* Frantic, I looked around, but there was nothing in that empty world I could use to put out the fire. I tried to reach into the fire, but each time I touched the flames, my hands began to melt. I couldn't bear to stare uselessly into that tormented face, so I turned away, but now there were fires everywhere, and within each fire, a child's face, pleading. I looked upward, so as not to see, and there was another face, this one huge and dark, dimly illuminated by the glow from all those fires. *Help them,* I cried, but there was no response, no change of expression; the eyes were turned toward me, but they were so vague, I didn't know if they could see. Suddenly, there was a flash of color, and a feeling of unendurable pain, and I realized that I, too, was burning.

I WOKE WITH a gasp, bolting upright, my heart pounding in my chest, the plea *No* echoing through my head. I sat rigid, struggling to breathe, as the beating of my heart became less fierce. I was covered with sweat. I made my way across the moonlit room to the sink and toweled off. I returned to the bed and sat there for a time, breathing deeply, trying to rid my mind of the images from the dream. When I began to feel more relaxed, I lay down and closed my eyes. Just as I started to drift off, I got jolted awake by a glimpse of the nightmare. I sat up again, knowing now that I wasn't going to sleep. I turned on the light and looked around for something to distract me. Seeing Havens's book on my bedside table, I picked it up and began to read.

Night after night I sat alone in my apartment, in darkness, drinking, going over what I had done. I kept putting myself back into that hallway, into the fierce heat and acrid smoke, at the moment when I heard those children scream.

I had saved three children and let my son die. Had that really been wrong, saving the greater number? I hadn't even known Ricky would die—I had had to weigh the certainty of three deaths against the chance of my son's death. How could I have done other than I did?

Then again, Ricky was my own child—a child who had loved and trusted me. Didn't a parent have a special obligation to save his own child? But how far would that obligation go? It might be right to save one's own child instead of one other, but one's own child instead of two? Three? Ten? A hundred?

Or was I missing the point with these abstract calculations? Where was my love for Ricky in all of this? Maybe there were times when feeling should have priority over ethical principles. Maybe a loving father would have said to hell with ethics and run toward his son. Maybe the fact that I had saved those other children showed that I hadn't really loved my son.

When I wasn't going over the ethical questions, I was going over the what-ifs. What if I'd simply pulled that girl out into the hallway, gotten her out of danger, then run to my apartment. Maybe I could have saved Ricky and come back for the other boys. No, there wouldn't have been time for that. If I'd gone for Ricky, I'd have ended up trapped in the apartment, and Ricky and I and those boys down the hall would all have died. But maybe, being in the apartment with Ricky, I could have helped him survive—and maybe the firefighters could have gotten to the other children in time. But if firefighters could have saved the boys, then I had let my own son die to save just one other child, and that stuff about saving the greater number was all wrong.

Eventually, exhausted by the endless questions, I would force myself to imagine Ricky's pain and the pain those children would have felt dying, trying to weigh the one against the other as if I were a human scale, hoping some truth would emerge from my torment. After a time I would lose the thread, and simply sit there hurting, like some Jesus taking on the pain of the world, except that I wasn't trying to redeem the world, I was trying to redeem myself.

As my nights degenerated into obsession and alcohol, my days went on as before, at least for a while, my work self having a momentum that my solitary self didn't have. It's amazing how a hundred habits can carry you through a day.

Creativity, however, isn't a habit, and mine had disappeared with Ricky's death. Still, I managed to get by without it for a while. It wasn't necessary to my administrative assignments. As for my own ad campaign, I had already developed the basic ideas and had only to fill in the details.

The people at work, like the work itself, provided distraction, but no comfort. I had developed a superficial friendliness with my fellow workers, which now yielded a superficial sympathy. My colleagues reacted as I would have reacted in their place, making an effort to be supportive and say the right things, while feeling more than a little uncomfortable with the idea of death and mourning—wishing I'd get over my grief as quickly as possible so things could get back to normal.

At night I continued to obsess, but these obsessions began to take a different turn. Unable to convince myself I had made the right choice in choosing to help those other children, I tried to transfer the blame I felt onto the situation that had forced me to make such a choice. That burning hallway, the girl's clothing on fire, my son in danger, everything happening so fast—what could anyone have done in such circumstances? What if I had saved Ricky instead of the others? Wouldn't I be feeling terrible guilt for having let those other children die? There had been no right choice. What had happened hadn't been my fault, it had been the fault of the situation in which I had found myself.

To try to save myself from guilt, I began to cultivate an anger that kept taking on a larger scope, moving outward from that burning hallway to other tragic situations until it encompassed life itself. Life had doomed us to suffering and tragedy, to situations in which any choice we made could cause pain and death. The world was a terrible place. It wasn't my fault if I was caught in the middle of it. (I didn't know if I believed in God or not, so didn't know if my anger should be directed toward God or the world itself. But I was perfectly ready to be angry at either one.)

It doesn't take much thinking to see through those simplistic explanations of suffering that try to make all or most of it our fault—the result of our free will. If human beings were really as free to choose good as evil, there would have been much more good over the course of human history—and much less suffering. Watching nature programs for an evening makes it obvious how much aggression, suffering, and death are built in to the world. We're the products of that world, not creatures exempt from its laws. Even if one does believe in free will, there is so much suffering that comes from forces over which we have no control—earthquake, fire, flood, and disease.

Even those familiar Sunday-school stories that trace suffering to the Garden of Eden admit that now, because of our degraded nature, it's virtually impossible for us to choose, and do, good. But we're supposed to be responsible for these tendencies because of the Fall. However, apart from the general implausibility of the Garden of Eden story, the idea that we should be blamed for, and forced to suffer the awful consequences of, one ancestral wrong is such a morally ludicrous idea that it turns the world (and any being in charge of it) into a horrible joke. The world is not our fault.

This generalized anger of mine began to spill over into my day world in an odd sort of way. I had always been a doodler, and the habit had served me particularly well in advertising, as a prod to continual brainstorming. I was always jotting phrases and sketches for possible ads. The problem was that I didn't have ideas anymore—at least not any constructive ones—and I was now being assigned new ad campaigns. I would scribble down ideas, hate the results, cross them out, write down others, then cross those out. When my frustration level became high enough, the scratching over would turn into defacements that were angry, even obscene. Eventually these defacements would take on a life of their own until I was filling pages with dark fantasies. I might be trying to develop ideas for an insurance ad, hinting at disasters the way they do without having the bad taste to spell them out. Nothing useful would come, and after a while the hints of misfortune would turn into a horror show of outlaw bikers or mad terrorists attacking my bland suburban family ("Because you never know what tomorrow might bring"). The parodies would become more cosmic, and God would get into the picture, and I might end up with Jesus selling Rugged Cross Insurance ("You'll never be lost, with a piece of the Cross")— God loosing evils on the world in an attempt to boost the premiums, while a pair of hapless philosophers ran around trying to convict him of insurance fraud.

At a certain point, as punishment for my by-then obvious slump, I was handed a dog of an account that I'll call Honest Archie's TV and Appliance Warehouse. Archie was one of those urban hillbillies with the cowboy hat, suit, and string tie who yearn for celebrity even more than sales, and who yuk it up on TV with various animals and family members (two groups not always easily distinguishable). Archie's family consisted of a boozy, buxom blond wife who came on to any male around her, and a twenty-year-old son who was in his shoplifting phase. I don't think I even tried to come up with any real ideas—whatever they would have been. Instead I got right into ads with Archie chattering in the foreground, with his family behind him—the kid with his hand in the till, and the wife with her hand in some customer's pants. Other ads showed Al performing lewd and lascivious acts with his various animals, while voicing some version of his trademark "Come on down." These ads were all sophomoric and mean, but in my dark mood I wasn't trying for good taste.

The problem with thinking on paper is that you risk someone reading your thoughts. In the beginning I was careful how I disposed of my scribbles. Eventually I stopped being careful because I stopped caring. How copies of the ads started circulating around the office I'm not quite sure. Presumably someone spotted one in a wastepaper basket and then went looking for more. I think the discovery of the ads, some of which were really vicious, were met by my fellow workers with as much relief as consternation. They had long ago become irritated and impatient with me. The ads—proof that I had overstepped the line—removed any obligation of sympathy and gave my colleagues permission to vent their anger. Management was sick of me as well. Out of a lingering sense of propriety, they dismissed me with vague references to possible future reconsideration if and when I'd had sufficient "professional help." But as we said good-bye, I think we both knew we wouldn't be seeing each other again.

I had no income, but I did have some money put aside. Without the distraction of work, I could go home, pull down the shades, open a bottle, and consign myself to continuous night. I could get on in a serious way with the job I had been working myself up to all this time—the job of destroying myself.

I woke up groggy, my mouth and eyes dry, my body hot under covers too heavy for the midmorning heat. I could hear the phone ringing in the kitchen. I stumbled out of bed, tipping Havens's book off my chest onto the floor. I jogged down the narrow hallway and got to the phone before the answering machine kicked in. I grabbed for the receiver and mumbled something into it.

"Dave?" came the response.

"Yeah," I said, doing a little better this time.

"This is Sylvia Bennett. Are you all right?"

"Yes," I said, working some saliva into my mouth. "I just woke up. I was up pretty late."

"Another child's been murdered."

"I know. I was there."

"You were there? What do you mean?"

"I was with a police officer when she got called to the scene. She had to take me along."

"Was it terrible? It must have been."

"Yes. Have they identified the boy yet?"

"It was in the newspaper. Just a second." I heard a rustle of paper. "Tony Sestriere, age seven. His father, Carlo, is a lawyer in town. The poor family."

"Yes."

She cleared her throat. "The reason I'm calling is that there are a couple of things you need to know about. John doesn't have to worry about that accusation anymore. He—both of us—were with people last night when that child was supposed to have been killed."

"Where were you?"

"We went to a lecture together at UC Santa Cruz, to hear a psychiatrist friend of John's. There was a reception afterwards. We were with people the whole time."

"Good. You must feel pretty relieved."

"Yes, but something else has happened. John just received another threat."

"When?"

"This morning. I talked to him a few minutes ago."

"Is he still being casual about the threats?"

"No, I think he's finally getting worried. He's beginning to see that whoever's sending the threats might be serious."

"Does John still have the new letter?" I asked.

"Yes. He's going to turn it over to the police next week. He says they have enough to worry about this weekend with this new murder."

"I'd like to look over that letter before he gives it to the police. I haven't had a chance to see an original. I better give him a call."

I had in mind something more involved than just "looking over" the letter, but it wasn't something I wanted to discuss with Mrs. Bennett.

She said, "I told John I'd call him back as soon as you and I talked. I can ask him to hold the letter for you, if you like."

"Thanks. Tell him I'll phone him later. Right now I have an appointment with the Raleys."

After we'd hung up, I began looking up the phone numbers of local sanitation companies. I wanted to find out some garbage-collection dates. Such dates are easy to get. You just call the company, tell them you're buying a house on such and such a street, and ask what day the garbage is collected. Since I had to ask for two dates in Granite Valley, I told the company I was a realtor calling on behalf of two clients. The dates I collected were these: Monday, the Caldwells, Granite Valley; Tuesday, the Malanders, Bear Creek; and Thursday, both the Raleys, Granite Valley, and Ruth Havens, Soquel.

If one of those people was sending the threatening notes, it was possible that the materials from which the recent note had been constructed would be tucked away in this week's garbage; if found, such materials could be matched with the note. I was particularly interested in checking out Ruth Havens, but the others were worth checking as well.

Investigators spend a lot of time dealing with garbage, and not just metaphorically. Those cans that people leave out in the street are the best and easiest source for the most intimate information—from financial records to love notes. And it's all admissible. The Supreme Court ruled some time ago that people have no reasonable right to privacy with garbage. California law disagrees, saying that people have a reasonable right to privacy with garbage until it's been commingled with other garbage. But the citizens of California, disagreeing with the law, passed one of their frequent propositions, saying that any evidence admissible in federal court is admissible in California courts.

I wasn't really thinking about getting admissible evidence. According to the California penal code, Section 422, threats of death or great bodily harm, even without intent to carry out the threat, are punishable by up to a year in jail. But there are conditions, and I figured that the chances of prosecution, let alone conviction, based on garbage gathered by a private detective, were chancy at best. If I could just learn who was sending the threats, I could evaluate the threat and, if necessary, try to scare the person off.

I shaved, showered, and dressed. As I was preparing to leave, I noticed the light blinking on the answering machine and realized a call had come in while I'd been in the shower. I punched the playback button.

"Strickland," said a voice it took me a moment to recognize as Witmer's. "About your note, there was nothing down there, but we took the impression. The forensics guy I talked to said there was a definite nick in the blade. Maybe it will help somewhere down the road. Thanks."

I gathered up my things, locked the house, got in my car, and drove down the drive. At the gate I waved away the Bouffer, who was lurking there in the hope some careless delivery man or meter reader would give him the chance to slip out. I shut the gate behind me, then drove off toward Granite Valley.

The note Witmer had referred to was one I'd handed her as I was about to be driven away from the murder scene in a departing patrol car. The note was about something I'd noticed earlier after being ordered back to Witmer's car by the patrol officer. Just off the dirt road, within the span of the car's interior light, there had been indications of digging. It looked as if someone had dug up a few shovelfuls of earth, turned them over, then broken them up with the shovel. The disturbed earth could have been unrelated to the murder scene, but it had been newly dug, and from what I could see with the surreptitious use of a small penlight I always carry with me, there didn't seem to be any other digging nearby. It was possible the murderer had buried something there, but that seemed unlikely. The digging had looked too shallow, and the spot too obvious. It had occurred to me that the digging might have been an attempt to obliterate a tire print. The dirt road itself was hard and covered with twigs and decomposing leaves. It was unlikely to pick up tire prints. The digging had occurred on a softer, grassy area and formed a rough arc that went off the road, then back again. It was possible that the killer, feeling his vehicle hit softer earth— or maybe just checking the area prior to leaving—had found a tire print and tried to obliterate it. It was just a possibility, but worth checking.

I doubted that any kind of tire print would be salvageable from the broken-up earth, but an impression of the shovel might. It was not something the cops, or even the forensic people, would automatically think of—at least not before someone started digging up the dirt to see what was under it. There were so many things that could be matched in a lab, one cut end of something to the other cut end, the cutting implement to the cut. The shovel-impression idea was just a different version of the latter. I'd mentioned the idea in my note to Witmer.

When I'd been dropped off at Witmer's place to get my car, Sarah had emerged from the house; I'd given her a quick report before driving off. I had then retraced the route to the crime scene, checking any obvious dumpsters along the way for discarded material that might relate to the crime. It was such a long shot as to be a fairly stupid idea. But I was wound up and wanted to do something. Also, having seen that same plastic at the crime scene that I'd conjured up in my mind, I'd wanted to see if the killer and I might be on a similar wavelength when it came to disposing of gloves and other such items. Nothing

115

had come of the search but loss of sleep. I'd finally gotten to bed about four A.M.

I CAME OUT OF my reverie as the highway dropped down out of the mountains into Granite Valley. I took Vista View Road and turned left just short of the shopping center. The road went past a trailer park, then ascended into some low hills. Just beyond a sandy hillside carved with graffiti, I spotted the Raley place. The house was just up the hill to my left at a bend in the road, built in stages to accommodate the slope, like three railroad cars taking a downward curve. The two lower sections had two stories, the other section had one. The house was attractive, white wood with a blue composition roof, decks built all along the back of the house. A large motor home was parked in the drive.

I made a U-turn at the end of the street, maneuvering carefully to avoid some young children who were riding bikes. I parked just above the house. The view was pretty nice. There were some less-than-attractive glimpses of town—the dull, blocklike roofs of the shopping center and the trailer-park roofs looking like so many silver dumpsters. But the large trees set against the sky were beautiful, and so were the distant hills.

I got out of the car and descended to the house's front entrance, a two-story porticolike arrangement with a large, bomb-shaped lantern hanging from a chain. Standing in front of two polished wooden doors with small stained-glass windows, I rang the bell.

After a few moments, Karen Raley opened the door. Makeup had moderated the dark circles under her eyes and brightened her face, but she still looked exhausted, as well as slightly shrunken in a blue summery dress that had obviously been bought in healthier days.

She acknowledged my appearance with a thin smile and gestured me into the house. I followed her through the hallway to a large sunken living room with plush carpeting and overstuffed furniture. The room was done in subdued pastels, mostly beige and blue, with occasional suggestions of brown or pink. Across the room were picture windows looking out on backyard and trees.

"I'm sorry if we got off on the wrong foot at John's house the other day," I said as we faced each other in the middle of the room. "I felt like I got caught in the middle of things."

"You did," she said. "I definitely overreacted. I guess I was really tired. I apologize. Would you like some coffee?"

"If you're having some."

"I have some made," she said.

Karen left to get the coffee, and I gave myself a slow tour of the room. There was a white brick fireplace over which hung an abstract painting, easy on the eye, but unremarkable, probably chosen by the decorator for some beiges and blues that matched the main colors of the room. On either side of the fireplace were built-in bookshelves painted the same whitish beige as the walls; the bookshelves were used to display glass figurines and silver dishes and occasional small groupings of books that had a fake but tasteful antique look.

Among the things on one of the shelves, pushed back as if to make it blend with the other items, was a picture of the Raleys with their daughter. Judging from the age of the girl, the photograph had been taken not long before her death.

The photo was one of those studio portraits where everyone is sitting on different-sized stools in front of a mottled backdrop, told to lean this way, no that, try the hands here, no there, all the time being ordered to relax and look natural. The instructions hadn't worked well with Karen Raley, whose smile was stiff. But I was struck by how much better she looked in the photograph, with her body filled out, with clothes that fit, and with a healthy flush to her skin.

Ken Raley was confronting the photo proceedings with a small ironic smile that seemed to fit naturally on his face. He was conservatively dressed in a charcoal suit, a white button-down shirt, and a subdued and subtly patterned maroon tie. The girl, a cute thing with a round face, large brown eyes, and dark hair, was wearing one of those ultrafeminine dresses with the lace and bows that adult females long ago ceased to wear but still love for their young daughters. There was laughter in the girl's eyes and a near giggle on her lips. The mirth could have been coming from something the photographer was doing, but I guessed it had more to do with her father's fingers, which seemed to be pressing into her rib cage—perhaps that little joke was the real reason for his smile.

"That's us in better days," said Karen Raley from somewhere behind me.

I hadn't heard her come back, but then I'd been absorbed in the photograph, and the carpeting in the room was very thick. I turned around and saw her standing in the middle of the living room, holding a coffee service.

"Your daughter was a beautiful little girl," I said.

"Thank you," she said. "I'd put more pictures of her around the house, but Ken is having a problem with pictures right now." She walked over to a glass-and-metal coffee table and set down the tray. "Cream or sugar?" she asked.

"A little sugar, please."

As Karen prepared the coffees, I made my way around to the picture windows. To my left, I saw a couple of boys coasting down the hill on their bikes. The voices of the children outside had been a constant since I'd entered the house, mostly low and steady, sometimes elevated into shrieks and taunts. I looked off at the view for a moment, then glanced down at a broad tier of land just below us. It suddenly occurred to me that something was missing.

"You weren't living in this house when your daughter died," I said.

"Of course we were. Why do you say that?"

"There's no swimming pool."

"It's under the ground." Her voice was almost a whisper. "We buried the damn thing."

I heard a rattle of china and a small curse, and I turned to see Karen dabbing at some coffee that had spilled onto the tray.

"Sorry," I said.

"It's all right." Karen finished mopping up the coffee, then said. "Neither of us could bear to look at the pool after Terri died. But it's not as if we destroyed it. It was filled in professionally; it will be easy enough for the next owners to excavate."

She gestured me to take a seat on the couch and handed me my coffee. The couch was a sectional. She took a seat at a right angle to me.

"Are you planning to move?" I asked.

"We wanted to move right after Terri died, but neither of us had the energy at the time. And the real estate agent told us we'd be losing lots of money if we didn't wait a bit. Then Ken got sick—he's been in no shape to go anywhere. As soon as we can, we'll leave this place. Actually, if Ken stays off work much longer, we won't have any choice."

"Ken's an accountant?"

"Yes. He has his own firm. That's the only thing that's saved us so far—the percentage we get off the other accountants. But the money keeps diminishing—the firm is losing clients without Ken there. I have my job, of course, but it isn't enough to make the payments on this house."

"It must be really rough on you, having to deal with the financial pressures and your husband's illness on top of your daughter's death. There must have been a lot of times when you were tempted to just sit down and give up."

A momentary suggestion of a smile appeared on her face. "Oh, I did sit down and give up," she said. "Lots of times. But I guess I just can't stand sitting that long."

"Good for you."

"Actually, I'm not sure how much of the credit I deserve," she said. "I don't know what I would have done without John and the group to help me."

"How did you hear about John?"

"Ken did some work for the Sullivans—the first couple in John's group. They recommended John to us. And us to him."

"You and your husband started going to the group together?"

"Yes. At first Ken was really positive about what we were doing in the group. But at that point, I think, he was getting by on fantasy and denial. Once the shock gave way to real feeling, he just fell apart, he couldn't handle anything. He loved Terri so much."

Karen Raley paused, thinking something over. "It's not that Ken loved Terri more than I did," she said. "It's that he needed her more. He invested more of himself in her. He really blossomed when Terri came along. Before that, a lot of people thought of Ken as a caricature accountant—stuffy and unfeeling. He wasn't, though. He had a real sadness in him you could sense if you were close to him. That's one of the things that attracted me to him, I think—the caregiver needing someone to care for. I got the impression that Ken's childhood was really awful, though he would never talk much about it. I think his choice of accounting and the role of accountant was an attempt to make the world and himself seem orderly and intelligible. Numbers are clean and precise."

"But he changed when your daughter was born?"

Karen smiled. "Oh, yes. But I don't want to give the impression that the change was night and day. I didn't fall in love with a robot. Ken always had a dry sense of humor that came out when he was relaxed. He could be a riot. Though there were times when he could seem closed up and kind of angry, he could be very sweet and gentle with me. But knowing what I did about him, I wasn't prepared for the changes that occurred in him after Terri was born. I'm sure he wasn't either. He hadn't wanted children and only agreed to have one to satisfy me. But with Terri, he just blossomed. Having a child must have opened up parts of him that had been closed since those early years. He loved Terri so much. They could be like two kids together, with their games, and make-believe, and secret messages. When she died, well . . . you'll see."

"Tell me more about your husband's condition."

"He's still grieving, of course, but after almost a year, it seems to have gone beyond that. He suffers from what they call agitated depression. There are times when he feels sad and totally exhausted. He cries, or at least looks like he wants to. He doesn't have much appetite. He sleeps a lot. Other times he is very nervous—or angry in a hopeless sort of way. Sometimes he'll seem okay, and talking to him is like old times. But those good times never last long, especially if I try to talk to him about getting help."

"Why doesn't he want help? It sounds like he's really hurting."

"He is hurting. But to him it's all the result of losing Terri. He's partly right, of course—it is from that—but he doesn't see that it's gone on too long. He's just burrowing himself further down into his misery. It's as if all his efforts are going toward holding on to his pain. And toward justifying it. I realize such thinking is at least partly the result of his depression, but it makes dealing with all this very frustrating."

"I heard you say at the meeting the other night that he takes care of himself all right while you're at work."

"Yes. He's not feeble, and he's not crazy. I work from four to midnight, and he takes care of his dinner, if he's got any appetite. In the morning, while I'm sleeping in, he'll dress himself and shave if he can find the motivation. He even goes out by himself sometimes if he feels up to it."

"Where does he go?"

Karen shrugged. "To get coffee. Maybe drive around or take a walk. I assume most of what he does is brood. I've seen him out walking a few times when I was coming home from doing errands, and he was too lost in thought to notice the car. He always looked sad."

"Do you think he'll talk to me?" I asked.

"I don't know," she said, "but tell me something. If you find out who's sending those notes, what will you do?"

"First, I guess I'll talk to Sylvia and John and see what they want to do."

"You wouldn't immediately go to the police?"

"Not unless I thought there was immediate danger."

Karen nodded, looking away for a moment. When she looked back at me, her eyes locked on mine. She said, "You're wondering if my husband is sending those notes."

I just blinked at her, giving myself a moment to think. She was right, of course. Apart from what Malander had told me, Karen's own description of her husband's mental state at the group meeting would have made anyone want to check him out. I had just hoped that she wouldn't be thinking along those same lines. I started to formulate some phony reply, but something in her eyes made me discard it. I said, "I wonder about everybody—that's my job—but maybe about your husband more than some of the others. Do I take it from your question that you're wondering, too?"

"Yes."

I was surprised both by her admission and the directness with which she'd made it.

"Mr. Strickland," she said, emphasizing the formality as if she were putting some kind of protective barrier between herself and me, "I am one hundred percent sure that John is in no danger from my husband. If nothing else, Ken wouldn't have the energy for a violent act. I am

121

ninety percent sure Ken isn't sending the notes, but that's a little less sure. If he is sending the notes, I'd like to know that so I can get Ken some help. It would be just what I'd need to get him into a hospital. Of course, I'd also like to take the worry of those threats off John's mind but I don't want to get Ken into trouble with the police. I'm willing to let you talk to Ken on one condition. If you get any indication it's him sending the notes, you talk to me about it before you talk to anyone else."

"I'm sorry," I said, "I can't do that. My first obligation is to my client."

"Then I can't let you talk to him."

"How about this? If I find any indication that the person sending the letters is Ken, I'll tell Sylvia and John I promised we'd discuss the situation with you before deciding how to proceed. In practical terms, that comes to the same thing. The person you have to trust isn't me, it's John. You know him better than I do. Do you think he'd want to throw Ken in jail, or otherwise hurt him, if there was no real threat? Do you think he wouldn't be willing to work with you on this?"

"No," she said, quickly. "I trust John. He's a nice man." She took a deep breath. "All right, I'll let you talk to Ken. That is, I'll let you try."

"Thank you," I said. "But before I talk to him, tell me why you're wondering if your husband is sending those notes."

"I assume you know that Ken got furious at John just before Ken left the group," she said.

"I heard something about it," I said. "But that was several months ago. If you're worried about your husband, that must mean you think the animosity is still there."

Karen gave a tired sigh. "All my husband's animosities are still there. These days he doesn't get over being angry. But except for an outburst at me now and then, the anger just sits inside him, feeding his black moods. That's why I'm so sure he could never be a danger to John."

"Yet you think it's possible he could send those notes."

"It's not likely, but it's possible. It wouldn't take much energy to mail the threats."

"Have you seen the letters John's been getting?"

"I've seen the copies."

"You know how they were made?"

"With the cutout letters, you mean?"

"Yes. Do you remember ever seeing cut-up pieces of magazine on your husband's desk or in the trash?"

"No."

"Tell me more about this outburst of your husband's."

"I told you that when we were first in the group, Ken was running on denial, trying to stay 'up,' put everything in a positive light. That was why he was so enthusiastic about what John was saying. At times he was too 'up' for the rest of us. We were there to grieve, as well as to try to make the best of it.

"Then the grief hit Ken all at once, hit him hard. He turned from being all enthusiastic about what John was saying, to being angry. Now we were the ones who weren't taking grief seriously enough, we were the ones who were making light of our children's death. John didn't do anything to Ken, he just represented a viewpoint Ken was reacting against. Ken was shooting the messenger."

"What did Ken say?"

Karen winced. "Awful things. About how John deserved to have his child die. The rest of us, too. It was vicious, but it was also the anger of a grief-stricken man who had no sense of what was happening to him and was very frightened. After that he quit the group and came home and just sank into himself."

"And you think he's still angry at John for that . . . philosophical disagreement?"

"It's a little more personal than that. Ken resents the fact that I still go to the group, that I still like John, and that I'm trying to develop the attitude that John suggests. I think Ken would like me to be a willing companion in perpetual misery."

"Has your husband ever expressed any jealousy toward John?"

"There's no reason for him to be jealous," said Karen, stiffening slightly.

"That doesn't preclude him *feeling* jealous. If your husband is badly depressed, he must be feeling pretty lousy about himself. If you admire John, agree with his point of view rather than your husband's, it wouldn't be that odd for Ken to develop some kind of jealous fantasy."

"Ken has never expressed anything like that to me. What his secret fantasies might be, you'll have to judge for yourself. Come on, I'll take you to him."

14

KAREN STOOD ABRUPTLY, and I had to hustle to follow her as she marched into the hallway, then up a carpeted staircase to the second floor. She turned left at the top of the stairs and waited for me at the open doorway to one of the rooms. I saw, as I caught up with her, that the room served as a study or office. The right side of the room held a desk and some wooden tables, all covered with computer equipment. Behind the desk were built-in bookcases filled with what I took to be professional books—large cloth-bound volumes in dull colors, often grouped in sets. On the opposite side of the room, just ahead of us, was a sitting area—a small couch, easy chair, and straight chair forming three sides of a square, with the easy chair in the middle, facing the picture windows at the rear of the room.

Ken Raley, I saw, was sitting in the easy chair, the back of his head toward us. Karen and I walked into the room and moved around to the other side of the chair until we stood side by side, facing Raley. He was freshly shaved, his jaw nicked in two places; his hair was newly cut, with just enough rough spots to suggest a home trim. He was dressed in freshly pressed khaki slacks and a blue button-down shirt. But if these things suggested that he was ready for a visit, his body language gave the opposite message. He was sunk down in the easy chair as if he wanted to hide in it, his arms were wrapped tightly around his chest as if in protection. His face was glum, showing hints of both aggression and timidity. His eyes were filled with a dull flame, like a fire that had spent its energy, but refused to die.

"Ken," said Karen, "this is Dave Strickland, the detective I was telling you about."

Raley just glared at me.

"Hi," I said.

"I told my wife . . . I didn't want . . . to see you," he said. Raley's speech was flat and effortful, as if he were having trouble getting breath.

"But you agreed to talk to him anyway," said Karen.

"I don't . . . remember that," said Raley.

Karen opened her mouth as if to argue, then apparently changed her mind. She looked over at me.

"Don't worry, we'll be fine," I said.

"No, we won't," said Raley.

"I'll leave you then," said Karen.

She gave me a look that seemed to be part apology and part encouragement, then turned and left the room. I took a seat on the straight chair, at a right angle to Raley, facing the couch and the wall. He was staring toward the windows.

I sat silently, not rushing things. After a few moments, Raley said, "Have you ever noticed . . . how hard it is . . . to get people . . . to leave you alone?"

"Yes," I said. "On the other hand, how does it feel when they go away forever?"

I hadn't calculated the remark. If I'd thought about it first, I probably wouldn't have made it. It seemed to hit Raley like a slap. He looked stricken.

I felt the impulse to apologize, but I held it in check. If I was going to get through to this man at all, I'd have to put a little pressure on him, break through some of his defenses.

"It feels terrible," said Raley, his voice a whisper. It was a whisper full of tears. For a moment Raley's face showed a pain that was almost childlike in its purity. Then the sullenness slipped back into his face and the hopelessness into his eyes.

Watching him, I felt a sudden stab of panic, a sense of falling, an impulse to grab for something. It was over in an instant, and I knew what it was. I had been where Raley was now, and the depression was still buried inside me, like an old well that had been covered over, but

126

not filled in. From time to time, it felt as if some ground inside me was giving way, and my foot was slipping, and I was about to sink back into that darkness. I never wanted to be there again.

I saw that Raley was turned toward me now, his angry eyes fixed on mine.

"That was a terrible . . . thing to say. It's . . . so easy . . . to be smug about other people's pain. Especially . . . when it's a kind of pain . . . you know nothing about."

"Speaking of smug, I find it interesting that people who are hurting often think they're the only ones who know what pain is."

"You don't know what this pain is," he said.

"I guess not. Not unless it has to do with feeling as if you have the worst kind of flu, and so little energy that it's hard to imagine ever moving again or ever wanting to. Except that two days, or even two hours later, you're all revved up with an awful nervous feeling and you couldn't stay still if you had to."

"That's only . . . part of it," he said.

I noticed that he had begun to wring his hands.

"Let me guess the rest," I said. "Maybe that constant weight on your chest that makes it hard to breathe or speak. The weight seems to be made up of anger and tears that are all impacted together, festering— and nothing ever really releases that weight, not even crying or getting mad. You want to fight and gain control, but it feels like there's so little 'you' anymore, and what's there keeps getting battered by those waves of awful feelings, and it seems like it can't be long now before you drown in them, and just disappear."

Raley's body gave a small shudder, as if a short burst of electricity had just gone through him. "So you read books," he said. "You . . ." He stopped as a look of suspicion came into his face. "You're some shrink, aren't you?" he said accusingly, moving forward in his chair. "This is all a damn trick to—"

"No," I said. "Look."

I pulled out my license and showed it to him. The sight of it seemed to key him down a bit. With the talking paused, I became conscious of the children's voices again. They seemed to be close. The children's moving about had brought them to the area of the street just above the part of the house where we now sat.

"So you're not a shrink, and maybe you . . . get in bad moods some-times," he said. "So, what now? I get the . . . usual pep talk that I'll get over it in time?"

"I'm fresh out of pep talks. Anyway, I don't know if you'll get over it or not."

"But you're telling me I . . . should try."

"I'm not telling you anything. What you do is your business."

Raley seemed a little startled by my laid-back response. Maybe he was used to pushing back those who were pushing him. When the other steps away, it can throw you off balance.

"If you're okay the way you are, why change?" I said.

"I'm not *okay,*" said Raley, his voice bitter. "This hurts, and it's scary, like you said. I didn't choose . . . to be like this. It's something that happened to me."

"There are doctors who could help make it easier on you."

"No," he said, shaking his head hard. "I don't want anything to do with doctors. Those shrinks think sadness is some kind of disease. Like having the flu, or something. You're supposed . . . to do whatever you can to . . . get over it as fast as possible. They don't realize sadness can come from seeing the way things are. They don't care that you might have to lie to yourself to feel better. My daughter died. To me that's horrible. Why should I try to feel good about it?"

Raley had become more animated. This animation seemed to have freed his breathing and made his speech more natural.

"Do you think that's what Havens is saying?" I asked.

"I *know* that's what he's saying."

"I understand you were in his group for a while."

"Yes."

"I heard that you liked the group at first."

"I suppose I did," said Raley. "Until I found out what pain really was. Then I realized Havens was all wrong."

Some loud screeches came from the children outside. Havens glared toward the street side of the room. I noticed that he was working his hands again.

"How is Havens wrong?" I asked.

Raley looked back at me, and said, "It's easy to talk about all the wonderful things that pain can do when you're talking about other people's pain. Once you've felt it crush you, the whole thing looks different."

"Whatever you think of Havens, he has been through it himself."

"Then let him stick to his own pain and not tell me what I should think of mine."

"I don't really know what Havens's philosophy is," I said. "But maybe all he's saying is just that if you hurt, it's better to use it for something constructive rather than simply letting it destroy you."

"He's saying more than that," said Raley. "He's saying we should accept the world as it is. Well, I don't want to accept the world as it is; I don't want to accept what happened to my daughter."

"Your wife seems to feel differently."

Raley's eyes narrowed. "That's because Havens is manipulating her. He—"

Raley jumped as a sudden burst of screeches and yells erupted from outside. He looked furious.

"Goddamn kids!" he said, glaring in the street direction again. "They never shut up!"

I waited for Raley to calm down. In a moment the kids and their argument moved away. He slumped back in his chair.

"I assume you know that someone's been threatening Havens's life," I said.

"Yes."

"Do you have any idea who might want to kill or hurt or scare Havens?"

"No," said Raley, still angry. "And I don't much care."

"Do you have any idea why someone might want to hurt him?"

"Maybe someone figures that if he likes suffering so much, they want to help him by giving him more."

THE REDS AND yellows and grays of sunset were smeared across my rear- and side-view mirrors like finger paints on miniature canvases. Ahead of me the sky blanched, and the mountains darkened, and lights went on in houses clinging to the mountain ridge.

I turned off the highway onto a small mountain road, the evening growing darker as the road dipped down among the trees. As I drove,

I scanned the houses on either side, noting the progress of occasional renovations. Some of these were related even now to the earthquake of 1989—so long had it taken some of the people to get the financing, the permits, or the will to rebuild. The mountains had been hard hit, houses shifting off foundations, outbuildings collapsing, cracks and crevices appearing everywhere. Power had been out for a week or two, and water for at least that long, since most of the houses up here had their own wells. For those whose wells had collapsed, the wait for a new one had been two years. I'd gotten off pretty easily in terms of the larger things. The barn had nearly collapsed, several water lines had ruptured, and the driveway, front steps, and veranda had been full of cracks, but the well and the house had stayed intact. The inside of the house had been another matter. Everything had fallen to the floor— TV, VCR, computer, mirrors, dishes and glassware, and the contents of every shelf and cupboard. It makes for an interesting situation. There you are, with darkness falling, no power or water or prospects of any, the kitchen covered with broken glass, spilled flour, molasses, salad dressing, oil, jam, and a hundred other things, and all you have at your disposal is a broom.

The earthquake had been in October, and Katie had died the previous May. The quake itself had felt like the end of the world, and in my mood I hadn't much cared if it was. But the end of the world isn't much fun if you have to clean up afterward.

I slowed for a stop sign and warning markers, where half the road had collapsed and the two-way traffic had to take turns with the single remaining lane. You find these spots all over the Santa Cruz mountains, missing pieces of road that were torn off in the earthquake or washed away by some heavy winter rains. The danger areas are marked, then left alone, sometimes for years, by the cash-poor county.

Since I could see that there was no traffic ahead beyond the short, one-lane stretch, I slid through the stop sign and continued on. Farther ahead, I passed a small fundamentalist church, which, with its notices for Bible camps and teen groups, always evoked in me a pained nostalgia for my born-again childhood. On the announcement board, along with the times of the services, was a Bible verse, "Our God is a consuming fire, Heb. 12:29." It seemed the fundamentalists were doing their own take on the deaths of the children.

When I arrived at the house, I petted the Bouffer, then mounted the steps, walking along the tiled veranda toward the French doors of the kitchen, through which I normally enter the house. The cute cat from next door was lying on the tiles, torturing a lizard. I chased the cat away, saw that the lizard was beyond hope, and administered the coup de grâce. I thought suddenly of Havens's book, and his bitter comments about the cruelty in us and in nature.

The sunset was magnificent now. I stepped out into the yard, away from the overhang, to get a better look. Overhead wisps of clouds hung like pink streamers in the darkening sky. Along the horizon, streaks of red tinged with yellow and orange looked like flame. Lower was a smear of darker red, the color of blood.

This is a world that can inspire awe and anger in equal measure. Someone once argued that if you looked at the world with eyes clear of any doctrine or dogma, you'd decide that there exists a God who is a brilliant engineer, a sensitive artist, and a moral savage. Of course, few outside the mental wards and the drunk tanks actually believe in a God like that. Either we try to explain away the apparent evil or explain away the apparent design.

The last bits of color disappeared from the sky. I turned and went inside, turning on the lights against the dark. The message-machine light was blinking. I pressed the play button and began to look over the mail.

A black postcard fell out of the stack, the Montana version of the old joke, "Nighttime in . . ." I turned the card over, smiling as I saw it had been written in Becky's hand, the looping script with the circles dotting the *i*'s.

"Dave, hi," said Janet's voice, and I looked up at the machine. "We're here, and we're fine. We've spent most of the time just settling in and saying hi to some neighbors. Yesterday one of Dad's friends took us on a motorboat ride that was lots of fun. Afterwards we had a barbecue. Becky gets her first horseback ride today and is totally thrilled. We both sent you postcards, and I'll write a letter soon. I miss you. We both send our love."

A good antidote to grim thoughts.

15

THE USUAL MIDSUMMER late-Sunday-morning beach traffic was doing its bumper-to-bumper crawl over the mountains to Santa Cruz. Rap and rock and roll filled the air, legs and arms dangled out car windows, horns and middle fingers urged the traffic on. Kids argued in back seats, maybe making Mom and Dad wonder how they'd gotten talked into this again. Sunning had already begun in the convertibles, with the low-cut halters provided rubbernecking diversion for passing shut-ins.

I slipped gratefully out of the traffic at the first Granite Valley exit and stopped in the left turn lane. To my right, two lanes away, was an old beat-up Dodge sedan with Earl Ritchie at the wheel. He wasn't looking in my direction, he was too preoccupied with his passenger, a pretty young blond. She was sitting sideways in the seat, laughing and poking at Ritchie, while he laughed and tried to fend her off. Seeing their sexually charged fun made me think of Janet and wish she were back.

When the arrow turned green, I took a left, then a right, working my way toward the Caldwells' house, which sat within a broad strip of land that ran between Granite Valley Drive and a parallel ridge. Many of the houses in the strip were ramshackle and haphazardly placed, harking back to a time before the developers and city planners had taken control. There were old trees and occasional patches of woods; a small stream and footpath meandered through the area.

The Caldwells' house was a small white bungalow almost hidden by the six-foot hedge that surrounded it. The hedge brought to mind

Ruth Havens's place, but here the house and the yard were much smaller, and there was no sign of flowers.

I parked in front of the house. As I got out of the car, I eyed the two plastic garbage cans sitting out on the street, their lids held tight against roving animals by taut bungee cords. Some fifteen or so hours from now I'd be back for the garbage. It was too bad I couldn't take it now.

I walked up the front path and rang the bell. Through a front window I saw Lisa get up off a couch and come toward me. I felt my stomach tighten as I remembered her misery of a few days before. But as she greeted me, I felt myself relax. She looked much better. What surprised me wasn't the modestly stylish blue dress, or the makeup, or the carefully brushed hair; she and Craig had been crisply dressed the other evening. What surprised me was Lisa's face. The eyes that had been red with pain were clear and calm. She seemed rested, almost peaceful. She even smiled when she saw me.

"Hi, Dave, come in," she said.

She moved aside, and I entered the house, stepping directly into the small living room. Like the living rooms of a lot of younger couples, this one was dominated by electronics—big-screen TV, VCR, CD player, floor speakers, and shelves of CDs and video tapes. But the rest of the furniture wasn't just for camping out. The fabric on the couch and easy chair looked expensive, the coffee table and end tables were oak, and everything was sitting on a Persian-style rug.

"Can I get you something?" asked Lisa. "I just made some coffee."

"Coffee would be great, thank you."

I followed Lisa to a small ordinary-looking kitchen enlivened by new appliances, some well-tended plants, and two framed posters, one of mushrooms, another of herbs.

"You look like you're feeling better," I said as Lisa, her back to me, took some cups down from a cupboard shelf.

"Thanks," she said. "I am."

As Lisa set the cups down alongside a pot of coffee that had a fresh-brewed smell, I found my eye drawn to a wall phone tucked into a back corner of the kitchen. I wondered if that was the phone Lisa had been using when her daughter, Corinne, was taken. My eye drifted to the backyard. On the neglected grass was a toddler-size swing set.

Lisa must have seen my gaze and so read my mind.

"I'm sure you'll have questions about Corinne," she said. "I don't think I'm up to those yet. Craig can tell you what you need to know. He had to run down the street for a minute, but he'll be right back."

"Okay."

"But I am willing to talk about John, the threats, anything like that."

"Good."

"Please, have a seat and help yourself."

I sat down at the table where Lisa had set out the coffee, cream, sugar, and a plate with slices of cake. Lisa sat down with me. The cake was good, tasting of a flavor Lisa told me was cardamom.

"I'm glad you're feeling better," I said.

"Thank you. Me, too. I was feeling such bitterness. I'm sorry for the way I acted at the last meeting. I was hurting a lot."

"I understand."

"I'm still hurting, but I feel like maybe the bitterness isn't there anymore."

"That's good."

"A really nice thing happened to me," she said. She smiled, and her face took on a pleasant glow. "The last couple of days I've been talking to this nice woman who lives down the street. She's been talking about how much her religious faith has meant to her. This morning she and her husband took us to church. I didn't want to go, but I felt I owed it to her for being so kind. The service was nice—with the singing and the prayers. I really liked the minister and what he had to say. I guess Cathy—that's the woman's name—told the minister about me because he told the congregation there was a young woman attending who'd lost a child, and he wasn't going to say my name or point me out because he didn't want to embarrass me, but he wanted them all to pray for me. And he talked about how awful it is to lose someone you love, especially a child, and how easy it is to get bitter, but God loves us and has a plan for us and one day we'll see how everything works together for good. Then everybody prayed for me, and there was music, and—I don't know—all of a sudden I felt really peaceful. Does this all sound crazy to you?"

"No."

"I mean, I've never been religious before. I don't know anything about it. Some of my friends were into New Age things, but I never went to Sunday school as a kid, and I never thought about God or anything like that. It all seems very strange—but nice, you know?"

"Yes."

"Cathy and her husband took us out to Sunday dinner after church. It was the first time I've been able to taste my food since Corinne died."

There was a noise, and I looked up to see Craig coming through the back screen door. He was dressed in a beige summer suit, white shirt, and a relatively conservative brown-and-green tie. He greeted me and apologized for being late, then sat down and turned his attention to Lisa.

"How're you doing, hon?" he asked.

"I'm doing okay," she said, and put her hand over his.

Craig looked much as he had the other night—tired, sad eyed, and a little confused. He squinted at his wife as he studied her face, as if she, too, confused him. I wondered how he was taking these changes in her.

"Maybe you two should talk now," said Lisa, removing her hand from her husband's and sitting back in her chair.

"In a minute," I said. "First let's take care of the kinds of questions we talked about the other night. Do either of you have any enemies you know of?"

They both shook their heads.

"Was there anybody you thought had a strange reaction to your daughter's death?" I asked.

"No," said Craig.

"Was there anyone who seemed to blame you for Corinne's death?"

The two of them glanced at each other. Craig said, "My mother. But that's just her."

"What was her reaction?"

"Snide comments," said Craig. "That's generally her reaction to anything. She said some things that hurt—particularly to Lisa. Finally I told her to get the hell out of here and go home."

"Where's home?"

"Illinois."

"Does she know about John and the group?"

"No."

"Anyone else?"

"No."

"Do either of you have any idea who might be sending those notes?"

The two of them shook their heads, but I thought I caught a hesitation this time.

"It doesn't have to be anything definite," I said. "It might just be something you'd want to check out if you were me."

I saw Lisa glance at Craig. He caught the glance and cleared his throat.

"There're a couple of people from the group I'd want to check out if I were you," he said. "I don't mean to be accusing anybody. Just as a precaution, you know?"

"Who?"

"The thing is, we're not supposed to talk about what we hear in group."

"But, of course, these are special circumstances," I said.

"Maybe," said Craig. "Anyway, I was thinking, I don't really have to violate any confidences to give you what you want. In fact, you can probably guess one of the two people from what you heard the other night."

"Ken Raley?"

Craig nodded.

"Because of his emotional problems?" I asked.

"Yes."

"Any other reasons?"

"No." Craig looked uncertain. "You don't think that's enough?"

"I think it's plenty. Who else?"

Craig looked thoughtful for a moment. Then he said, "You wouldn't know about the other person from the meeting the other night. But . . . well, I assume you're doing a routine background check on everyone in the group."

"I haven't so far."

"I bet the police have—with the accusation and all."

"What kind of background check?"

"You know—things people might have done in the past."

136

"Craig, are you telling me that someone in that group has a criminal record?"

Craig just looked at me.

"Come on, Craig," I said with a sudden flash of annoyance. "Let's not be cute with this thing."

"Don't attack Craig, Mr. Strickland," said Lisa. "He's just trying to help you. He didn't have to say anything. Maybe he shouldn't be saying this anyway."

I felt the impulse to argue, but I held it in check. There was no point in alienating these two. If I had trouble getting the information, I could always come back at them later.

"Okay," I said. "Thanks."

When they continued to give me glum looks, I decided I needed a more congenial subject. "I just realized I don't know what kind of work you do," I said. "Do you both work?"

"I'm a computer programmer," said Lisa, "but I cut down to part-time after Corinne was born. Craig writes computer games."

"The kind where the cartoon characters keep jumping over things and trying not to get bonked?"

"Some of those," said Craig with a smile. "But mostly logic games."

"Craig's been talking about getting more into educational software," said Lisa.

"The idea sort of evolved out of the kind of discussions we have in John's group," said Craig. "After what happened and all, I decided I'd like to do something more serious with my life—but still with computers—and with kids. Most of the money and time goes into the entertainment stuff. I'd like to see what I could do to make the educational software better."

"Good for you."

"Do you have any more questions for me?" asked Lisa.

"No," I said.

"Then I think I'll excuse myself."

Craig and I both stood as Lisa got up. When she'd left the kitchen, I asked Craig to show me the spot where Corinne was taken. He nodded and led me out the screen door to the small back porch. Like the front yard, the backyard was surrounded by a high hedge, though the hedge had some gaps here and there. Through the gaps could be seen a low picket fence. There was a large tree near the house, just off to the right. Craig pointed at the area near the tree.

"There," he said. "That's where Corinne was taken from."

"How old was your daughter?" I asked.

"A year and a half. A toddler."

"She was taken while Lisa was in the house to answer the phone?"

"Yes. She—well, come here, I'll show you."

I followed Craig down the back steps and over to the other side of the large tree.

"Here," he said. He had maneuvered himself to a spot behind the tree where there was only a partial view of the kitchen windows. I noticed that there was a gap in the hedge to the side of us, revealing a small side gate in the picket fence.

"Corinne fell asleep on her blanket, and Lisa wrapped it around her," said Craig. "The phone rang, and Lisa went to get it in the kitchen. It was her mother, upset about something as usual. Lisa says that after a couple of minutes, she told her mother to wait and went out on the porch just far enough to see that Corinne was still asleep. She went back to talking to her mother, but kept looking out the window, thinking she was seeing Corinne's bundled-up feet. Lisa says it was probably two or three minutes until she went out to check on her again. But it could have been more. I know how it is when her and her mother get going. She wasn't worried because she thought she was seeing Corinne. When she went out to check again, she found the bundled-up blanket with no Corinne in it. She also found the gate unlatched. She thought Corinne had wandered off. She went running around looking for her. When she couldn't find her after a few minutes, she called the police."

"She didn't notice a strange car in the neighborhood or anything like that."

"No. None of the neighbors did either. The police think that the man might have parked on the other side of the stream back there and walked over. People take walks along there sometimes. The neighbors wouldn't tend to notice."

I stepped out through the small side gate. Between the hedge here and a small, wooded vacant lot next door, the killer would have had all the privacy he needed. If the inhalant had worked quickly, he could have wrapped the child up in something, even put her in a specially prepared sports-style bag, and been out of there pretty quickly, without being obvious. As always, it would have been very risky, it would have taken luck. One had to hope that before the next child died, the killer's luck would run out.

16

I WAS BACK ON the highway, heading home. It was only four. It would be at least a half hour before the great mass of sunburned, sand-speckled humanity began the reverse crawl home from the beach. After leaving the Caldwells, I'd stopped at Denny's for a hamburger and a coffee, but I hadn't dared stay long. I was in no mood for a bumper-to-bumper reprise of that morning's torture.

There was lots of traffic, but it was moving at a pretty good clip. I slipped into the right lane and set the needle at sixty, letting the speedsters fight for the left lane. I wanted a minute to think over the case.

I had been on the job for five days. I'd talked to Sylvia, John, Jack Malander, Karen and Ken Raley, and Craig and Lisa Caldwell—everyone in the group but Susan Malander, whom I'd try to see tomorrow or the next day. I'd also talked to Ruth Havens.

If I'd had to guess, I would have said that Ruth Havens was sending the threats. She'd half sounded as if she were admitting it, though I didn't know how seriously to take her remarks. If it was her, though, someone else had to have called in the accusation, which had been made in a man's voice. Raley was my leading candidate for anonymous caller, as well as being another possible letter writer. I'd be collecting garbage all week, checking on everyone but John and Sylvia, seeing if any of them had thrown away scraps of paper that might connect them with the latest note. It was a long shot, and I didn't really expect results, but it was always possible that the person threatening John was more angry, or arrogant, than careful.

I would also check with Witmer tomorrow to see if she'd done background checks on the people in Havens's group; if not, I'd do my own. Then I'd see who had what record and whether it seemed to have any impact on the case.

If nothing came of any of that, I'd focus more specifically on Ruth Havens and Ken Raley. Deciding what to do would be tricky. To push those two could be dangerous if one of them was on the edge. I didn't want to identify the person sending the threats by finding him or her standing over Havens's dead body.

Of course it was entirely possible that the person sending the threats was neither Havens's wife nor anyone with a connection to his group. But so far I had no information that would lead me in some other direction.

I slowed for a pickup truck hauling a trailer, glanced in my sideview mirror, waited for two cars to pass, hit my turn arrow, and eased into the left lane. At the same moment a dark blue Camaro two cars behind me jerked into the passing lane, gunning his motor, then hitting the brakes to avoid rear-ending me. He leaned on the horn, moving up on my tail as I moved past the trailer.

I was looking at the idiot in the rearview mirror when it happened.

Something seemed to explode inside the car, and suddenly I couldn't see. I blinked frantically, getting only a blurry impression of road and car. My eyes stung, they were thick with liquid, and I had to fight to keep the lids from blinking shut. I had the sick, panicky feeling that I'd been badly hurt, but I was distracted from that fear by the thud and jarring of my car caroming off the cement median. I rebounded into the pickup to my right and then got slammed from behind, at which point my straight-ahead vision disappeared entirely as the safety glass in the windshield spider-webbed into one huge blur.

I couldn't see to maneuver, all I could do was hit the brakes and hang on. I hit the median again and then another car before I came shuddering to a stop. I braced myself for a blow from behind, but it never came. I was seized with the fear that I'd been badly hurt, that maybe I had terrible injuries that shock wouldn't let me feel. I looked down through what I now realized was one barely functioning eye, relieved to see that my arms and legs seemed to be intact, but disturbed by the sight of blood covering my chest and stomach. I leaned toward the rearview mirror, trying to get a look at my face. There was blood covering the left side of my face, though I couldn't determine its source through a right eye that kept twitching like crazy and trying to close.

I felt suddenly claustrophobic. I pushed at the driver's door only to feel it hit cement, then fought to move in the other direction before I realized the seat belt was holding me back. I undid the belt and maneuvered myself across the passenger seat. As I pushed the door open, I heard a male voice, close, urging me to stay in the car and not try to move, but I wasn't having any of that. I kept going and felt a strong hand clasp my right upper arm and guide me around some kind of vehicle and across the other lane. I was taken to a shady spot and urged in a gravely male voice to lie down. I was helped to a sitting position, which was as far as I was willing to go.

"Can you see what's wrong with me?" I asked in a voice that sounded shaky to my ears.

I lifted my head to give whoever it was a better look. Through the twitching and tearing, I could see a male with long blond hair and some kind of colored pattern on his T-shirt. I couldn't make out his face.

"The only thing I can see, man, is a cut over your eye," he said. "But you may have head injuries. You want to stay quiet. Someone's called for an ambulance. I'll get you a cloth for that head."

He got to his feet, but I was no longer paying him any attention. The phrase "head injuries" had set off some sickening flashbacks—my smashed-in skull, my half-paralyzed body, the moments of terror and depression waiting for surgery. I wrenched my mind back into the present. Focusing on those memories would almost certainly send my nervous system into full panic.

"Here," said the man's voice again.

A cool, wet cloth was pressed against the left side of my face. A hand lifted my left hand and pressed it against the cloth.

"Hold that there," he said.

"Can you see what's wrong with my right eye?" I tried to force the eye open for inspection. It kept blinking shut.

"I can't see," said the man. "You might have gotten some glass or something in their. Try not to touch it."

"Okay."

I felt a pat on my shoulder.

"Hang in there, buddy," he said. "The ambulance will be here soon."

"Anybody else hurt?" I asked.

"Looks like the guy driving the Camaro broke his arm. Everyone else seems to be okay—just a little shook up. Hang on to that cloth. I'll be back to check on you."

I tried to get a look at the accident scene out of my uncovered right eye, but it was still stinging and watering and trying to twitch shut. I got a glimpse of my car against the median, and the pickup, the trailer, and the Camaro all tangled together in the right lane, before I had to give up and let the eye shut.

I removed the cloth from the left side of my face and got a fresh spurt of blood. With my left hand I pushed the top of the cloth back against the eyebrow area, which seemed to be the source of the blood. Using my right hand, I wiped my left eye with the lower part of the cloth, then pushed that part of the cloth aside. The eye was sticky with blood and kept tearing up, but there was no pain and the vision was good. I felt a wave of relief.

Traffic seemed to be stopped in both directions. Through the smashed cars I could see a small audience on the other side of the median—some teenagers in a kind of dune buggy who seemed to find the situation pretty cool, a man and woman who were giving me sympathetic looks from the front seat of a utility vehicle, and a very young girl, looking out a back seat window, who was sucking her thumb and observing me with big serious eyes.

To my left a line of cars stretched down the mountain. I could imagine the mood of the beach crowd with their sunburns and stomach aches now facing a drive home that had just been downgraded from awful to unbearable. They would start by cursing Life (that this should be happening to them), then the county of Santa Cruz (which, to promote low growth, had refused to broaden the road), and finally each other. There'd be a few relationships in danger of breaking up before the day was over.

About twenty yards to my left sat the guy from the Camaro, a heavyset guy in tank top and jeans. He was cursing and moaning and clutching his left forearm to his chest, while the young blond-haired man told him he'd feel less faint if he'd just keep his head down. I wasn't

143

glad the guy was hurt, but I was glad that if someone had to be hurt, it was him rather than someone else. He'd set himself up, tailgating me the way he had.

A highway patrol car was almost to us now, its lights and sirens urging cars to either side as it squeezed its way along the center divider. It moved over to the shoulder and stopped just short of the man with the broken arm. As a pair of cops got out of the car, the volume of the injured man's voice went up, sending out curses about his "fucking car" and his "fucking arm" and "that fucker over there . . . caused the whole thing . . . probably drunk . . . they should lock him up."

Now I was glad he was hurt.

One of the cops, a female, came over to me. She knelt down to look me over, but also, I knew, to smell for alcohol. She asked me how I felt, and I told her about my eyes, and she said the ambulance would be there soon.

"What happened?" she asked.

"I don't know."

"You don't remember?" she asked, the skepticism obvious enough under her official voice.

"I remember it all right, I'm just not sure what it was. I was driving along, and it was like something exploded inside the car, and then I couldn't see, and I hit the median, and then there were other collisions."

"Which car is yours?"

"The blue Taurus."

"I'll be right back."

I watched the officer cross the roadway to my car, but then got distracted by the sight of the ambulance pulling up behind the patrol car. I was glad that medical help had arrived, and I was anxious to get my eyes attended to, but I wasn't looking forward to the ambulance ride. The ambulance people give you two choices, find your own ride or go with them and get strapped into a gurney. It doesn't matter if you have nothing but a bruised shin, and it won't help if you offer to sign a release—you get strapped down or you don't go. It doesn't sound bad, except that you can't move your legs or your arms or even your head—there's a strap for your forehead as well. If you have any tendency toward claustrophobia, or if your nerves are just jangling from

144

the shock of the accident, you can find yourself in the middle of a panic attack. For what ails you, they have two remedies—giving you an oxygen mask or flipping you upside down. For many people, the ambulance ride is the worst part of the accident.

I was thinking about that when the officer came back and told me I was a lucky man.

"How do you figure that?" I asked, sarcastically.

"That explosion you mentioned. It was a bullet going through your windshield. From inside the car it can sound like a bomb going off."

"A *bullet?*"

For the moment, everything else was forgotten.

"Someone fired through your windshield," she said. "My partner's calling the sheriff's department in to check it out. It was probably some idiot taking rifle practice and missing his target. Some of these people move into the mountains and think they're back in the Old West."

I looked toward the Taurus sitting crunched against the median. I still couldn't quite believe what the officer was saying.

"Like I said, you're a very lucky man," she continued. "The bullet went through the driver's side of the windshield. It should have taken off your whole head."

T HE CEMETERY WAS a stretch of grave sites the size of two foot-
ball fields, bordered by a Spanish-style funeral home to the east and
Highway 1 to the west. The eastern half of the cemetery was the old-
est and most interesting part, with large headstones, some ornate as
chess pieces, spread out over the lawn as in some cosmic game. The
western half of the cemetery looked empty until you were close
enough to notice the flat gravestones. Either there was some ordinance
minimizing the cemetery look near the highway or the people with
the budget stones got consigned to the noisy end.

The cemetery sloped down from south to north, sometimes in terraces. Beyond the northern perimeter were woods, a river, an ugly
construction yard, and, in the distance, beautiful rolling hills. I stood
in the southeastern sector of the cemetery, looking down at the service already in progress. I had come here to find Witmer, but it also
felt good to pay my private respects to the small boy, Tony Sestriere,
whose burned body I'd seen, whose funeral this was.

About seventy-five mourners, mostly in black, stood around the
open grave, listening to a service being read by a priest. To the side of
the group, on a small paved path, was the hearse that had brought the
casket, a white Cadillac done up with fake chrome lanterns. Behind
the Cadillac, a small stream of cars flowed along the path into a pond-
sized parking lot.

I noticed Witmer below, her back toward me, observing the funeral. She was holding something black in her hand that looked like
a camera. Not far from her were two observers, bulky men in suits I

guessed to be sheriff's detectives. That a cop should be here to see who might attend the funeral, I could understand. That there were three cops here might indicate some official gesture of support, a gesture probably meaningless—or worse, bitterly ironic—to the mourners themselves.

I made my way down an upper terrace filled with tall monuments shaped like stone spikes. Just below the terrace was a small mausoleum in the form of a Greek temple, its inner wall full of burial vaults that lay one upon the other like so many bunk beds. Farther on was a group of black headstones belonging to a single Italian family whose death dates went back to 1910. Several of the older headstones held framed photographs, black-and-whites showing stiff poses and grim faces, the kind you can see on headstones all over Italy, that turn cemeteries into old family albums.

I noticed Witmer say something to the two male cops. They were standing a few yards away from her, but turned toward each other in a V formation, as if shutting her out. Witmer's remark didn't make them break formation. The one with his back half toward her responded by glancing back over his shoulder, shrugging, then resuming the conversation with his partner. I wondered if this was emblematic of what Witmer had meant when she'd said that cooperating didn't mean they had to take you seriously.

I moved down to the lowest level, keeping several yards behind the cops. Nonetheless one of the men saw me. He nudged his partner, who turned and looked in my direction. Witmer turned as well, saw me, nodded, then turned back and shook her head at the other cops. They lost interest and resumed their conversation.

I turned my attention to the ceremony, frustrated by having the use of just one eye. Something, presumably a piece of safety glass thrown off by the bullet, had scratched the cornea of my right eye. Such a scratch sends the eyelid into protective spasms and causes the tearing up of both eyes. All that, together with the blood spurting into my left eye from the cut over my eyebrow, had all but eliminated my sight during the first few seconds of the accident—before the shattered windshield had made sight irrelevant.

My eye had been attended to at the hospital and a patch put over it. The patch now protruded out of one side of my sunglasses, adding

147

another feature to my winning appearance. Fortunately, the cornea heals fast, and I was told I should be able to remove the patch in another day.

Looking at the ceremony, it was easy to identify the dead child's mother and father—the mother a small woman in black dress and veil, huddled up with pain, and the father a husky, young, brown-skinned man who supported her, or clung to her, it could have been either. Another young woman in black, maybe a sister, stood close to the grieving mother. She held a small child by the hand but in back of her, and away, as if to keep the child from the contamination of death. A heavyset grandmotherly looking woman stood on the far side of them, weeping. An older couple, perhaps more grandparents, stood close to the dead child's parents, their backs to me, the man white haired, with a strong physique now bent in sorrow.

I bowed my head, remembering the small burned figure, hoping there had been little pain in his death, hoping his few years of life had been happy ones.

I raised my head and looked around. Behind me the spiked monuments stood like faceless Easter Island figures, testifying to the silence of the past and the mystery of the lives lived in it. I looked at the headstones close by, all inscribed with name and duration as if, in the end, the length of time one had survived was the one salient thing. The saddest graves were of those who had lived so little, the infants and the small children, whose dates alone could break your heart. Nearby was a small relief of St. Anthony holding a child. There was a small flat stone, For Our Baby, and in front of it, four small teddy bears, weathered and worn.

I looked out over the cemetery and the community of the dead. We all wish they could have gone on to some happy place. But what if we had to choose, right now, whether to let the graves open and the dead emerge, half to heaven and half to hell, or to leave the dead where they lie, without consciousness, forever? Apart from doctrine, most of us, I think, being kinder than Calvin's God, would leave them to eternal rest. This is one of my consolations for no longer believing in an afterlife, that the damned are, in this way, saved.

The funeral service was concluding now, the mourners moving slowly by the family to offer words of sympathy. The family members were turning around to face the others, and I got glimpses of faces I hadn't been able to see earlier. My eye passed over the face of the white-haired man, came back to it a moment with the sense of its being a face I knew, then moved on again as a quarter-profile view convinced me otherwise. I wouldn't have paid him any more attention if he hadn't stepped full faced into my line of vision as I was looking at someone else. My eyes locked on his face, but even then it took me another few seconds before I realized who he was. The recognition brought a sudden rush of adrenaline. I moved over to where Witmer was standing.

"I need to talk to you," I said as I stepped up next to her.

"Wait till the people have left," she said.

"This can't wait. Do you see that guy with the white hair standing over there?"

"Judge Brera?"

"You know him?"

"I know of him," said Witmer. "He consults for the county and teaches a course at UCSC."

"Isn't he a San Jose judge?"

"He was—he's retired now. He and his wife moved here last year to be closer to their daughter and grandson. Brera is the grandfather of the deceased."

"He's the judge who sentenced Earl Ritchie."

Witmer's head jerked toward me. "You're bullshitting me," she said.

"No. That's him. Check the file."

"Jesus." She was silent a moment, then she said, "We need to talk, but not here. Can you meet me at my house in, say, an hour? We can put together some sandwiches if you're hungry."

"Okay." I nodded toward the detectives. "Do we tell your friends over there?"

"No," she said quickly. "I need to process this first. Look, I've got to get back to the station to check on some things. I'll see you in an hour."

Witmer went over to the detectives, said a few words, and then rushed off. I followed more slowly, walking back up the terraces of land, among the tiers of graves. My eyes moved over the low hills beyond the roads. If Ritchie had done this thing, he might well be watching from somewhere, taking pleasure in the family's pain.

Suddenly my image changed from Ritchie watching to Ritchie aiming. The image startled me, and I stumbled slightly. Could it have been Ritchie who'd shot at me the other day? My mind began racing with thoughts and counterthoughts. I told myself I was jumping to conclusions and inventing meaning out of coincidence, even while explaining how it might all make sense. I told myself that at least he wouldn't try it again here, not with all these people, not with cops here. Yet, in spite of this attempt at reassurance, I felt my feet move faster as I headed for my rental car.

WITMER AND I were sitting at the dinette table where we had eaten dinner the other night. Bread, deli meats, cheese, lettuce, pickles, mayonnaise, and mustard were spread out in front of us, along with the remnants of the sandwiches we'd made and eaten. I was sipping a beer, Witmer had a diet Coke.

"You think it could have been Ritchie who took the shot at you yesterday?" asked Witmer.

"It's possible," I said.

Prior to the funeral I'd considered a different alternative to the stray-shot theory: Ken Raley. I'd even called Karen the previous evening, learning that Raley had not been home at the time of the shooting and that he'd once done some hunting—though Karen claimed there had been no guns in the house since the birth of their daughter. Now Ritchie had pushed Raley virtually out of the picture.

"It could have been a stray shot like the cops are proposing," I said. "It would have been kind of tricky to set up a shooting like that. On the other hand, if someone knew I was in Granite Valley—had spotted me or was tailing me—he'd know I'd be coming home before too long. He could have set up along the highway with a pair of binoculars. He'd have known my car; with the long slope of highway there he'd have had plenty of warning. The advantage of the setup is that no one need have suspected I was the intended victim."

"The grandson of the judge who sentenced Ritchie is burned to death, and then someone takes a shot at the investigator who gathered the evidence. If I were in your place, I don't think I'd be wasting any time on any stray-shot theory. I think I'd be focusing everything I had on Ritchie."

"What's your point?" I asked.

"I'd like your help with something."

I'd figured something like this was coming, otherwise why would Witmer be sitting here talking to me instead of running off to the task force? But I didn't know exactly what was coming or whether I'd like it. I waited for her to tell me. She waited, too, perhaps hoping I'd volunteer my cooperation.

When I didn't, she said, "I'm really grateful for the information about the judge. I suppose we'd have made the connection eventually, but it might have taken valuable time. The problem was, we'd worked Ritchie so hard for the first two murders, we'd pretty much eliminated him. Now, of course, he's back, front and center."

I nodded and Witmer went on. "We need to recheck Ritchie's alibis for the first two murders. I'd like you to take a look at the people who gave him the alibis—see if any of them look familiar to you. We can look over Ritchie's file, check out other sources, but not everything's going to be there. You spent a lot of time following Ritchie on that old case. Maybe something will ring a bell with you that wouldn't mean anything to us. And, who knows, maybe if you keep your eyes and ears open, you'll find out a thing or two about Ritchie that we don't know."

"Do a little investigating."

"Yeah, but carefully. We don't want to tip him off that we're suspicious."

I studied her a moment. "In other words, you want to cut the task force out of this and have the two of us do the investigating."

"I didn't say that."

"You didn't have to. If this were a task force thing, you wouldn't want me within a million miles of Ritchie or his friends. Maybe to take a glance at a couple of faces, sure, but that's it."

"That's all I want," said Witmer. "I just meant if you happened to see anything . . . well, you know."

"No, I don't. Look, Witmer, I might be willing to help, but only if you're straight with me."

"I am being straight with you."

"No, you're not."

We looked at each other across the table. Finally Witmer lowered her eyes. Suddenly she looked very tired. "They're taking me off the task force," she said softly.

"Why?"

"Because Ed—that's the other detective I told you about—is coming back from disability leave. The chief says he has more experience."

"That's stupid, taking you off after all this time. You know the case, he doesn't."

"That's what I told the chief. It didn't go any good. Ed has buddies on the task force. And, of course, he's a man." Witmer winced. "Shit, I didn't mean to say that. Maybe that isn't even it. Maybe I just didn't impress anybody. But, hell, no one else has done much either. Damn it, I wanted the chance."

"How long before you're off?"

"A week. Ed comes back next Monday. I'm on till then. Except that I'm not really on, because I'm just holding a place for him."

"The others on the task force know about the change?"

"I think they knew before I did."

"So what's your idea?"

"To work this thing with Ritchie a little bit before I turn it over to the others. I could run to them now with what you gave me, and they'd pat me on the head and say thanks—and then they'd totally forget where they got it. What I'd like to do is work it for a couple of days, put together some other data, then hand in a formal report. If it doesn't keep me on the task force, at least they'll know I did something good."

"It could backfire on you big-time if they figure out you've been holding things back."

"I think the chance of that is pretty slim. I can pretend I didn't figure out about the judge and Ritchie until tomorrow or the next day. I'll say I put it together when I was going over the notes I have to turn over to Ed."

"And if they find I've been messing in things?"

"You could . . . tell them you were upset about getting shot at. You weren't buying the stray-shot theory. A man you helped put in jail was working in town. Of course you'd want to check him out."

"Do I know about the judge?"

"No," said Witmer. "That way they can't say you knowingly meddled in a murder investigation."

"Okay."

"Look, in terms of your doing a little investigating—I guess I'm trying to walk a fine line here. Not tipping off Ritchie is the number-one thing. But I sure could use anything you can get me short of risking that."

"One thing that helps—if I run into anyone from Ritchie's old days, they're not likely to recognize me under all this hair."

"Just don't run into Ritchie. I don't mean just because of the case. I mean because of you. I don't want to see you get shot."

"That's reassuring. Tell me, does it bother you that what you're doing here will delay the task force investigation—including a search of Ritchie's place? Where does he live, by the way?"

"In a trailer park across the street from where he works. As for the search, today's Monday, the boy was murdered Friday—Ritchie has had plenty of time to dispose of evidence. Anything there is likely to stay there a couple more days. Beyond that, anything we can develop could help the task force make more intelligent moves."

Witmer was treading close to rationalization; nonetheless, her reasoning made some sense. It was a flip of the coin either way.

"Will you help me?" she asked.

"On two conditions," I said. "One, that you agree to turn in a report to the task force by Thursday morning."

"Okay."

"Two, that you let me in on the details of the murders."

Witmer shook her head hard. "I can't do that, Strickland. You know that. All that stuff's confidential."

"You're already breaking rules here. You can break that one, too."

"For Christ's sake, Strickland, you're representing a possible suspect. Like we were saying when you first came in, Ritchie may have done all three or just this one or none at all. Your client isn't close to being off the hook yet."

"If you end up charging my client, you'd have to disclose the evidence anyway."

"Maybe. But not before we'd used it to build a case."

"I have no interest in protecting Havens if he's killing those children."

"It's more complicated than that and you know it. What if we think he did it, and you think he didn't? You'd use it. You'd have to."

"I see the problem, but I'm not just going to run errands," I said. "I'm not going to work in the dark. If you want me in, you have to let me in. We're talking about a guy who may be trying to kill me."

"Strickland, I can't give you all those details. I just can't. I'm sorry."

"Then I'm sorry, too. I'm just not willing to work with you on those terms."

I sat back in my chair, and so did Witmer. We looked at each other across the table. Her expression was stubborn and so, no doubt, was mine. I'd meant what I'd said, but I did want to help Witmer—I figured I owed her one—and I certainly wanted to help myself. I figured it would be worthwhile trying to look for a compromise.

"Let's try this," I said. "You go over with me whatever's public knowledge about the case. I'll see what else I need to feel okay about this. Maybe you can give it to me vaguely or indirectly—without feeling you've given away too much. If I can get enough to feel comfortable, I'd be happy to help. If I don't, you haven't given me anything important."

Witmer thought about it. "Okay," she said. "Let's give it try."

"You say Ritchie has alibis for the first two killings."

"Yes."

"What are they?"

"The first time he was supposedly playing cards with three guys in a band he plays with now and then. The second time he was with a girlfriend. I'll give you their names before you go."

"The girl a blond?"

"No. Dark haired. Why?"

"I saw him with a blond the other day. She was real pretty, and it looked like they had a thing going. Any idea who she might be?"

"No. I sure wouldn't mind finding out."

"Did Ritchie have an alibi for the third murder?"

"We didn't even ask," said Witmer. "The first time we took him, and that rental trailer of his, apart, he was still on parole—we didn't need a warrant. The second time we got a warrant. We didn't find anything. We checked both alibis pretty carefully. None of these characters are the most reliable people in the world, but none of them have records. It was a little hard to believe they would lie to cover someone who might be burning kids to death. Maybe we made a wrong assumption."

"Ritchie's alibis—did they cover time of death, the times the kids were snatched—what?"

Witmer thought for a moment. "Times of death, with a healthy margin for error. He didn't have alibis for the times the kids were taken."

"So that means that if those alibis were good enough for you, then you must have been convinced that no timing device was used that would have allowed Ritchie to take the kids, but be somewhere else at the time they were burned to death."

Witmer didn't say anything.

"Let's try a slightly different tack," I said. "The other day when you were telling me what was public knowledge, you said one witness noticed a trail of burned rope that looked like a kind of fuse."

"Yes."

"I saw the same thing. A fuse made out of rope would be pretty crude. It would indicate a real amateur or someone trying hard to look like one. To make a fuse out of rope you could coat it with gun powder and glue or soak it in gasoline. But those would burn so fast they wouldn't give you time to go anywhere. What they would do is allow you some seconds to move back from the body so you wouldn't get singed when all the accelerant on the body ignited."

Witmer just looked at me.

I said, "Of course, if you also wanted to be a little farther away—say, in your car ready to drive, or observing from a couple of hundred yards—you could slow the burning of the rope by soaking the rope in a mixture of gasoline and fuel oil. The more oil, the slower the burn."

"You could do that," said Witmer, finally giving me something.

"Let's assume I'm the investigator and I know the killer used a gas/fuel-oil mixture on the rope. I guess I could be pretty sure that the killer would hang around to make sure the fire ignited. Such a fuse would be pretty unreliable—in wind, for example. It would be risky to leave the scene before the body ignited—especially if the victim had seen your face."

"It would," said Witmer.

"On the other hand, I don't think I'd dare base everything else on the assumption that the killer would need to stay until the fire ignited. The fuse might work just fine if the weather was good. The killer might even have developed a halfway decent time frame if he'd done enough experimenting burning rope with different fuel mixtures. He might risk it—especially if he were a little nuts and if he knew the child had never seen his face."

"How would you determine that the killer was at the scene when the fire ignited?"

I thought about it a moment, then said, "One way would be if forensics would tell me the mix of fuel oil and gasoline the killer had used. I'd also need to know the length of rope—but I'd think forensics could determine that from the ash. Then I—or they—could duplicate the fuse and see how long it took to burn."

"What else might help you?"

"I suppose . . . if I had evidence that the fuse had, in fact, gone out. That either the fuse had been relit or something else was used to ignite the body."

"Let's just leave it at that."

"Okay," I said. "But, though concocting a crude rope and fuel oil fuse wouldn't take any expertise, it might take a little experimentation. Seems possible a neighbor might have noticed that kind of burning. If not, at least it's something you might find traces of if you find the right person."

Witmer shook her head.

"We know where he—or she—did the experimenting. After the first body was found, we did a search of the quarry. At the opposite end we found remnants of a camp fire, and with it, strings of burned rope half covered with sand. Forensics said the different strands of rope had different concentrations of gasoline and motor oil and that burning of those ropes predated the first killing. Apparently that had been our killer, experimenting."

"He found the place such a good place to practice that he brought his first victim there."

"Seems so."

"I assume you tried to trace the materials found with the bodies."

"We figured it was going to be hopeless with the tape and the rope. That would be a one-time purchase, and who would remember that? We thought we might have a chance with the gas cans—maybe several had been purchased at one time or each on different occasions from the same store. But we checked on some stores in the immediate area, and sent notices to some others, but we didn't get any leads. There's no way we could cover all the possible stores in the Bay Area, let alone a larger area than that. But we tried."

"Let's go on to the next thing. When we were talking over lunch, you seemed open to the idea that this fourth murder was either a copycat or just another one of the string. That's got to mean that there aren't significant discrepancies between this murder and the others."

Witmer gave a vague nod.

"But shouldn't that be prima facie evidence that they were all done by the same person?" I asked.

"It would be, except for a couple of things," said Witmer. "First of all, a number of details about the other murders were published. We tried to get the people who witnessed the scene to shut up, but these days that's hard to do. The other thing is that details vary from one murder to the next—as if the murderer were tinkering. So if certain details are a little different from three to four, well, there were some earlier discrepancies as well."

"With the inhalant as well?"

"Yes."

"What about the numbers?"

"What about them?"

"When we talked at Denny's, you said witnesses said there were numbers next to a couple of the bodies that looked like the kind of numbers you buy for front doors or mail boxes. That's what I saw next to the Sestriere boy. They were brass colored. I take it there were numbers next to all four bodies."

Witmer hesitated, then nodded. "Yes," she said. "Though the colors and materials varied."

"The number I saw next to the Sestriere boy was three-two-three-two-one-nine."

"Yes. The others are confidential."

"Come on."

"Why? You don't need them."

"Look. You're asking for my help because I know a bit about Ritchie. You think I might recognize a face you wouldn't. Maybe I'd spot something in the numbers, too."

"That seems unlikely."

"Do you know what Ritchie's favorite music is?" I asked.

"I can guess from where he plays that it would be country."

"Okay, but that's not something that would have popped into your head."

"No."

"Can you name one of this favorite songs?"

"Of course not."

"Well, I can. Look, I'm not saying I'm an expert on Ritchie, but I know more about him than you do, and I know people who know even more about him. Suppose those numbers had to do, for instance, with song lyrics. That would never cross your mind."

Witmer looked at me hard for a moment.

"Damn it, Strickland. You'd have to promise that these numbers are just between us—no matter what."

"I promise."

"Okay," she said. She looked down at her notes. "The number next to the Malander boy was two-two-one-two-two, the Caldwell girl, two-one-two-nine-one-oh, and Kiedrich, one-four-one-two-one-three."

"Anybody have any ideas on what the numbers might mean?"

"No. None that are worth a damn."

"Okay," I said. "I think I've got what I need. Let's just go over the possibilities in terms of Ritchie's involvement in the killings. One is that he wasn't involved at all, that someone else killed all four children, and it's just coincidence that one is related to the judge who gave Ritchie a hard sentence."

"That's too much coincidence for me."

"Me, too. A second possibility is that one person did the first three killings, and Ritchie did a copycat for the fourth to cover up what he was doing. A third is that Ritchie did all the killings."

"Let's hope it's the last one," said Witmer. "That we can get Ritchie and be done with it."

"If Ritchie did do all of them, why?"

Witmer shrugged. "Maybe he was just setting up the fourth one," she said.

"Too elaborate and too strange. There have to be easier ways to cover up a killing."

"Maybe Ritchie didn't do the first three in order to cover up the fourth. Maybe he was just doing them and then included the judge's grandson as a bonus."

"I like that better," I said. "But why's he doing them at all?"

"I don't know. For whatever reason sick people do sick things like this. He's an arsonist and he's hung up with fire—maybe prison pushed him over the edge. You said he lost his child when he went to jail. Maybe that has something to do with it."

"I suppose another possibility is that there's some connection between Ritchie and the families of the first three victims."

"I've already got that down to check out."

"Good."

Witmer picked a piece of paper off the top of the pile in front of her and handed it to me. "Here are the names of the people who gave Ritchie his alibis, along with whatever information we have on them. You know, we really need to rush this thing."

"I'll start tonight," I said. "Oh, I almost forgot a question I was going to ask you. Did you do background checks on the people in Havens's group?"

"Yes."

"Does anyone in the group have a criminal record?"

Witmer smiled. "That sculptor . . . what's his name? . . . Malander," she said. "About eight years ago, after he got dumped by his girlfriend, he tried to scare off the new boyfriend by waving a gun around and shooting it in the air. He was bombed at the time. Apparently he had a hell of a drinking problem. He pleaded guilty to a misdemeanor and was given a suspended sentence on condition that he go into AA and do community service. He did both and hasn't been in trouble since. I couldn't see how that was relevant to the murder investigation."

"Probably not. But it could be relevant to the matter of someone threatening Havens. Especially since I know that Malander is drinking again."

THE BARROOM WAS long and dark, a tunnel opening onto the light and noise of the stage. I was sitting at the back, near the blackened pool table, in the darkest corner of the room. Near me were the quiet couples and the brooders; the hooters and hollerers were closer to the front. The band was belting out some country rock, and the tiny dance floor was packed with cramped dancers who could only bounce in place, jiggle their forearms, and yell a lot. The dancers ranged from real bikers to fake cowboys, and they all seemed to be having fun.

I'd just come from a movie theater where I'd suffered through a blood-splattered teen horror film and some grease-splattered popcorn to get a couple of looks at the good-looking, dark-haired female usher behind the snack bar who'd given Ritchie his alibi for the second killing. I hadn't gotten a flicker of a memory of ever having seen her before.

I had only come into the bar after making sure Ritchie's car wasn't outside—and after removing that absurdly conspicuous patch from my eye. No one had shown much interest as I'd entered the bar, only the waitress who'd been too harried to give me more than a quick smile as she'd taken my order. I sipped at the draft she'd delivered. It was ice-cold and tasted very good.

I was watching the bandstand through the thick trails of smoke that floated like streamers beneath the colored ceiling lights. The bandstand was set low, and I had to strain to see the band members over the bobbing heads of the dancers. The band was now playing one of Hank Williams, Jr.'s chip-on-the-shoulder country songs about how he loved God and guns and living free in the U.S. of A. and if you didn't like it, he was going to shoot you in the eye. Or something like that. The crowd loved it.

The drummer, the bass player, and the singer, according to Witmer, had given Ritchie his alibi for the first killing. I was positive I'd never seen either the singer or the drummer before. Both had distinctive faces I was sure I would have remembered. The bass player, with his long dusty blond hair and short beard, looked so generic that I'd never know if I'd seen him before or another just like him. Who notices bass players anyway?

The one person I did recognize was the waitress working the front of the room. She was the blond I'd seen in Ritchie's car. Since Witmer wanted her identity, I decided I'd come back at closing time and either get her license plate number or follow her home. By the time I'd finished checking on her, it would be time to get the Malanders' garbage; I could then go home and get some sleep before sorting through the mess. I'd been through the Caldwells' garbage that morning and had gotten nothing out of it but a lot of old fish smells. I was hoping the Malanders were carnivores, or vegetarians.

I took another sip of my draft and was about to leave when the singer climbed down off the stage and a familiar face took over. Actually, a familiar face and girth. This, I now realized, was the regular singer. He was thanking "Sam" for sitting in. This was Bob Smith, with the heavy body, handlebar mustache, and cowboy hat. I was kicking myself for not having recognized the name, but its commonality had thrown me off. Also, I'd known him best as Poky, a nickname not noted on the information sheet Witmer had given me.

Smith and Ritchie had been buddies back when I'd been investigating the arson. Smith had been a heavy drug user at the time and I'd suspected he and Ritchie might be into some things together, but since I'd had no reason to think Smith was involved in the arson, I hadn't considered the rest my business. Anyway, I could have been wrong. As Witmer had indicated earlier, Smith still had no criminal record.

Whether Smith being part of an alibi meant anything, I didn't know. The friendship might have given him motivation to lie for Ritchie and get his friends to do the same—especially if they'd all gotten hit with some hard-luck story about how the cops were on a vendetta against Ritchie to get a fast arrest. On the other hand, maybe Ritchie really had been playing cards with Smith that night—and their friendship was the reason why. In any case, the information would provide an extra flourish for Witmer's report. The task force could work it out from there.

I'd gotten what I'd come to the bar for—more if you added in the waitress—and it was time to go. There was no point risking having Ritchie walk in while I was there. I left a dollar on the table, got up, and went outside.

The night was beautiful—cool and clear, with a moon that was nearly full. I walked up the street toward my rental Accord, trying to decide what to do next. I had a couple of hours to kill before the bar closed—not enough time to make it worth going home and coming back. I had Havens's book in the car, so I decided to find someplace to sit and read. A block farther down the street I came across a small restaurant/coffee shop that was going to be open for a while. Inside, I ordered coffee and pie.

I flipped through the rest of Havens's book just to see what was there. The last half of the book seemed to consist mainly of library research and interviews Havens had conducted to determine current thinking on stages of grief and techniques for dealing with them. There was a middle section of the book on various philosophies of suffering. The book began, of course, with Havens's story, and I had almost finished that part. I flipped to my book-marked page and began to read.

I continued to sit alone in the darkness, drinking hard, cursing this world of suffering where I could end up in a burning hallway, faced with the cruel choice of saving my child or other children, where, no matter what choice I made, children would die. In my bitterness I would create fantasies of better worlds—not as pleasant escapes, but as contrasts, to show how miserable this world of ours really was.

It's child's play to imagine a better world than this one. If we can imagine it without contradiction, then God could have created it, and we can blame Him for not having done so. If there is no God, we still know these better worlds might have happened by chance instead of this one, and like the gambler, we can curse the turn of the wheel that ruined us.

Many of the arguments people give to defend suffering are weak because they assume one aspect of this world to argue for the necessity of another, instead of considering broader possibilities. They say we'd be unhappy no matter what kind of world we lived in because we get bored with whatever we have; but we might have had a different psychology. They say that death is necessary to limit population without ever considering the possibility of a world in which creatures had a different reproductive urge or access to greater resources.

Adding free will to the mix makes things trickier, but not as tricky as the free-will fanatics like to suppose. It's easy to imagine creatures who have free will along with a tendency toward good and a limited ability to destroy. People who would argue this isn't free will are the same ones who describe us as having free will and a tendency toward evil; if one is free will, so is the other.

Maybe free will would inevitably bring about some suffering; maybe some amount of suffering is desirable for contrast. But even if this is true, by limiting our ability to hurt or be hurt, the suffering could be kept to the level of flu and tooth aches and mild bad moods.

In the darkness of my apartment, I could see those better worlds so clearly, more hospitable worlds in which people made with gentle natures existed in bodies that were less able to be hurt and had much stronger recuperative powers. Worlds in which people were made to be happy. The clearer I could see those worlds, the more I hated this one, and the more anxious I became to leave it.

I continued drinking heavily, seeking self-destruction by the slow alcoholic numbing of my mind and body, death by anesthesia. But I hit a snag. Instead of oblivion, I began to find sickness, nightmares, and episodes of pure terror. I tried to blot out these things with harder drinking, but that just made everything worse. To dull myself into death would have been fine, but the feeling that I was going crazy or sinking down into some true hell where terror could never be stopped, that I couldn't take. I knew I had to reverse my course.

But only so far. I had no thought of ever being happy or reconciled or even sober. I just wanted to go back a little, to find a level of inebriation I could live with. But it turned out to be too late. However I modified my drinking, the fear was always with me.

After a while, in desperation, I went to see a therapist, hoping to get some advice on how to handle my panic. The therapist agreed to see me on the condition that I stop drinking. I agreed, though I had no intention of stopping. The trick was to go easy the evening before my appointment and show up shaved and showered and in fresh clothes, then I could hit the bar as soon as the session was done. Sometimes I'd get angry and quit the therapy, but after a week or two, not knowing what else to do, I'd return.

I was living in a kind of frightened suspension, unable to go either forward or back. The way to destruction had been cut off and the way to salvation seemed both impossible and undesirable. I didn't want some Pollyanna acceptance of a world I hated or the loss of the son I'd loved.

And yet, along with my anger and my bitterness, there was exhaustion and bad nerves and a longing for some kind of peace. I wanted to find a place in myself or in the world where I could find—not happiness, not acceptance—but distraction and rest. It was that, finally, that made me willing to take my therapist's advice.

She was always after me to focus on something other than myself and my past. At her suggestion I sought out other people, but I soon found their conversations hollow. How was I to put up with talk of everyday things, when such things seemed so irrelevant to the real issues of death and despair? I tried taking courses at a local college, but I could only get interested in the darker issues in literature and philosophy, and these only promoted more depression.

Next I tried charity work, volunteering first at a homeless shelter, then in a nursing home. These activities were good in that they got me out of my apartment, gave me some kind of a routine, and made me focus on things outside myself. But none of them engaged me emotionally. The chores were routine, and often the people I dealt with were whiny, depressed, and ungrateful. I know this reaction is a weakness in myself. I admire those with a greater capacity for sympathy or a greater sense of what needs to be done. But for someone who was drinking and depressed, these were not the tasks or the people who were likely to help.

Then came the children. At a certain point in my ever-changing volunteering, I began working in a children's cancer ward. I took to it almost at once. My job was to play with, read to, and talk with the children. I found that I was good at these things and that the children seemed to like me. I know I liked them, and that this liking was the first positive feeling I'd had since Ruth had left me. My feelings for the children sometimes brought forth painful memories of Ricky, but I was so tired of depression that almost any other feeling was preferable.

There was much misery in that hospital ward, and it was painful to see. But in spite of this, or maybe because of it, I felt profoundly at home. Psychologists tell me that people sometimes seek out unpleasant situations because those situations conform to some preexisting view of the world. The abused seeking abusive situations would be one example. For me that children's ward, with the suffering of those innocents, exemplified the awfulness of the world with particular clarity. Here, among these children, any talk of the benefits of suffering seemed ludicrous and incredibly mean. Also my being there felt like a small gesture of revolt against such a world.

There were a lot of children I really liked (and a few I didn't), but the one who had the greatest effect on me was a boy I'll call Stephen. He was nine—slender and dark haired—and he was dying of leukemia. He was a normal enough boy, active and impatient, often mischievous, sometimes peevish. But he had courage and a good heart, especially with regard to his parents and his eight-year-old brother, Bobby, a Down's syndrome child. Throughout the course of his increasingly difficult and decreasingly effective chemotherapy, Stephen was protective not only of his brother, but also of his parents, who were frantically denying the reality of Stephen's situation.

What crying Stephen did, he did with me. We made friends right away, and as things got tougher for him, I became like a safe third parent, one who could handle his weakness and his disease. To play this role for him, I had to pretend a lot, particularly as I came to care for him more and more, and as his condition got worse. Sometimes after calming and comforting him, I would head off to the men's room to cry. There were many moments when I was sure I wasn't up to this, but his own courage was an example for me.

I came to like Bobby, too, with his sweet disposition and the well-documented tendency in Down's syndrome children to feel happy. I felt, like Stephen did, the desire to protect that handicapped child, though in some ways he was in less need of protection than the rest of us, having a disposition that already protected him from a lot of unhappiness.

One day Stephen slipped suddenly into a coma—mercifully, because it saved him from a lot of fear and pain. But his parents suffered terribly, all the more, I think, because they realized that their denial had left their son to face his death alone. I hurt, too, but the pain felt clean, not polluted by the sort of anger and bitterness I had felt in the past. I think it was the first time I'd suffered a serious loss without overpowering feelings of guilt.

During the week Stephen was in a coma, I tried to help his parents by taking care of Bobby. Bobby was concerned because everyone else was unhappy, but along with his concern, there was puzzlement, too, as if he couldn't quite understand what those feelings were about. It was easy to distract him, and we had fun playing together. The hours I spent with him felt like a small gift I was giving to Stephen. I enjoyed Bobby's peace of mind, grateful that he could be spared the suffering of the others.

And yet . . .

It occurred to me soon enough that in some essential way, Bobby represented the world I'd been wishing for all this time, a world of people limited in ways that made them happy and peaceful. Such a world wouldn't have to be filled with Bobbys exactly. No doubt a God could create people like Bobby who were more conventionally attractive, who had a greater intelligence and a greater range of interests. But I also realized that such aspects were more cosmetic than essential. If happiness and peace were what I was after, everything else was secondary. Bobby was happy and Bobby was gentle. That was what I had wanted of people in my world. (To note that Down's syndrome children could not survive by themselves in our world would be beside the point. An all-powerful God could create a world that protected and nurtured them.)

I liked Bobby and cared about him very much. But I loved and admired Stephen. I kept asking myself if I would really want a world in which Stephen wasn't possible. I realized I

167

wouldn't. And yet for Stephen to be possible, so would everything I hated in this world, all the misery and the pain.

I thought about these questions by the hour, as I played with Bobby, as I went to check periodically on the comatose Stephen and his grieving parents. As many had been before me, I was caught in a dilemma. To have people I could love and admire, I would have to accept a world I despised, a world that could destroy those people. Hard as it was for me, I finally decided that I couldn't give up people like Stephen, no matter the pain it might cause his parents or even Stephen himself. Or me, or Ruth, or even Ricky.

It's pain that makes possible our humanity—with its grandeur and its pettiness, its heroism and cowardice, its saints and its sinners. What we are is bred in suffering and would disappear without it. Even the hating of it is part of it. It is right that we should hate suffering, that we should struggle with everything in us to defeat it, to try to relieve the pain in our lives and in those of others. But even as we fight it, in philosophical moments we must temper our bitterness with the knowledge that we need this suffering, that forced to make the most fundamental sort of choice, we would have to choose this world all over again. It is this knowledge, finally, that can save us from despair. Like Jesus, all of us must suffer and die for a world in which it is possible to be human. When Jesus said in the Nineteenth Book of John, verse thirty, "It is finished," he meant simply that it was finished for him. For us, however, it is only beginning. . . .

THE BLOND'S HOUSE was off the first Granite Valley exit, a quarter mile from where Ritchie worked. The house sat in the crotch of a Y formed by the sharp-angled intersection of two roads. The busier road, which formed the base and left arm of the Y, was like a two lane country highway; farther on it would pass a stretch of open land, ascend to the crest of a hill with a panoramic view, then dip down into miles of woods. The road that formed the right arm of the Y, was a quiet, suburban street, lined with apartment houses, a park, and a school.

The property looked like a piece of a poorer yesterday that the bulldozers had missed. Watered by a creek bed and neglected by its owner, the property was a thick tangle of vegetation that stood in sharp contrast to the mowed weeds across one road and the prim lawns across the other. The house, a run-down ranch-style dwelling, would have been an eyesore without its trees and bushes; half-hidden by all that green it had a slightly romantic, if still impoverished, air.

The house was constructed in the shape of an L, the base a jutting garage; the inside of the L faced the smaller street. To the left of the house, alongside the garage, was a fenced-in yard where thin grass and a few pathetic flowers fought a losing battle against the ever-present shade. The outside of the L was outlined by the creek bed, now dry, and the main road. A small footbridge crossed the creek bed to the house's back door.

The blond's name was Sheila Yeager. I'd heard her first name spoken in the bar. Her full name had emerged from both a cross-directory check of the address to which I'd followed her the previous evening and from a motor vehicle check of the license number of the Mustang that had been sitting in the drive. The blond hadn't actually driven the Mustang the previous evening. At closing time, she had seemed to look around for a ride that hadn't shown—Ritchie?—then had gotten a ride home from the other waitress. I'd sat in my car down the street from the blond's house for an hour to see if Ritchie would show later; he hadn't. Finally I'd driven back to Bear Creek to collect the Malanders' garbage. Sorting through it at home I'd found nothing of interest.

Witmer or her task force could do whatever checking needed to be done on Sheila Yeager. My only remaining interest was to determine if Ritchie was staying in the house part of the time. Or more exactly, if some of Ritchie's belongings might be there. If they were, the eventual search warrant should include the Yeager house. Since there wasn't time to stake out the house, I would have to interview some neighbors. Normally this would have been tricky, even with the woman gone, as she was now; one of the neighbors was bound to tell her about the interview. But given the position of Yeager's house, I thought I might be safe. Along the main road, the only building visible from the back of Yeager's house was a small apartment building across the road set a very steep fifty yards up a slope. I couldn't see Sheila Yeager struggling up that slope to borrow a cup of sugar, yet the residents would have a good view of her house from their rear balconies. On the suburban street, where sociability seemed more likely, the only building directly across from the Yeager house was a day-care center. The buildings up the street were apartments, and I figured the occupants would look within their complexes for neighbors to visit with.

I started with the apartment building across the main road. I drove to an upper street, parked in front of the building, then walked around to the backyard, which overlooked the Yeager house. An older couple that I'd spotted from below were planting some flowers on the slope just below their ground-floor patio. The woman was wearing a blue smock and a straw gardening hat. The man was wearing blue cotton slacks, a yellow golf shirt, and a baseball-style cap with the logo for the De Laveaga Golf Course, a masochist's delight of thick woods and narrow, sloping fairways just down the road in Santa Cruz.

"Good morning," I said, as I approached the two of them.

The woman gave me a wary look. The man gave me a friendly brush-off.

"Sorry, young fella," he said, "we're not buying any."

"That's okay, 'cause I'm not selling any," I said. "I just want to ask you a few questions."

The man chuckled. "You mean like, 'Are we satisfied with our present vacuum cleaner?' "

"Nothing like that," I said. "I'm doing a security check—"

"We've got a security system," he said.

I took a deep breath. "I'm a private investigator," I said. "The woman in the house down below has applied for a job which requires that she be bonded. The bonding company has hired me to do a security check. It's routine, but it needs to be done."

"Well, that's a new one," said the man.

He looked at me expectantly, as if still waiting for a catch.

"I thought she was a waitress," said the woman.

"She is," I said. "But now she's trying for a different kind of job."

"I like that," said the man. "A young person trying to better themselves."

"I hope it's a day job," said his wife. "It's not good for a young girl to have to come in so late."

"It is a day job," I said. "Do you know her well?"

"We don't really know her at all," said the woman. "We said hello to her a couple of times when we were out walking—that's all. We don't go walking down there anymore, there's too many cars."

"Have you been to where she works?" I asked.

"No," said the woman.

"Then how did you know she was a waitress?"

"Because of those outfits she wears. Black skirt and white blouse."

"When you met her walking, did you get any kind of impression of her?"

"Not really," said the woman. "But she seemed nice enough."

"How is she as a neighbor?"

"We hardly think of her as a neighbor—with her being so far below," said the man. "Sometimes she has parties kind of late, but they don't bother us up here—not if we keep the windows shut."

171

"Does she live alone, do you know?" I asked.

"I think there was another woman living there, but I haven't seen her for a while," said the woman. "She's usually got a boyfriend hanging around, but I don't know if any of them actually live there." She frowned. "Was that all right to say? I don't want to get her in trouble."

"No problem," I said, with what I hoped was a reassuring smile. "Bonding companies aren't that old-fashioned anymore. Is there a boyfriend around at the moment?"

"I think so," said the man.

"What's he look like?"

"Thin. Dark haired. Wears an earring. I know because I was driving by the other day when he was coming out of the house. I think that's the same guy I've been seeing around for a couple of weeks now. It's hard to tell. They all tend to look alike to me."

"I know what you mean," I said.

I hung around for a couple of minutes of small talk—their flowers, his golf game—then thanked them for their help and went around to the front of the building. I figured I'd gotten about as much as I was going to get from people up here on the hill, but, just in case, I tried the other three apartments. Two didn't answer, and the third yielded a glimpse of a woman who told me curtly over the chain lock that she had no time to talk.

I drove back down to the right fork of the Y, parked in front of one of the apartment buildings, and began walking the street. I stopped a man in a dark suit, but he turned out to be an insurance adjuster who was just in the neighborhood on business. I stopped two kids on skateboards to ask if they knew where my friend Earl Ritchie lived. They didn't know the name but said they'd seen a man matching the description I gave them hanging around at that "pretty blond lady's house" down the street.

As I continued on, I saw a middle-aged woman in shorts and a T-shirt wheeling a garbage can out to the street. I tried to be as nonthreatening as possible as I greeted her, but I needn't have bothered. She watched my approach with the stiff confidence of a bureaucrat who knows she has all the power she needs to deny your piddly petition if she's so inclined.

I gave her the same story I had given the older couple.

"But I hardly know the woman," she said.

"That's all right. As long as you live in the same neighborhood and know who she is." I smiled apologetically. "A lot of this is just routine."

"In that case, it sounds like you're wasting my time."

"It's not always routine," I said quickly. "One of our applicants turned out to be selling drugs. I got that information from a neighbor like yourself."

"I hope you turned him over to the police."

"We did give them her name," I said, straight-faced, adjusting my fiction to give her a little zing.

"That's good," she said. A faint smile played at her lips. "Do you have some ID?"

I showed her my license.

"Mr. Strickland," she said, comparing my face to the photo. She handed it back. "All I can tell you, Mr. Strickland, is that I don't know anything bad to tell you about the woman. She seems very nice."

"That's good to hear. Can you say the same for her roommate?"

"What roommate is that?" she asked.

"Some neighbors say that a wiry, dark-haired man wearing an earring seems to be living there part of the time."

The woman's face flushed slightly, and she gave me a disgusted look.

"Oh, brother," she said.

"What?"

"You're actually checking on the woman's sex life, aren't you. I don't believe you people. Hasn't anyone told you it's not the 1950s anymore?"

"I'm not concerned with her sex life," I said, making my voice sound mildly indignant. "I'm concerned with who this guy is. Suppose the woman were living with a convicted criminal. We'd be stupid to bond her."

"If you want to know who he is, why don't you just ask her?"

"That's the thing, we did. She said she lived alone. That's not what I'm hearing. So I'm wondering why she said what she did."

"How long ago did she file her application?" asked the woman.

"Several weeks ago. Why?"

"Well, that explains it," she said, looking pleased. "The man only moved in a couple of weeks ago."

"How do you know?"

"I saw him move in."

"You did?"

"Yes. He was carrying some men's things in on hangers. And I remember he put a bunch of boxes in the garage."

"Well, that clears that up," I said with a smile, glancing down the street at the closed door of the Yeager garage. "You've been a great help."

"I just hope you've learned a lesson from this," she said.

"What's that?" I asked, looking back at her.

"Don't assume the worst of people. You need to trust people more."

"Yes," I said. "I believe I do."

IT WAS COOL WITHIN the shade of the redwoods as I walked up to the Malander house. The door opened and Susan appeared, wearing something loose and old-fashioned and pretty. A sweet baking smell wafted over me, as seductive as perfume in its homey way. I was taken back suddenly to the days when I was first in love with Katie, when the idea of making a home with her had seemed so incredibly romantic. It had been, too, for a while.

"Smells good," I said.

"It's carrot cake," she said. "Come in and have a piece."

I followed Susan through the small living room, with its yard-sale furniture, into the tiny kitchen with its nicked cabinets showing layers of different paint. Through the back window of the kitchen I could see Malander moving in and out of his studio.

I was here to ask Susan the same questions I'd asked everyone else. But I'd just been given another assignment as well. Witmer had learned that part of Malander's community service had been spent teaching ceramics classes at the prison where Ritchie had done his time. There was no evidence indicating that Ritchie had taken any of those classes, but Witmer was still checking out a possible connection between the two men. She'd asked me to ask Malander about Ritchie.

Susan cut me a piece of the carrot cake and poured me a cup of coffee, and we sat down at the kitchen table. The cake was very good, and I told her so.

"I'm sorry I wasn't here the other day," she said. "I had to make a delivery. There's this new store over in Capitola, and they agreed to carry some of our things, and they were having this sale, and they wanted our stuff like right then, and I couldn't miss the chance."

"No problem," I said. "Anyway, it was my fault for being late."

"I don't know if it was worth your time coming back to see me. Jack and I talked about everything before you two talked, and then he told me afterwards what you talked about, and I don't think I have anything else I can tell you."

"Did Jack mention that he suggested I check out Ken Raley?"

"Yes," said Susan. "We talked about that before you came. We both feel kind of bad about bringing up his name because Karen has been so nice to us, and it feels like, you know, betraying her to say something. But with these kids dying . . . and you asked for our ideas . . . I don't know, I just felt we had to. Knowing what bad shape Mr. Raley is in and the fight he had with John."

"You did the right thing," I said.

"I hope you understand we're not accusing him. It's probably nothing. John doesn't seem to take the fight all that seriously, and he should know better than anyone. He says Mr. Raley was out of his head when he said all those things."

"What kinds of things did Raley say, do you know?"

"We weren't in the group then, but Karen's brought it up in group, and I heard Sylvia talking about it one time. I guess Mr. Raley said some really awful things, about how John should have saved his son and deserved to have him die. And how if John liked suffering so much, Mr. Raley hoped he'd get a lot more of it. There might have been some other things, but I don't remember what they were."

"On a different subject, does the name Earl Ritchie mean anything to you?"

"No," she said.

"Do you know anybody who works in a gas station over in Granite Valley?"

"I don't think so. Why?"

"It's probably not important. Just a detail that needs checking out."

I pushed my chair back. "I've taken up enough of your time. I'd better go talk to Jack. Thanks for the cake. It was very good."

"Dave . . . wait a minute. Can I ask you something?" The volume of Susan's voice had changed abruptly, becoming little more than a whisper.

"Of course," I said, leaning back toward her.

"It's something I can't get out of my mind," she said. "Burning the children to death . . ." Susan faltered, her eyes dropping. "I could understand the fire if the man were trying . . . to torture them . . . for pain. But to make them unconscious and then burn them. Unless the police . . . but I don't see why they wouldn't be telling the truth . . ."

I could sense the thing she feared lurking like a huge dark thing— the thought that the police might have lied, that the children might have suffered horribly after all. For the parents of the murdered children, that dark form must have continually menaced them from the edges of their minds, insinuating itself into their dreams.

"They wouldn't lie about that," I said.

Susan's expression didn't change. I had thrown out the answer without thinking, then realized that talk of police honesty wasn't likely to convince her, or anyone else, these days.

"They wouldn't dare," I said. "They have to make a case against the killer when he's caught. If they lied about something as important as the inhalant, they'd risk screwing up their whole case."

I was simplifying. Even if the police weren't lying, there were possibilities other than no inhalant/terrible suffering or inhalant/no suffering—but I didn't want to think about those gradations myself. The important thing now was the relief I saw in Susan's face.

"Thank you," she said.

"Strange as it is to say, I don't think the children were the main objective of the killings. What I mean is, the children were killed to make some sort of point. Making them suffer wasn't part of the agenda. In fact, it looks as if the killer tried hard to make sure they wouldn't suffer."

"What was the point then?"

"I wish I knew." I studied her pale face for a moment. "Are you all right?"

"I'm trying to be," she said.

I said good-bye, went out the back, and walked to the garage. As I approached, I heard things being banged around and Malander cursing. I stood outside for a moment among the garden sculptures, giving Malander a chance to calm down. When he didn't, I called his name over the noise.

"Yeah, what?" he asked angrily as he came stomping outside. He saw me, and his anger level dropped. "Oh," he said. "It's you."

"Hi," I said.

"This isn't a real good time for me," he said.

"I just have a couple of quick questions."

He looked at me irritably. Then he nodded. "Okay, come on back."

He turned and charged back into his studio. I followed. Malander was rattling things again by the time I joined him.

"Some days I can't find a fucking thing around this place," he said as he kicked aside some metal gadget on the floor.

The alcohol smell I'd caught vaguely on Malander outside was a lot stronger in here, and as I glanced around I noticed a half-full pint of whiskey partially tucked behind an unfinished clay figure on a corner of a work table. I reminded myself that I wasn't there to represent the Temperance League. Day drinking might not be the best antidote for grief and depression, but that was Malander's business, and anyway, I'd tried the same medicine myself for a while. What was my business was whether his past trouble had any bearing on the present case.

"Excuse me a minute," said Malander.

He pushed open a door that went back to a third section of the garage I hadn't noticed before. As Malander disappeared, I looked around at his work, still fascinated by the disfigured creatures with their aura of evil and decay. In particular, my eyes were drawn to the figure fallen in front of the dark god. My dream of the other night had invested this sculpture with a special power. I looked closely at the faint impression of the face on the stone, trying to read its expression. I saw that the face was not just remote, but ambiguous as well: that, depending on the angle, it could seem either cruel or benign.

"Not quite," Malander was mumbling to himself as he came out the door. He stopped in front of me. "What was it you wanted to ask me?"

177

"Do you know a man named Earl Ritchie?"

"No. Am I supposed to?"

"He works at a gas station just off the Granite Valley Drive exit. Once in a while he sings at the country bar here in town."

"I hate country music," said Malander. "What about him?"

"I thought you might know him. He was in prison when you were teaching your ceramics classes."

Surprise, then anger, showed in Malander's face. "Who the hell told you about those classes?" he demanded.

"No one had to," I said. "Background checks are standard in any kind of investigation."

The anger slowly left his face. "I was young and stupid," he said. "What was the guy's name again?"

"Earl Ritchie."

"Doesn't ring a bell. But it was a long time ago. You're thinking he was in one of my prison classes?"

"I was wondering if he was. Take a look at this."

I pulled out a photograph of Ritchie that Witmer had given me. Malander looked at the photograph for a few seconds, then handed it back.

"I don't remember him. And I didn't keep any records from those classes."

"The prison has records. They're checking them out."

Malander nodded, seeming to think something over. "Is he a suspect in the murders?" he asked.

"No," I said, lying. I didn't want Malander or anyone else descending on Ritchie. "It's a related matter."

"Oh. Well, I'm afraid I don't know him." Malander glanced behind him. "Just a minute."

Malander went into the back room again. I let my eyes fall on his dark sculptures, thinking. In having me ask Malander about Ritchie, Witmer had to be considering the possibility that Malander was involved in the killings. It seemed a long shot: That Malander had had some trouble with drinking and anger when he was younger, that he might have taught a class to Ritchie in prison, and that his art showed an obsession with disfigured, possibly burned, bodies seemed a fairly weak basis for suspicion. But, of course, it had to be checked out.

I noticed that the door to the back room had been left partially open and that it was possible to see inside. I took a couple of steps closer to the door. I saw Malander checking a gauge on something that looked like a small, stainless steel, top-loading washing machine.

"Do you mind my asking what that thing is?" I asked, from the doorway.

"What? Oh, it's a kiln."

"I thought kilns were big brick ovens."

"They used to be—you can still make them like that. This is a small electric one. I've just been waiting for the temperature to cool a few more degrees so I can take some pieces out. Come in if you want."

I stepped through the doorway and walked over to where Malander was standing.

"How do you manage to do all your pieces in something that small?" I asked.

"Actually I don't fire many pieces. The garden pieces are all cement. You just let them set. The bronze pieces I take to a foundry."

He glanced at the gauge again.

"Have you talked to Raley?" he asked.

"Yes."

"What did you think?"

"I don't know. He's not in very good shape. Whether he's the one threatening John—we'll have to see."

Malander glanced at the gauge again. He released the lid and lifted it up. I felt a blast of heat against my face and heard Malander curse.

Two heads showed at the top of the kiln; one of them had cracked from the heat. The one intact was an older man with a short beard. His face was gaunt, the skin stretched tight over jutting bones. His thick nose was flattened slightly, as if it had once been broken. His brow was wrinkled, his lips, compressed, his eyes reflective and sad. There was a magnificence to the face, a sense of wisdom and courage, a sense of the man's having faced tribulations and come through. The broken face was that of a youth, its gentler lines shaped by softer flesh. Yet the flesh was contorted; the eyes and mouth were open hollows. It was as if the youth, defenseless and stunned, were watching some terrible

179

thing about to engulf him. Or something that had engulfed him, if you counted as part of the sculpture the broad crack that ran down one side of the face.

"The heads are beautiful," I said. "It's too bad about the one."

Malander shrugged, apparently reconciled to the damage. "It's a crapshoot," he said. "When you subject pieces to this kind of heat, some just aren't going to be strong enough to make it."

20

THE LAST REMNANTS of sunset had disappeared from the sky, and a full moon was starting to rise. The lights in the apartment houses had gone on; the street was quiet. The Yeager house was dark, the driveway empty. Sheila Yeager was at work, I knew. I'd driven by the bar a half hour before and seen her Mustang there.

The house was vulnerable now. I wasn't planning on breaking and entering—just sneaking into the side yard. I was hoping a glance through the garage window would confirm the existence of those boxes the neighbor had mentioned. With the garage door closed, I couldn't do my confirming from the street. I also felt a nagging curiosity about a shovel I'd seen leaning against the inside of the fence; I wanted a look at the blade to see if it had a nick like the one used to cover over a tire track at the scene of the fourth murder. That done, Witmer could report whatever we had and let the task force do its thing. If Witmer hesitated, I'd force her hand: The delay had been profitable, but it had gone on long enough.

I walked up the drive, then turned and looked back. The day-care center across the street was closed, a single night-light showing in the empty main room. Only two apartment windows were visible from where I stood, one showing cracks of light from behind a pulled-down shade, the other full of light, but empty of any human face. Feeling safely unobserved, I slipped through the side-yard gate. The yard, with its tall fence and wild shrubbery, seemed a world apart, but I knew that was something of an illusion. Any light I used could be glimpsed from outside if I wasn't careful to shield it.

I waited a moment to let my eyes adjust to the dark, then moved up to the wall of the garage. I put my penlight against the window, cupped it with my hands, and turned it on. Sure enough, there were several boxes stacked inside the empty garage. I turned off the light, waited for my eyes to adjust again, then moved toward the back of the yard where I'd seen the shovel leaning against the fence. The shovel was still there. Turning on the light, but touching nothing, I examined the blade. The edge was nicked in a couple of places. That didn't mean this was the shovel Ritchie had used at the murder scene, but it meant that it might be.

I turned off the penlight, waited again, then moved back the way I'd come. Suddenly I froze, as bright lights seemed to sweep over me. No, the lights had only swept the trees overhead. Still, a car had just pulled into the drive. Was it the cops? Ritchie? Had I been spotted?

I moved to the back fence to look for another gate. I couldn't find one. Then I remembered the impression I'd had that morning—how the back of the house had seemed almost sealed off, as if to make it less vulnerable to intruders who might think of entering it from the more anonymous main road. I put a foot on the fence, to scale it, then heard the garage door open. I stepped back down. There had been no police radio and no voices; no one was entering the yard. Maybe I hadn't been spotted, maybe this was just someone coming home.

A light went on inside the garage, sending an elongated rectangle of light out across the thin lawn. I heard a single set of footsteps walking about, then duller sounds, as if things were being moved. Feeling more curious than threatened now, I moved along the fence until I had taken a ninety-degree angle and was opposite the garage window, able to observe the window from behind some trees. I didn't take long to realize what was going on: Ritchie was loading the boxes into his car. Suddenly the problem wasn't my getting away—it was his getting away.

How important were those boxes? If they'd been brought here two weeks ago, they couldn't contain anything used during the most recent murder, however they could contain things related to the earlier murders or used in preparation for the fourth murder. More likely, the boxes contained high school sports trophies and yearbooks—or simply cold weather clothing—brought here because of the limited space in Ritchie's trailer. What was important was simply knowing where Ritchie's things were, just in case. Ritchie might be moving these boxes back to his trailer. But if they were going somewhere else, I wanted to know where.

Still, it would be tough to follow him. I'd be stuck here in the yard until Ritchie drove off, and then I'd have to get to my car up the street. I could scale the back fence now, but that would gain me nothing. I couldn't get to my car from the main road without walking all the way around the house and passing in front of Ritchie. The only thing I could do was to see which way he went, run for my car, then try to find him on the road. The odds weren't good. If I did lose him, though, I'd drive to his trailer, hoping he'd simply gone there.

I waited where I was until I heard the trunk lid shut, the car door open and shut, and the motor start. Then I moved across the yard, keeping low, and crouched behind the gate. I watched the car turn right out of the drive, stop at the corner, then turn right on the main road. That last right turn had given me my best chance, I knew, as I raced for my car. The road ahead ran through open land, where even cars taking side roads would be visible from some distance away. But I had to get out there fast enough to take advantage of the view.

A minute or two later, I spotted two cars a mile or so ahead, one tailgating the other. There was traffic coming from the opposite direction, making it difficult for the rear car to pass. A little farther on, the front car showed a left turn signal, and both cars came to a stop. I strained forward as I closed in, trying to figure out which car was Ritchie's, but I couldn't get close enough. The left turn was made, and now the cars were simply two separating sets of lights, one traveling perpendicular to the road, the other traveling straight ahead at increasing speed. Had Ritchie been the one in back, held up by a slower car in front? Or had he been the one traveling slowly, perhaps made cautious by his load? I couldn't decide, but inertia kept me going straight.

Then I got a break. Another car approached, its lights dimly illuminating the interior of the car ahead of me. There were bulky shadows in the back seat that could well have been boxes. It wasn't definitive—it was possible that neither of the two cars had been Ritchie's—but I felt my confidence lift as I continued to go straight.

The road climbed a hill to a crest that yielded a view, to the left, of dark hills sprinkled with lights, set against the moonlit sky. Then we dipped down into woods, where occasional window lights marked houses set back from the road. Eventually the road flattened out as it followed a valley between two pine-covered hills. I wondered how long I could keep this up without being too obvious, and almost at once I found out. We came to a Y, with the main road going right and another road, marked Caution, One Lane, going left and uphill. The car in front took the left, and I kept going right, knowing that my taking that left would have given everything away. I hit my brights before I passed the intersection—a driver impatient to see the dark road ahead. The lights showed me the familiar Dodge sedan, with boxes piled high in the back seat. Okay, at least now I knew that was Ritchie. I'd also caught a glimpse of a small sign telling me the name of the road was Mountain Crest.

I slowed as I drove past, watching the lights of Ritchie's car climb the ridge. In a few moments his lights disappeared, and I could assume I was out of Ritchie's sight. I made a U-turn and drove back to the intersection, trying to decide what to do.

It looked now as if Ritchie were planning to store or dump those boxes in some isolated spot. How was I going to find out where? Even if Ritchie didn't necessarily suspect the next set of headlights he saw, he certainly wouldn't do what he intended to do with other headlights in sight. My only chance was to follow without lights. If it could be done.

I pulled off onto the shoulder just short of the intersection, cut my lights, and let my eyes adjust to the night. There seemed to be enough moonlight seeping through the pines to let me to drive without lights. Still, my brake lights could give me away. I flipped the trunk lid, got out of the car, and removed the bulbs from the lights inside the trunk. I also took my Colt and holster from their hiding place in the trunk and strapped them on. I got back in the car, picked up my cellular phone, and dialed Witmer's home number. Her message machine took the call. When the beep had sounded, I said, "Witmer, Strickland. Ritchie has those boxes from his girlfriend's garage in his Dodge, and he's driving them up Mountain Crest Road. I'm going to try to follow him. In case anything goes wrong, I wanted you to know. One other thing. There's a nicked shovel in Sheila Yeager's side yard that should be checked out."

I tossed the phone onto the seat, turned onto the one-lane road, and began making my way up the hill. Driving without lights was trickier than I'd thought it would be. Here on the ridge, the trees were thicker and let less moonlight through. The road and the shoulders were a bit grayer than the terrain to either side, but similar enough that I had to go very slowly and concentrate—especially since the road here was mostly a series of bends. I knew I might meet a car coming the other way, but I wasn't worried about that. In this darkness, approaching headlights would be easy to spot. And my headlights were still usable in case I needed them to warn someone off.

The road became level for a time, then descended in a series of curves, then leveled out again. I had just started to speed up when I had to hit the brakes. There were taillights ahead, and they weren't moving. I showed no lights as I stopped, but still felt obvious, sitting there in the road. However, I was half-hidden by one bend, as Ritchie was by another, and his night vision, after driving with lights, shouldn't be good. Maybe he wouldn't notice me.

What was Ritchie doing? Most likely, he was hiding or dumping his boxes. But it was also possible he'd stopped to see if he was being followed. In that case, either he didn't see me and would go ahead with his plan or he did see me and would abandon it. I'd just have to wait and see.

Then I got another image: of Ritchie, armed, working his way back toward me along the dark hill to my left or along the slope below my vision to the right. I felt my hand move to my gun while I was telling myself the image didn't make sense. Even if Ritchie did know someone was following him, he couldn't know who it was. It would most likely be a cop, and I couldn't see him shooting a cop when all he had to do was move on. On the other hand, if he knew there was something incriminating in those boxes, maybe he'd be willing to do anything to make sure he didn't get caught. As I peered nervously into the night, I reached up and flicked the switch for the interior light of the car so that it wouldn't come on when the door was opened: If I had to get out of there fast, I wanted it to be in darkness.

I felt a wave of relief when I saw the taillights begin to move again.

The lights disappeared, appeared, then disappeared again as the car took some curves. I eased down on the accelerator and began to follow. As I took that first curve, I was looking toward the spot, some yards ahead, where Ritchie had stopped. But had my focus been on what was just in front of me, I'm not sure I'd have seen it in time—that huge missing piece of road.

I hit the brake, even while knowing it was too late to do me any good. In what seemed an instant of suspended time, my mind took it all in. To my left, the intact portion of the narrow road, along with the broadened shoulder that made passage possible. Straight ahead, a jagged half-moon tear in the road, perhaps fifteen feet long, as if some monster had sunk his teeth into the side of the hill and taken a bite. To my right, dark air.

Terrified, I braced myself, knowing I'd be dropping onto a landslide with a slope that could be anywhere from vertical to fairly steep and with a height of anywhere from five to a hundred feet. The car skidded, dipped, seemed to hang for a moment, then fell. I could see the slope now, it was fairly steep, and maybe fifty feet high. The car fell, the impact jarring me so hard, in spite of my seat belt, that it took me a moment to realize the car wasn't rolling. Amazed, I saw that a few feet of plateau and some large, well-placed rocks had allowed the front of the car to dig in and hold.

Then I saw that the relief I felt was premature. The car, in addition to being tipped forty-five degrees forward onto the small plateau, was leaning far to the right, toward the slope; the position seemed awfully precarious. Getting out of the car wouldn't be easy. On the driver's side, all but the roof and a few inches of window were below the road and close to the first, nearly vertical, cut of hill. There wasn't enough room to open the driver's door or even squeeze out the window. The only possible exit from the car was out the passenger door, which hung over the slope. There was no problem with the drop, it was only a few feet. The problem was that shifting weight to the passenger seat might be all that was needed to dislodge the car. If the car started rolling just after I'd unfastened my seat belt and started crawling across the seat, I'd end up banging around inside the tumbling car like a die in a dice cup. If the car started rolling just after I'd gotten out on the slope, I'd be crushed. It might be best to stay where I was—until morning, if necessary—when I could honk down a motorist and have them get help. Eventually, with a tow truck cable hooked to the car, I'd be able to slip out the passenger side without danger. If the car did go during the night, at least I'd be seat-belted in.

I glanced down the slope. At the bottom was a moonlit streambed, with a small trickle of water and a wide bed of white gravel. Beyond the gravel were heavy woods, but the car wouldn't roll that far. The slope itself was clear of things the car could smash into. Maybe I could survive the fall if I were belted in.

I started feeling dizzy as I stared down the slope and forced myself to look away. My eyes came back to the roadway, and I jerked upright. A dark figure was moving toward me along the road, a rifle gripped in front of him with both hands. I'd imagined Ritchie long gone, unaware of what had happened behind him. I had the sudden feeling that Ritchie was behind all this, though I couldn't see how that made sense. In any case, there was no time to think about that now.

I undid my seat belt and began to slide over the hump of the automatic transmission toward the passenger seat. I did so too slowly, in partial paralysis, almost as afraid of what I was about to do as of what was coming toward me down the road. But then the explosion of Ritchie's bullet filled the car, and the paralysis was gone. I pushed open the passenger door and threw myself out. I slid and tumbled down the slope, past construction cones and a broken stop sign, flailing wildly, my movements a confusion of trying to control my descent and make it faster. I was in panic, listening for another shot and for a sound I feared just as much, the sound of the car beginning to roll.

I tumbled to the bottom, then scampered to my right, getting myself behind a thick tree with heavy brush to either side of it. I took a deep breath and slowly leaned my head out. The car was still where it had been on the slope; Ritchie's face was above and behind it, looking down in my direction. My hand went to my holster, fumbled around, and found nothing.

No gun.

I patted at my body and then at the ground around me, my movements becoming more frantic. Where the hell had the gun gone?

"Strickland, you should learn to drive a little better," said Ritchie with a laugh.

I extended my reach to the ground beneath the bushes around the tree, leaning out as far as I dared. Nothing. I backtracked with my eyes, moving up the probable path I'd taken down. Still nothing. I cursed myself for not having protected the gun better. Without it, what chance did I have?

"You should learn to look behind you," said Ritchie. "I been on your tail since Monday night. I described you to some friends, and they called me when you went to the bar. I followed you when you followed Sheila home. When I saw you at Sheila's tonight, I figured it was time we took a little drive. I knew if I took some things, you'd come after me. How do you like my little trap? It just occurred to me on the spot. Pretty good, huh?"

What should I do? I looked around. My surroundings were as I'd seen them from the car—the landslide, the creek and gravel bed, and the woods. The slope to either side of the landslide, I noticed, was heavy with vegetation. I would stay behind the tree until Ritchie started down the slope. At that moment, when he'd be off balance, I'd run like hell, trying to keep the tree between me and Ritchie. The odds of success were small, especially with my lame leg. But it was the only chance I had.

"You don't have to be shy about talking to me, Strickland," said Ritchie. "I know where you are. You're right *there.*"

On *"there,"* he fired, the bullet slamming into the side of the tree trunk just above me, sending a shower of bark down into my face. It occurred to me that I could help my odds a bit if I could make Ritchie think I had a gun.

"Ritchie, if you get a kick out of shooting up the tree, be my guest," I said. "But come any closer and I'll blow your goddamn head off."

There was silence, what I figured was thinking-it-over time.

"I don't think you got a gun," he said.

"Then come on down."

"You wouldn't want to squeeze off a round, would you?"

"What's this? The amateur hour? You'll hear the gun fire when you feel yourself fall."

I hoped Ritchie couldn't hear my voice shaking under all this gunfighter bullshit. I figured he'd have to assume initially that I had a gun. That didn't mean he wouldn't come after me, it meant he wouldn't come straight at me. He'd walk some distance down the road, slip down the slope there, then work his way back toward me, looking for a shot. If I could catch a glimpse of him at his maximum distance, that would be the best time to run.

I got to my feet behind the tree. I saw Ritchie back away from the edge of the road, then move to my right and disappear from view. Something told me to run now—that I'd gain the time it took for Ritchie to get down the road in addition to the time it would take him to come back. But I resisted the impulse, just in case, and it was good I did. About twenty seconds later Ritchie appeared suddenly at the road's edge, his rifle pointed, ready to shoot. It had been a trick, and if I'd bought it, he'd have had me. Ritchie cursed, then laughed— the laugh of a gamesman whose first move has failed, but who has plenty more. He disappeared from view once again.

For the next half minute my eyes darted back and forth along the slope to either side of me, looking for some sign of Ritchie climbing down. As I waited, poised to run, my fear kept telling me that I'd waited too long, that he'd already made a descent I hadn't seen and was now moving toward me. I started counting slowly, telling myself that at ten I'd have to gamble and go.

At the count of eight, I spotted him on the slope about seventy-five yards to my left, the south, the direction from which we'd come. I turned and ran, trying to keep the tree between Ritchie and me as I splashed across the stream and crunched my way across the gravel. I'd planned that part okay, Ritchie didn't even fire a shot.

As I reached the edge of the woods, I glanced back quickly, double-checking Ritchie's position. As I began to turn back, a dull glint of metal caught my eye, and I saw it then, my gun, lying on the slope, about a third of the way up. The gun was just to the right of some hunks of dirt that had made it impossible to see with my earlier line of vision. The impulse to go for the gun lasted no more than a second before I rejected it and ran into the woods. There was no way I could have made it across the stream and up the slope, given where Ritchie was.

The running quickly stopped as thick brush impeded me and twigs tripped up my bad foot. I had to settle for thrashing my way ahead at the pace of a fast walk. I knew I'd be all right for another few minutes: I had a head start, and the number of trees between us would make it difficult for him to get a decent shot. But I also knew that as soon as he closed in on me—as he was bound to, with two good legs—I'd be an easy target. There were too many patches of moonlight interspersed with the shadows for anyone's movements to go undetected. My only hope was that somewhere not too far ahead would be a downslope or a small hill or a pile of boulders—anything that would give me a chance to change my course with his view of me blocked.

I found what I needed some fifty yards ahead—a ravine deep enough for a man to move in unobserved, if he crouched. I scrambled down into the ravine and found the bottom full of large stones. They'd be easier to move over without noise than the brush of the woods.

The ravine paralleled the road here, running north and south. I moved north, away from Ritchie's approach, which would come from the southwest. When Ritchie did reach the ravine, he'd have to think twice about which way I'd gone. Maybe he'd guess wrong. But even as I expressed that hope, I decided he wouldn't guess wrong. In his place, I would have guessed that I'd gone north. To have gone south would have taken me closer to the approaching hunter—against all the instincts of the prey.

I followed the ravine, moving as quickly as I could. After fifty or sixty yards, the ravine curved west, back toward the road. I stopped, found a spot where some rocks on the upper edge would disguise my head, and straightened up, looking back in the general direction from which I'd come. I saw Ritchie approaching the ravine about forty yards back. He looked along the ravine in both directions, then across it, seeming to study the terrain. He was deciding where to go, and I waited, barely breathing, to see where that would be. After a moment, he turned and came toward me.

But not right toward me, I saw, in the next second. He was on a course that would cut across the bend of the ravine like the base of a triangle, but not an equilateral triangle. A thick tangle of brush would prevent him from cutting much of the corner. He'd reach the ravine about fifteen feet ahead of where I was standing now. I could be well past that point by the time he reached it, but I would have lost a lot of distance. So I did what I should have done before, but what my gut begged me not to do: I doubled back.

190

I could feel myself trembling as I began to retrace my route along the ravine. I was moving in Ritchie's direction now, and even though he was angled away from me slightly, we would pass very close to each other. If he decided to take another look at this section of the ravine, I was dead.

I heard him start to run, and I froze. That running seemed to come right at me—until the moment I realized that he had just run by. Ritchie had obviously decided I didn't have a gun, and there was going to be no creeping around on his part. I had to move fast, and it was safer to do so now, since Ritchie's noise would hide my own. Ritchie would follow the ravine in the other direction for a bit, but then he'd be rushing back. By that time I had to be out of the ravine and away, forcing him to make another guess, and maybe guess wrong. If I could get him to make a couple of wrong guesses, I might just be able to slip away.

I passed the spot where I'd entered the ravine and continued on. Soon there was another bend, as the ravine angled slightly east, away from the road. I stopped and looked out. There was no sign of Ritchie. Which way should I go? The success of the last maneuver encouraged me to try a variant. I figured the last direction Ritchie would expect me to take was back toward the road, so I'd head there. There was one other attraction to heading that way: the gun.

I climbed out of the ravine and moved slowly toward the road, keeping low, trying to be as quiet as I could, stopping every few yards to look and listen for Ritchie. I would make my way back along the edge of the woods, just short of the streambed, then wait there as long as it took to identify Ritchie's position. If it was feasible, I'd go for the gun. If not, I'd slip back into the woods—maybe move south along the road and try eventually to cross it.

When I got close to the streambed, I stopped, keeping low and close to some heavy brush. Directly across the stream from me here was the slide—with the gun visible on the slope. If I did try for the gun, I'd go straight for it, then, gun in hand, move sideways toward that same tree. Then I'd try to move up the slope there, through the brush, with the tree to my back. To reach the road with that gun—what a relief that would be.

Suddenly headlight beams appeared, startling me as they must have startled Ritchie. I felt a reflex spurt of hope, even while knowing it was absurd. If I called out, the driver wouldn't be able to get the police here quickly enough to help me—even if there was a cellular phone in the car—since my calling out would give away my position and undo whatever maneuvering I'd managed so far. My calling out might even force Ritchie to kill whoever was in the car. I couldn't use the car's approach as a distraction to help me get the gun, since the car would only draw Ritchie's attention toward the slope. I didn't dare move off in any other direction until I knew Ritchie's position: I might just run into him. Better to lie low until the car had gone.

I saw the car appear, then slow, as its beams illuminated my disabled rental car. The other car crawled up to the rental car, then past, as the driver, no doubt, was trying to decide what to do. My thoughts urged the car to keep going, but after a few more yards, it stopped. Maybe the possibility that someone was hurt had been too much to ignore. I would stay still and hope Ritchie did the same. Let whoever it was look, and then go on.

The interior light of the car went on, and everything was changed. The face was Witmer's. Suddenly there was real hope. Witmer had a gun to keep Ritchie at bay and a radio to get help here fast. The thing was, she'd have to be warned before she made herself an easy target. But in warning her, I'd give away my position and make myself an easy target. I did the only thing I could think to do: I took off running across the stream while I screamed a warning to Witmer, hoping I'd catch Ritchie off guard, hoping I could make it to Witmer's side of my old tree before Ritchie had time to shoot. Once I was there, Witmer could cover me.

"Witmer, get back!" I screamed as I ran across the gravel. "Ritchie's got a—"

A shot rang out, and I winced against the expected blow, but it was Witmer who screamed and fell. I kept running, knowing I was committed, panic propelling me on. I felt the hopelessness of it. Ritchie had shot Witmer, so he must have a shot at me as well. I kept waiting for the bullet as I raced across the stream and started scrambling up the slope, but no shot came, and I began to feel a glimmer of hope as I got close to the gun, thinking how once I seized it, I'd throw myself to the side and roll—anything to confuse the shooter—as I struggled for the safety of my tree. As I reached out for the gun, there was a sudden explosion of sound and dust, and the gun wasn't there anymore—it was skittering down the slope.

"Gotcha," said Ritchie.

Frozen now in my crawl, I looked up. Ritchie was standing on the roadway, his rifle pointed down at me.

"Don't move," he said.

I saw part of a form I took to be Witmer's body lying near Ritchie's feet. He poked at the body with his foot, then poked harder. Satisfied, he stepped away and moved closer to the edge of the road, looking down at me over the hood of my car.

"Stand up, Strickland," he said.

I struggled to my feet, having to kick away some dirt to form footholds before I could keep my balance. My mind cast about for some desperate thing to try and quickly concluded there was nothing. I suddenly felt very tired. There comes an end to running.

"Why me?" I asked. "I'm not the one who sentenced you."

"You helped put me there, Strickland. Anyway, sitting there in the joint, you can learn to do a lot of hating."

Ritchie raised his rifle to shoot, but Witmer's arm lifted off the ground at the same moment, and the explosion that came was from her gun, not his. Ritchie screamed and grabbed for his leg, hopped sideways, then tripped, pitching forward off the cliff edge, falling spread-eagle down onto the roof of the car, his rifle skidding over the roof and landing on the slope just below.

The car shivered under the force of his weight and rocked once, sending tiny rivulets of gravel down the slope.

"Stay still, Ritchie," I said. I scrambled sideways, out of the path of the car, then started up the edge of the landslide, my eye on the gun in case the car didn't go.

Whether Ritchie's staying still would have helped him, I don't know. In his panic or his desire for the gun, he wasn't listening. He started to push himself up to his hands and knees, and maybe that one movement made all the difference.

The car shivered again and tilted downward. For a moment it

seemed suspended, like a tree just starting to fall. Ritchie was clawing at the car, trying to get himself free, but it was all useless motion. As the car went, he started to scream.

He pitched forward like a diver, headfirst, his back arched, so that as his body was caught between the car and the slope, it was folded in half, but backward, with a snapping sound I seemed to feel in myself as waves of nausea went over me. The night appeared to darken as the car went over and then thundered downward, leaving behind it that bloody thing on the slope.

I jerked my head away and fought the faintness. Then I scrambled up the slope toward the place where Witmer lay.

21

WITMER WAS SITTING up in the hospital bed, her left arm and shoulder packed into a cast. A tube flowing into her wrist was attached to some kind of intravenous drip. She looked pale and sweaty, her hair stringy against the pillow. I stepped aside for a nurse who was leaving the room, then approached the bed.

"Christ, Strickland," said Witmer before I got a chance to get a word out, "it took you long enough to get here." Witmer's voice was hoarse, but it had a surprising amount of energy, given how weak she looked.

"Your buddies have been keeping me busy," I said. "They're not real happy with us—as I'm sure you know. They didn't want us getting together until they'd questioned us separately."

"What did you tell them?"

"Something close to the truth. I figured it was useless to lie. With you passed out last night, there was no way to get our stories together—and what we talked about in your office wasn't enough to cover my looking at alibi witnesses and following Ritchie into the woods. Thanks, by the way, for coming to the rescue. I'm sorry you got hurt."

Witmer just grunted.

"Obviously you got my phone message," I said. "But how'd you get there so fast?"

"I called home from the car to get messages. I wasn't all that far away. Never mind that now. Tell me what you said."

"I stuck pretty close to the truth, but I tried to tell it in a way that made you look as good as possible. I told them how *we* spotted the

195

judge at the funeral. When I told them about your sending me to the movie theater and the bar, I kept emphasizing that you were putting together a report for the task force that you were going to turn in today. I told them that taking off after Ritchie and those boxes was my idea. I kept going on about what a hero you'd been to save my life."

"How did they react?"

"They didn't seem too impressed."

Witmer made a face, swore under her breath, and slumped back against the propped-up bed. The motion obviously hurt her, because she winced and grabbed at her shoulder.

"Well, you did better for me than I did for myself," she said after a moment. "It gives me a couple of things I can emphasize when they come back at me."

"So how's it looking with the investigation?" I asked. "They wouldn't tell me anything."

"It's looking like shit, Strickland. Do you know what they found in those mysterious boxes?"

"Nothing related to the murders, I assume."

"One box held a collection of beer mugs. Another was full of pictures and other things related to his wife and kid. They were all like that."

"The boxes were just a ploy to sucker me in. That was obvious from what Ritchie said."

"That's another thing," said Witmer. "We're a little short of corroboration here. We've got no chance of proving Ritchie shot up your car that day since no slugs or cartridges were ever found. You say Ritchie lured you out into the woods last night, but there's only your word for that. If Ritchie hadn't shot me, we'd have a lot tougher explaining to do."

"Thank God he did," I said.

Witmer gave me a sharp look.

"Joke," I said. "Bad joke."

"Ritchie's mother has already shown up with an attorney and dollar signs in her eyes, talking about how the police were harassing her poor son, who was trying so hard to go straight. According to her, his friends say he told them he was being hounded by the police. I don't see her getting anywhere with all that, but you never know with lawyers, and anyway that sort of thing always gets the department nervous—the possibility of negative publicity, if nothing else. Damn it, those forensics people better come up with something, or I'm in deep shit."

"Maybe the shovel."

"Your great shovel," said Witmer sarcastically. "They've already checked it. Your shovel, nick and all, does not—I repeat, does not—match the imprint at the scene."

"Too bad."

"That's the understatement of the year." Witmer glared at me. "Goddamn it, Strickland."

"Hey, don't start turning on me," I said. "I'm not the one who got me into this. I'm not the one who suggested holding out on the task force."

"No, you're only the one who had to go playing cowboys and Indians with our suspect and blow the whole thing."

"Witmer!"

"Scratch that," she said, holding up her one good arm. "Sorry. I hurt like hell, and I'm feeling cranky. And worried. I shouldn't take it out on you. I'd have done the same thing in your place."

"It's okay," I said. I reached over and squeezed Witmer's right hand. "Maybe you should try to get some sleep."

"Maybe I should."

"Is there anything I can get for you?"

"No, thanks. Sarah's taking care of that now."

"Okay. Try to get some rest. I'll check back with you later."

I HAD COME TO Havens's group again to tell them all about Ritchie, and I'd been talking for the last half hour. We were all arranged as we had been the week before—Havens straight ahead of me, Karen Raley and the Malanders to my right, the Caldwells and Sylvia to my left.

"He *may* be the one who killed those children," I said. "That's all anyone can say at the moment. We'll know more when the forensic people have done their analyses."

"How long will that take?" asked Karen.

"Different tests take different lengths of time—some, days, others, weeks."

A throb of pain went through my head. I put a hand to my face and rubbed my eyes. I'd had a headache and sore muscles most of the day, and in the last couple of hours I'd begun to feel feverish, as if I were coming down with something. Of course, I'd had a strenuous night and almost no sleep; maybe it was only that.

I became aware that Lisa had spoken, but I hadn't caught what she'd said. I apologized and asked her to repeat it.

"I was asking if you had any ideas why this man might have killed our children," she said.

"We have a possible revenge motive for the fourth killing," I said. "Why he might have killed the others is still a mystery. The police are investigating that now."

"You said this man was a convicted arsonist," said Malander. "Isn't that a kind of motive? I mean, if someone likes fire, likes burning things."

"It would relate, certainly, but it wouldn't explain everything. Arsonists don't generally go around trying to kill people. But who knows what happened to him in prison. He'd lost his own child when his wife disappeared after his conviction. That might have been a factor, too."

"Now he's dead, and we'll never know," said Malander.

"On the other hand, if he were alive, he'd be unlikely to say anything. Even if he did, a lot of times the explanation is just as crazy as the crime and doesn't satisfy anyone who's looking for answers."

"How do you explain something like this, John?" asked Lisa.

"If you're talking about why people do things like this, I don't have an explanation," said Havens. "Maybe one day we'll understand the workings of the mind better and be able to explain such things. Or maybe they come from free-will choices that are ultimately beyond explanation. I don't know. I wasn't speaking to that. What I was saying was that a world with suffering in it—including terrible, unexplained suffering—is better than a world with no suffering in it. It's something people have tried to argue for centuries. It's just that I had to come to it in my own way, through my own suffering. If you agree with what I and others have said, and you believe in God, then you can believe that God did the right thing in letting there be a world like this one. If you don't believe in God, then nobody planned it, but you can feel it was good that the world turned out this way rather than some other. But these are hard truths. The pain still hurts like hell. Sometimes everything in us is going to want to scream and curse the world. But if we can hold these truths in the back of our minds, they can give us some sense of meaning in the midst of tragedy, help us accept what we cannot change."

There was a heavy knocking on the front door behind me. Before anyone had a chance to move, the door opened and someone stepped into the room. I saw surprised expressions, and heard several people say "Ken" before I turned to see Raley standing there. He looked much as he had the other day, right down to the glower. I don't know what the others were thinking, but I was scanning him, looking for any sign of a weapon. His hands were empty, and there were no obvious bulges.

"Ken, I'm so glad to see you again," said Havens with a hearty, welcoming tone as he got up and walked toward the newcomer.

"Ken?" said Karen, with more concern in her tone, as she, too, approached him.

Havens and Karen converged on Ken at the same time, which might not have been the best thing. Ken glared from one to the other, as if their togetherness confirmed his reason for anger. It was obvious that Raley was not here for reconciliation. I stood up, ready to help out in case Raley started trouble.

"Ken, come sit down," said Havens. "Let me get you a chair."

Havens's demeanor was still friendly. Either he wasn't picking up on the signals from Ken or, more likely, he figured a little bonhomie was the best strategy for calming Raley down. Karen was on a different wavelength.

"Ken, honey, what's wrong?" she was saying, touching his arm.

"You're coming with me," he said.

"Ken—"

"You're through coming here," said Raley. "Thanks to *you*"— Raley glared at Havens—"and this group, people are saying that maybe my wife is a murderer. I won't have her subjected to that. If she doesn't have sense enough to see that, well, I do. I won't allow it."

Raley's voice was quivering, whether from his obvious anger or the stress of the confrontation. I noticed that his hands were shaking.

"Ken—" said Havens.

"Shut up," said Raley. "We're through listening to you—both of us."

"But Ken," said Karen, "all that gossip is done. The police think they've found the killer."

For a moment Raley didn't seem to have heard his wife, so focused was he on glaring at Havens. Then he blinked and turned toward Karen, a look of confusion coming over his face.

"What did you say?" he asked.

"I said, no one's going to be accusing me or John or anyone else in this group. The police have found the killer."

"What?"

For a moment, Raley just stared at her. Then his anger snapped back into place. He grabbed his wife's arm.

"It doesn't matter," he said. "We're going."

"Ken, you're hurting me," Karen protested, her free hand tugging at the captured arm.

"Ken, easy," said Havens, stepping toward Raley.

Raley let go of his wife and sprang at Havens, catching him off guard, sending him tumbling backward over an empty chair. Raley pounced on Havens, his fists flailing. Malander moved at the same moment I did, but I was closer. I grabbed Raley in a choke hold and yanked him back, though even then, I'd have had some trouble getting him off Havens without Malander's help, so frantic was Raley. When Raley was on his feet, I hauled him to the nearest corner and pressed him up against the wall. I had Malander pat him down for weapons. There were none.

All this was done amid general commotion and Karen saying over and over, "Don't hurt him, please, don't hurt him."

Ken Raley had become quiet in my hold.

"If I let you go, will you settle down?" I asked him, loosening my hold a bit.

"Yes," he said, coughing a little.

I moved Raley to the side for a moment and had someone set a straight chair in the corner, facing the room. I eased Raley down into the chair, then stepped back, standing guard in front of him. Raley wasn't going to be jumping anyone from that sitting position, and if he tried to get up, I'd have leverage to stop him. But it looked as if the fight had gone out of Raley. He had a hand to his throat, and he looked pale. He was staring down at the floor.

"John, how are you?" I asked.

I took a quick glance back to the right. I could see Havens sitting on the couch, a hand to his head, Sylvia and Susan seated to either side of him.

"I'm okay," said Havens, his voice shaky. "Just banged up a little."

"Do you want me to call the police?"

"I'll leave it up to Karen what she wants to do."

Karen appeared at my side. "I just want to take him home," she said.

"Are you sure?" I asked. "A police report would help if you decide you want Ken held for psychiatric evaluation."

"I don't want the police," said Karen. "Anyway, I have plenty of witnesses here, don't I, if I ever need to bring this up?"

"I suppose so. Do you want me to help you get Ken home?"

"No, I'll be okay," she said. "But I'd appreciate it if you could help me get him to the car."

"Sure."

Raley was still staring at the floor. I moved closer to him.

"Ken," I said, keeping my voice soft.

Raley lifted his head and looked at me.

"Did you send those threats to John?" I asked.

I waited. Raley just stared at me.

"Did you call the police with that accusation?"

Raley wasn't going to answer. His face tightened, and his eyes turned hard. It might have been my imagination, but I thought I saw a small smile cross his lips.

IT WAS FOUR in the morning, and I was feeling groggy and sick: I hadn't gotten any sleep, and my cold or whatever it was had gotten worse. I'd spent the early hours of the morning collecting and going through the Raleys' garbage; I'd found nothing of interest. Now I'd pick up Ruth Havens's garbage and, results or no results, would finally get some sleep.

I cruised by Ruth Havens's place, seeing no lights or hints of activity in her house or the other houses nearby. I U-turned, made a last visual check for any approaching cars, then pulled up to the curb. A single garbage can was there by the street, plastic, with a bungee cord snapped from handle to handle over the top to keep the garbage safe from prowling dogs. I flicked the trunk lid of the rental Ford and jumped out. Going to the garbage can, I snapped back the bungee cord and flipped the top onto the grassy strip between the sidewalk and road. I picked up the garbage can with one hand, moved to the car, and lifted the sprung trunk lid. I dumped the contents of the can onto the heavy tarp with which I'd covered the interior of the trunk. I pushed the can back up on the curb, shut the trunk, got in the car, and drove off.

I took the back road home, winding through heavy strands of trees, slowing once for another stop sign marking some collapsed piece of roadway, but otherwise making good time on the dark, empty road. Bouffi started barking as I opened the gate, setting up a sympathetic cacophony from other dogs in the neighborhood. As usual, no one seemed to pay any attention.

The sensor light over the carport came on as I got to the top of the drive. I gave Bouffer a pat, then shooed him away as I pulled an empty garbage can out of a carport cupboard. I opened the trunk of my car, folded the tarp around the garbage, and lifted it out. I put the tarp on the ground and unfolded it, displaying the garbage, which was mostly in paper grocery bags. I got a flashlight out of the car to supplement the garage light and sat down next to the tarp.

The first bag seemed to be mostly fish parts and mail. The mail took some time because even though it was all black and white and could have nothing to do with the cut-out letters of the notes, I wanted to make sure I didn't miss any notes or correspondence that might have some bearing on the case. As I finished with the pieces, I threw them into my own empty can.

Out of the second bag came bits of celery and banana peel, a crushed milk carton and cereal box, a crumpled piece of foil, and then . . . some cut scraps of paper, a scissored magazine, then another.

I looked up from the magazine and smiled.

"Gotcha," I said, aloud.

I SHIFTED UNCOMFORTABLY in the phone booth, trying to squeeze myself into the thin strip of shade that slanted across one corner of the booth. The temperature of the day had climbed above ninety, my own temperature, above a hundred: In the eighteen or so hours since the confrontation with Raley, I'd developed a real fever along with a worsening of yesterday's symptoms. The heat of my body and the heat of the day were working together in a miserable synergy.

Witmer's voice came on the line. "Strickland, is that you?"

"Yes."

"They've nailed down Ritchie for the fourth murder," she said excitedly. "They've got just one piece of evidence so far—I'm sure they'll get more—but even if they don't, we're okay now. It was definitely him."

"What evidence?"

"You know the strip of tape Ritchie put across the victim's mouth? They've matched one end of it with one of the strips of tape on those boxes in Ritchie's car. Thank God some sharp lab technician thought of checking that."

"But the boxes must have been sealed a week or two before . . ." I stopped and laughed, realizing what must have happened.

The criminal takes his tape (or rope or whatever) and uses it to bind his victim. Being wise to forensics, he knows that the end of the roll of tape in his possession can be matched microscopically to one end of the last strip of tape he used in the crime. So he carefully disposes of the roll of tape. There's just one problem: He's forgotten that the

203

last piece of tape he used before committing the crime—perhaps several weeks earlier—is sitting at home on a pipe or a box, and it also can be matched up.

Had Ritchie been trying to dispose of the boxes because he'd known that the matching piece of tape was on them somewhere? I doubted it. If he had known, he'd have disposed of the boxes earlier—and then only the boxes, not the things inside. If he'd been decoying me that night, as he claimed, why use real evidence when I wouldn't have known the difference? He'd probably had no idea he was carrying around something so incriminating.

"The chief came by a little while ago," Witmer was saying. "He was in a really good mood. The people on the task force may be pissed, but I think for the chief, the fact that someone on his staff cracked the case is going to outweigh any . . . irregularities."

"I'm happy for you."

"Oh, I almost forgot. One of the dicks on the task force cracked the number code for the fourth victim."

"What was it?"

"Nothing too complicated. The numbers were three hundred twenty three thousand two hundred nineteen. The first three give the date he was married—March twenty-third—and the last three the day his child was born—February nineteenth. That's a pretty clear message of revenge, isn't it?"

"Yeah—for the fourth one. What about the other three?"

"They're going to check the numbers found near the other bodies against whatever other numbers they can find in Ritchie's life."

"What about Ritchie's alibis?"

"They've got people working hard on those. Ed Vogel—he's one of the guys on the task force—says that the singer has been going on about how Ritchie told him the cops were trying to frame him for the killings because of his record. Ed thinks the singer may be about to come clean and is trying to lay down a rationale for having lied. Ed's going to keep at him. We've got people going back over every detail of the first three cases. If there's a connection there, I think we'll find it this time."

"I hope you do. It would make life a lot simpler if he did all four."

"Strickland . . ."

"Yeah?"

"Thanks for your help."

"Thanks for yours."

"I think I might just let you call me JoAnn now," she said, a teasing tone in her voice.

"Terrific," I said with the expected sarcasm. "That makes it all worthwhile."

Witmer laughed. It was good to know she was going to be okay.

After I'd hung up, I moved out of the airless booth into a day that didn't feel as if it had much air in it either. For a moment I felt a little dizzy, but the dizziness quickly passed. It was a miserable day to be sick. I wanted so badly to be home in bed, but I was close to the end of what I'd been paid to do, and I wanted it done.

I left the store parking lot where the phone box was located and walked up the street to Ruth Havens's house. She was in her garden, as she had been before, wearing, if not the same clothes, another old set just like them. She was still trimming the hedge, but she'd worked her way around it so that she was almost to the gate. The stepladder she was standing on boosted her head above the top of the hedge. I watched her watch me as I approached.

"Hello, Mr. Strickland," she said as I stopped just outside the gate.

"I need to talk to you," I said.

"Go ahead."

"I think ground level would be better. This is something serious."

She looked more closely at my face and at the manila folder in my hand. "All right," she said.

She stepped down off the ladder, and I walked through the gate.

"You don't look so good," she said as we faced each other on the front path.

"I'm coming down with something. You probably shouldn't get too close."

"Let's get you a seat in the shade."

I followed her up the front steps onto the small porch. On one end of the porch was a white metal table covered with a flowered tablecloth; on the cloth sat a bowl of flowers. There were three metal chairs with green seat cushions around the table. Mrs. Havens seated me in one of the chairs.

"How about some iced tea?" she asked.

"No, thanks."

"It's all made. I'm going to have some, and I'll bring enough for both of us. You need liquids."

"Okay, thanks," I said.

I felt as if some momentum were shifting away from me, and for a moment regretted that I hadn't delayed this meeting until I was feeling better. But then I reminded myself that no psychological shifts would undo what I had in the envelope.

I looked out toward the street. From where I sat, I could see the whole gorgeous garden set against a background of the ratty yard next door, the gray street, and the pleasant but plain condominiums across the way. The garden was like a rich fantasy life built against a very bare reality.

"Here we are," said Mrs. Havens as she emerged from the house. She put a tray with two glasses and a pitcher down on the table, and poured us both tea. Then she sat down and sipped from her glass. "I don't have people here very often," she said.

"I wish this were a social visit," I said, wanting to tone this down before we ended up having a real tea party.

She ignored me. "When I was a young lady, and during the first few years of my first marriage, I had people around me all the time. I loved parties, I loved to visit. I never would have thought I could end up like this—all alone."

"You could change that," I said. Immediately I regretted the remark. It was not the tone I wanted to set today. Beyond that, I'd found over the years that suggesting life changes to people is almost always a fruitless exercise. Anyway, I knew from my own experience how difficult changing could be. I could feel my own residual bitterness that I hadn't been able, or willing, to give up, could feel its striations like veins of coal in my heart.

"It's too late," she said.

We lapsed into silence. I took a sip of my tea, then held the glass against my cheek, letting its coolness sink into my skin. Finally, I put the glass down and said, "I know you're sending those threats to your ex-husband."

"That's nothing new," she said. "You claimed to know that before."

That ironic, game-playing look of the other day was back on her face.

"I wondered," I said. "But I didn't know."

"And now you do?"

"Yes."

"Let's suppose you're right, and I did send those notes. What good does it do you, this supposed knowing, without any proof?"

"That's the thing," I said. "Now I have proof."

Her thin smile wavered for a moment, then held. "I hope you're not going to try to tell me that my fingerprints were on the notes," she said. "I know better than that."

"No," I said. "It's something a little different."

I lifted the manila folder off the chair and put it on the table. Ruth Havens's expression stayed fixed, but I saw her eyes narrow.

"What's that?" she asked. "Or am I supposed to guess?"

I opened the envelope and tilted it down, letting some of the contents slip out. There were partial sheets and scraps of magazine, all cut up, like the mess left by a child making paper dolls.

"These are the sheets from which the threatening letters were made," I said. "I matched these to the letters on the most recent note, using magazines I found in the library to confirm what the original pages looked like. Once I turn these over to the police, they'll confirm the match scientifically."

Mrs. Havens gestured toward the heap of paper. "What makes you think that stuff's mine?"

"Because it came out of your garbage can last night. Early this morning, to be exact."

"I hope you had a warrant, or whatever you need."

"I didn't need a warrant. Once you put your garbage out on the street, I can do whatever I want with it—including using it as evidence in court."

Mrs. Havens wasn't smiling anymore. "You're going to turn that over to the police?" she asked.

I didn't answer. I began pushing the scraps of paper back in the envelope. When I was done, I said, "This game of yours is going to cost you a year in jail."

She laughed derisively. "That's ridiculous," she said. "I haven't done anything. People get mad at people all the time and yell and maybe write letters."

"Yeah, but not a consistent pattern of anonymous death threats. That's what the law's about. Think about a year in jail. No flowers, just a lot of iron and cement. A cellmate you'll probably hate. A schedule you'll have to keep. I don't know about you, but when I felt really depressed after my wife's death, all I wanted was to be left alone. I can't imagine what it would have been like then, always being at the mercy of someone else, always with other people, always in the most depressing setting imaginable. It would have been horrible."

I was sketching an improbable scenario. It was unlikely she'd get prosecuted, let alone convicted. If convicted, the probable result would be mandatory counseling. But I wasn't trying for truth here, I was trying to scare her.

"They wouldn't send me to jail for a year," she said, though her voice sounded plaintive now—hoping, not knowing. "I've never been in trouble. I have reason to be angry. They'd take that into account."

"Let's say you're right about that. There'd still be the trial. You'd have to sit in that courtroom for days under the eyes of the jury. There'd be publicity, news people prying into your life. Do you really want that?"

"It would be a chance to tell my side of the story," she said. "Maybe people would finally understand what John really is."

Her face took on a tentative look, as if she were testing out the idea in her head. After a moment she smiled—a real smile, this time. It was easy enough to guess her daydream: a courtroom drama in which her husband would be exposed as the bad guy, while she, the martyr, finally got the acclaim she deserved. I'd been anticipating this point in our discussion. I knew I'd have to squelch this fantasy or I'd have failed in everything I was trying to accomplish here.

"Don't kid yourself," I said. "Your husband's a hero to a lot of people. He's already confessed to whatever crimes you'd accuse him of. He's raked himself over the coals more than most people would think he should have. He's worked his way through that to an outlook that most people want to agree with. They like to think positively, they like happy endings. If you try to make an issue of your bitterness, they're not going to feel sorry for you—not for more than a few minutes, anyway. You're going to be seen as someone negative, someone who's unwilling to grow, someone who wants to be bitter. And think about the charge: cutting out letters from magazines to form messages, like some kid playing spy games—sending anonymous threats, instead of standing up on your own. Do you think that's going to look like heroism compared to your husband's book? You'll just look like a crank and a fool. Maybe you can bring your husband down a notch, but that will be nothing compared to what you'll do to yourself. The whole thing will turn into a circus, and you'll be playing the clown. It will be humiliating."

I felt cruel, speaking to her like this, but I had to make an impact on her. I could see the remnants of her once-cool assurance deserting her. She seemed to shrink, as if lessened by the loss of her vindication. I was trying to help her ex-husband, but I hoped I might be helping her as well, by keeping her from making her life even worse than it was.

"What do you want from me?" she asked in a low, hoarse voice. "You must want something or you wouldn't be here."

"Were you planning to kill him?" I asked.

She gave a disconsolate laugh. "Me? How would I do that? A bomb? A gun? I don't know anything about such things. Rush at him with my garden shears while he's giving one of his speeches? I'm too clumsy. And too afraid. I'd just end up looking like a fool."

I watched her face, evaluating her, as I waited for her to say more.

"I think about how it would be to hurt him," she said. "I think about it all the time. I wish something awful would happen to him. Do you know what it's like, sitting here day after day with my pain, while that man, who let our son die, is getting all the sympathy—making himself out to be a hero. It feels like a knife in my stomach. A month or so ago I saw him on television, and I got so sick I had to vomit. I know I'm not capable of hurting him physically. But with the threats and the accusation, at least I could cause him some mental pain. I hope I have."

It almost went by me, this inadvertent gift she had just given me, the admission of having made the accusation. Yet the accusation had been made in a man's voice. I decided not to jump on the point. She might just back off. I'd work my way around to it gradually.

209

"How long were you going to keep up the threats?"

"I don't know," she said. "I didn't plan to send as many letters as I did. Once I started, I didn't want to stop."

"What were you going to follow up the letters with?"

"I don't know that either," she said. "I hadn't thought that far ahead."

"Tell me about the threats," I said. "You cut out the letters from those magazines. . . ."

"Yes. It felt pretty silly, but I couldn't think of any other way that would be safe. I used gloves."

"Where'd you mail them from?"

"Different towns."

"How did you address them?"

"I'd never thought about how you'd do that before," she said. "You can hardly put big cutout letters on the envelope. They wouldn't fit anyway. I thought of writing the address with my left hand or using some computer, but that would have taken away the whole point of using cutout letters in the first place. For the envelope, I used small letters and numbers of the same size, so they wouldn't look so odd. I made up the address, made photocopies, and then cut-and-pasted them onto the envelopes."

"How did you handle the accusation?"

"I called the paper, of course, and they wrote that article."

"What about the police?"

"What do you mean?"

"I mean, how did the police get involved?"

"Obviously the paper told them."

"The police said they got an anonymous call."

"I forgot about that," she said. "In fact, I never really thought about it. Like I said, I just thought the paper called them."

"Anonymously?"

Mrs. Havens just shrugged.

"Who did you talk to when you called the paper?" I asked.

"The man who's been writing the articles. Garza."

"Did you identify yourself?"

"No. And I called from a pay phone."

"What did you say?"

"Just what was in the article. I was nervous. I hung up as soon as I said those things. Does it make any sense that Garza might have called the police and not told them who he was? Maybe he was afraid that John would sue him if he started the story himself."

Garza wouldn't have worried about libel: Newspapers can report tips and rumors. But there might have been a different sort of advantage to the anonymous call. Given the known animosities between Garza, Mrs. Bennett, and Havens, Garza's reporting a tip might have raised some questions about his honesty or objectivity. But if the tip went to the police and the police investigated, then that would make Garza's role seem detached and professional.

Memories of my conversation with Garza gave the hypothesis further support. He'd seemed startled when I'd suggested the person who'd made the call and the person sending the threats might be one and the same. He'd made a point of arguing that they were probably not the same. His arguing that point made perfect sense under the assumption that he'd been the caller. He wouldn't want too much emphasis put on who the caller was. And maybe, realizing he was screwing up an investigation, he was trying to minimize the damage.

Also Garza had been totally uninterested when I'd suggested he follow up on who might have made the call. Such a follow-up should have been his basic journalistic instinct, whatever his animosities toward Havens and Mrs. Bennett. But the lack of interest would make sense if he had made the call himself.

I came out of my speculative haze to see Ruth Havens staring at me.

"What are you going to do?" she asked.

"I don't know," I said. "Are you going to stop these attacks on John?"

"What good would they do now that you know it's me? And how could I dare, given what you have there?"

She nodded toward the manila envelope.

"How do I know you won't try to hurt him physically now?" I asked.

"I told you," she said. "I wouldn't know what to do, even if I wanted to."

"But you said you keep thinking about wanting to hurt your husband. How do I know—how do you know, for that matter—that the desire won't get the better of you?"

"Because I don't want to hurt myself," she said.

I found myself inclined to believe her, but I didn't know if I should trust that inclination. During our first meeting, Mrs. Havens had talked admiringly of suicide. How much value, then, could I place on the sense of self-preservation she was now trying to give me as collateral? I remembered Karen Raley's firm belief that her husband wouldn't have the energy for a violent act—this, just before he jumped Havens.

"I'll have to think about it before I decide what to do," I said.

It would be up to Havens to make the decision, but I didn't want to bring up his name in case it should reinspire her rebellion. Knowing Havens, I assumed he would want to let the matter drop. In fact, the other options weren't all that terrific. Even if, against all odds, the woman could be convicted and sent to jail, that would only protect Havens for those few months she'd be in, and she might be madder than hell when she got out. Some pressure by the police, a restraining order, maybe some mandatory counseling—that might help or hurt. It all depended on Ruth Havens. If she decided to kill her husband, only luck or her own ineptness could stop her.

Would she try something? It was Havens's life and he'd have to decide. For myself, I didn't know.

23

IT WAS LATE AFTERNOON, and I was at a pay phone inside an air-conditioned coffee shop. But the way my body felt, I might as well have been standing out in the midday heat. I had just called John to tell him I'd be coming over. Now I had Karen Raley on the line and was asking her how Ken was.

"Not good," she said in a harried voice.

"Any more violence?"

"No, but he seems so keyed up. He's coming and going all the time, as if he's so restless he can't sit still. When he's home, he won't talk. He sits in his study, scribbling meaningless designs on paper. If I try to get near him, he yells at me to go away."

"What are you going to do?"

"I talked to a psychiatrist friend at work, and he's coming over this evening to take a look at Ken. I just hope Ken is home by then."

"He's not there now?"

"No. I'm hoping this friend can help me get Ken committed. I'm sorry I didn't take your advice about calling the police last night. Will you help me by testifying to what happened?"

"Of course. I'm sure you've already thought of this, but if you can get your hands on any of those designs, your psychiatrist friend might like to see them."

"I've saved a few. But I'm not sure they're going to tell him much. There're just numbers."

"He sits there and writes down numbers?"

"Well, he's not just writing them down. He makes them elaborate, as if he were doing . . . what do you call it when people take those special pens and? . . ."

"Calligraphy."

"That's it. Except it's not like he's trying to do careful work design. He writes in a fast, angry way, ripping off pages, then starting again. It's really obsessive."

"Series of numbers?"

"Sometimes."

I remember something Karen had mentioned the first time we talked.

"Karen, didn't you say something about Ken and your daughter writing secret messages to each other?"

"Yes."

"What kind of secret messages?"

"Number codes."

"How did they work?"

"Are you thinking that he's writing out some kind of messages on those pads?"

"It's possible isn't it, given his obsession with your daughter's death, that he might be writing out messages to your daughter—or just messages in the kind of code they used?"

"I never thought of that. I suppose it's possible."

"How did the code work?"

"There were a couple of them. You have to remember that Terri was only six so they had to be really simple. Sometimes the number would mean what number the letter was in the alphabet: one for A, two for B, like that. Ken would make a chart for Terri so she could just look instead of counting. Sometimes they'd change the numbers so one would be B, two would be C, and so forth. Just before Terri died, they tried using a book and having the numbers indicate the page, line, and what number the word was in that line."

"What book?"

"I don't remember. Whatever book Terri was reading."

"While Ken's out, will you please look around his work area and see if you can find anything Ken might be using as a code—a table of numbers or one of Terri's old books."

"Yes, of course."

"Please call me if you find anything. I'll be at John's house for an hour, and then I'll be going home. I'll give you my home phone. I'm not feeling that great, so I may fall asleep early, but leave a message on my machine and I'll get back to you as soon as I can."

"Why are you so interested in what Ken might be writing?"

"Because it might hold some clue to whether he's planning to do something to John."

"Of course—how stupid of me. I'll look around right now and call you."

I gave her my home phone number and hung up, excited by the information about Raley and those numbers. Ritchie might be guilty of all four killings, but it looked to me as if he was far from a sure thing: There was still the matter of having to discount his alibis and account for his motives. I wasn't too comfortable with the idea of Raley as the murderer, but certain things made him a real possibility: his anger toward Havens, his familiarity with Havens's past and book, his bitterness over his own child's death, and his psychological problems. And now there were the numbers.

I sat down on a small padded bench in the alcove where the pay phone was and pulled out a pad and pen. I wrote down the alphabet, then numbered the letters, putting 1 for A and going in sequence. I didn't have the number sequences Raley was writing now, but during the phone call, my mind had drifted to other sets of numbers— the ones placed next to the bodies of the murdered children.

When you thought of it, Raley was an intriguing suspect for the murders. He was mentally disturbed as a result of the death of his daughter; he hated Havens, whose son had died by fire; he hated Havens's philosophy and had said that he wished Havens could have more suffering; and he was an accountant, whose life was numbers and who had once written secret number-code messages to his daughter. I guess I hadn't thought of Raley before because I was focused on Havens's problems, not the murders, and because the initial descriptions of Raley had given me the impression that he was immobilized by depression.

I wrote down the number series that had been placed next to the body of the Malander boy: 22122. If the numbers were taken individually, the letters would be BBABB. But, of course, they didn't have to be taken that way. For instance, 2-21-2-2 would be BUBB, 2-21-22 would be BUV, and 22-1-22 would be VAV. Nothing promising there.

It was obvious that not knowing how the numbers were to be divided created a big complication. I got up and phoned Witmer at the hospital. Her voice was sleepy, she'd been just about to take a nap. I asked her if there'd been anything to indicate subgroups among the numbers next to the bodies. She said that question had come up before, and no, there'd been nothing like that. The five or six numbers had been set out evenly, with nothing marking divisions. She started to ask me more, but I told her to get her sleep and I'd talk to her later.

I went outside, getting a blast of heat as I opened the door. I had settled into slow-moving misery, but the sudden increase in temperature threw off my tentative equilibrium. I felt weaker and faintly nauseous. I got in my car, started it, and turned on the air-conditioning. I sat in the parked car until eventually the cool air revived me. Then I drove to Havens's house.

Sylvia was just getting out of her car when I pulled into Havens's drive. John had told me he'd call her. I said hello to her, then to Havens, who came out to meet us. The three of us went inside and into the living room, where I took a seat on the far end of the couch, near the bookcases. John sat in the easy chair, and Sylvia, heeding my advice not to get too close, sat across the coffee table from me in an easy chair.

I went over the latest developments regarding Earl Ritchie, then brought up the subject of Ken Raley.

"I don't want to alarm you," I said, "but if I were you, and I saw Ken Raley anywhere near this house again, I'd call the police right away."

"Do you really think he's dangerous?" asked Havens.

"I think it's possible. Karen has finally come around to the view that she's got to force Ken to get help. She'll probably tell the police about last night and ask us to verify it. In any case, if you see him somewhere else, stay away from him. If he comes here, lock the doors and call the police."

"You're really scaring me," said Sylvia.

"I'm sorry," I said. "There's probably nothing to worry about. I just want John to be on guard."

"So you think Ken Raley's the one sending the threatening letters?" asked Sylvia.

"No," I said. "The notes were sent by Ruth Havens."

The abrupt shift in names took a moment to sink in. Sylvia was the first one to speak.

"I knew it—I just knew it!"

"You're sure?" asked Havens, ignoring Sylvia's exclamation.

"Yes," I said.

I explained about my garbage hunt, and what I'd found in his ex-wife's garbage, and how my conversation with her had gone.

"I still can't believe it," said Havens. "I mean, why now?"

"Your book. She didn't say that right out, but it was obvious from what she did say. She hates you being made a hero. She hates the thought of you getting the credit for suffering when she thinks she's the one who's suffered the most."

"Poor Ruth."

" 'Poor Ruth,' nothing," said Sylvia. "Normal people don't send notes threatening your life. No matter how angry they are. And being that angry after all this time isn't normal either."

"Do you think Ruth will stop all this business now if we just let it drop?" Havens asked me.

"I'm inclined to say yes, but I don't really know," I said. "As for trying to prosecute her, that might add to the scare, but it could also energize her and make her more dangerous."

"Call the police, John," said Sylvia. "Ruth deserves it after what she's done."

"Do you have any idea who accused me to the police?" asked Havens.

"She was behind that, too."

"Does she really think I killed those children?"

"No. The letters and the call were just a way to cause you pain."

"John, you can't let her get away with this," said Sylvia. "It wasn't just you she was hurting—it was the rest of us, too. We should have some say in this. We have to make sure that woman doesn't do this again."

"Sylvia," said Havens firmly, turning toward her. "Ruth is a woman who's miserably unhappy. Whatever pain she's caused us, she's already paid for it many times over. I agree we want to try to see that she won't do it again, but you heard Dave—there's no guarantee that calling the police will accomplish that."

"But there's no guarantee that it won't."

It sounded like a discussion that was going to go on for a while. I tuned them out and leaned back on the couch, resting, letting my mind wander. John's and Sylvia's voices became blurred; in the background there were some distant traffic noises and occasionally the sound of a car pulling into the private road outside. I would leave in a few minutes, go home, get into bed, and sleep. Tomorrow or the next day, whenever I felt up to it, I'd call Witmer to check on how the police investigation was proceeding and call Karen Raley to find out if she'd found anything that might serve as a code for her husband's scribbles. The work I was paid to do was done, but I'd gotten involved in the larger case, and I didn't want to let go. Obviously the police wouldn't be inviting me to do any more, but while they were checking out Ritchie, I could be checking out Raley.

My gaze had been drifting lazily around the room and had come to rest on the bookshelves. The red-orange of Havens's book cover caught my eye. There were several of his books stacked on the edge of a middle shelf—maybe copies for giving away. An idea occurred to me. I got up and, as John and Sylvia continued their heated discussion, I walked over to the bookshelf. In order to reach Havens's book, I had to lean between the Bible and dictionary sitting on their separate stands in front of the bookshelves. I got my right hand on the book, but maybe because of my fever, certainly because I tilted the wrong way on my bad foot, I lost my balance for a moment and without thinking, thrust out my left hand to catch myself. To my chagrin, I felt a page of one of the open books rumple and tear under my hand. It was, I noticed, as I righted myself, a page of that beautiful Bible the Sullivans had bought Havens.

The noise I'd made brought Havens and Sylvia out of their chairs. I was clumsily trying to flatten out the rumpled page and put together the two edges of the torn word, "suffering," when Havens got to me and told me not to bother. I kept trying to apologize as Havens kept telling me that the book was not expensive and not to worry and that I didn't look well and I'd be better off sitting down. I gave in and let him lead me back to the couch.

"You look like you're burning up," he said. "How about if I get you some aspirin and a glass of water?"

I accepted. I was feeling worse, though I knew some of that was chagrin.

Havens gave a sudden laugh, and I followed his gaze down to the copy of his book that was still held in my right hand.

"Sorry," he said, "but it just occurred to me that I've been given the ultimate compliment. A guy has a headache, and the first thing he reaches for is my book on suffering."

I laughed, then winced at the pain in my head. Sylvia and Havens left the room, and, after a moment, when my head felt a little better, I opened Havens's book. An idea occurred to me. I'd wondered what code Raley might be using if he were the killer. What if he'd been using a book code referring to the book written by the man he hated? The irony was too good to resist.

I took out my notebook, blinking at it through watery eyes. I flipped to a page containing the numbers for the first three murder victims: 22122 for Jimmy Malander, 212910 for Corinne Caldwell, and 141213 for Peter Kiedrich. If I were going for page, line, word, without knowing how to divide the numbers, there would be alternate possibilities. But there would be certain limits—no page over 404, no line over 40, and no word number over about 15.

I looked at the first number, 22122. Page 2 couldn't work, because there couldn't be a word 22 to go with line 21. For page 22, line 122 couldn't work, so it had to be page 22, line 12, word 2. The word was "broken," from the phrase "broken man." Excited, I pushed ahead. The next number was 21718. Since the last two digits were too high to be the number of a word in a line, and 71 too high to indicate a line, it had to be page 217, line 1, word 8. The word was "then."

I heard the phone ring and Havens say hello. I glanced at the third number, which was 141213. Page 1 wouldn't work. But there were several possibilities. Page 14, line 12, word 13 was "here." Page 141, line 2, word 13 was "I." Page 141, line 21, word 3 was "always."

Broken then here? Broken then I? Broken then always?

219

"Here you go."

I looked up. Sylvia handed me two aspirins with one hand and a glass of liquid.

"I made you some lemonade," she said. "I thought it might be more refreshing."

"Thanks," I said. I swallowed the aspirins with a sip of the drink.

"We just got a call from an old friend," she said. "We'll just be a few minutes. Will you be all right?"

"Sure. No problem."

As she walked back to the kitchen I looked down at my pad. None of those three word combinations made much sense as a message. What had I expected to be in the message anyway? I supposed words like "anger" or "revenge" or "judgment" or "children" or "suffering" or . . .

I glanced over at the Bible, remembering the word I had torn. I got up and walked over to the stand. What I had torn was a subject heading at the top of the page that said "Share Christ's sufferings." Next to it was another heading that indexed the first verse on the page, "I Peter 4:12." I glanced down at my notebook: Peter Kiedrich, 141213. Could Raley have been using some kind of Bible code? One that worked off the first names of the victims? I knew there was no Book of Peter per se, just First Peter and Second Peter. The First Book of Peter had only five chapters. I Peter, Chapter 4, verses 12 and 13? I looked down at the verses.

12. Beloved, think it not strange concerning the fiery trial which is to try you, as though some strange thing had happened to you:

13. But rejoice, inasmuch as ye are partakers of Christ's sufferings; that, when his glory shall be revealed, ye may be glad also with exceeding joy.

I felt a sudden rush of adrenaline. What was this, Raley throwing Havens's philosophy back in his face as he mocked and mimicked the death of Havens's son?

I was getting too far ahead of myself—I didn't even know if this would work out as a code. The first names of the four murdered children were James, Corinne, Peter, and Tony. Tony and Corinne weren't the names of Bible books. But wait—I wasn't thinking straight. Tony had been killed by Ritchie and the numbers next to his body had already been interpreted in terms of dates in Ritchie's life.

What about Corinne? I glanced at the table of contents: Chronicles . . . no . . . of course, Corinthians. There were two Books of Corinthians, and so the first number in 2121314 must refer to the second book. I flipped to II Corinthians, Chapter 12, wondering about Raley's motives, when another thought occurred to me. If Raley was doing the murders, why was Havens's Bible open to the First Book of Peter?

"I'm sorry we're taking so long," I heard Havens say behind me. "We'll just be a few more minutes."

Havens? I thought. No, it couldn't be.

Nonetheless, as I turned and faced him, I got a sudden surge of anxiety, so that his simple physical presence felt like a physical assault. My aching head was full of conflicting thoughts, and I felt too weak to deal with them. I needed to get away from there and be alone.

"It's all right," I said, "but I really should get going."

"Can't you stay a little longer?" asked Havens. "I'd like to talk more about Ruth."

"Sorry—I'm feeling lousy. Tomorrow or the next day we can talk all you want."

"All right. If you're really feeling that bad."

I moved awkwardly around Havens, waved good-bye to Sylvia who was still on the phone, and went outside. Havens followed.

"You sure you feel all right to drive?" asked Havens, studying my face. "You don't look too good."

"I'll be okay. Really."

I got in my second rental car and backed up on the gravel drive, returning Havens's wave. I drove back toward the highway and then toward home, thinking over this new development. I still wasn't sure the Bible-verse code would work for the other numbers, but I had at least one Bible at home leftover from my religious days. In a few more minutes I'd be able to check. Suppose the numbers did refer to Bible verses? Who did this point to as the killer? I had thought the fact of the verses pointed to Raley—an emotionally disturbed man who had lost his child and who hated a man who tried to justify suffering. But if it was Raley, how did the Bible at Havens's house come to be open at that particular place? Could Raley have opened it? It was possible he could have snuck into the house. But what would have been the point? If he'd been trying to frame Havens, wouldn't he have been the one to call the police? Unless Ruth Havens beat him to it. Or unless he was working on a frame that hadn't yet been completed.

There was a loud honking, and I realized, suddenly, that I had drifted a few feet across the center divider. I jerked the car back into the slow lane, and the other car went by, the driver making some angry gesture. The incident shook me up, making me realize Havens had probably been right about my seeming too sick to drive. The rest of the way home, I drove slowly, keeping my mind and eyes on the road. When I reached the house, I felt exhausted with the effort—or maybe my day and my fever had finally done me in. I began shedding clothes the minute I hit the bedroom door, but my curiosity retained enough force to make me grab a Bible off a shelf of books before I climbed into bed. I turned to II Corinthians 12:9 and 10.

> 9. And he said unto me, My grace is sufficient for thee: for my strength is made perfect in weakness. Most gladly therefore will I glory in my infirmities, that the power of Christ may rest upon me.
> 10. Therefore I take pleasure in infirmities, in reproaches, in necessities, in persecutions, in distresses for Christ's sake; for when I am weak, then am I strong.

More approval of suffering.

The number for Jimmy Malander was 22122. Jimmy would be the Book of James, which, I noticed when I turned to it, had only five chapters. The reference, then, would have to be James 2:21 and 22.

> 21. Was not Abraham our father justified by works, when he had offered Isaac his son upon the altar?
> 22. Seest thou how faith wrought with his works, and by works was faith made perfect?

What did that mean? That Raley or Havens had killed his own child? But that was impossible. The Raleys had been away—and their daughter with a baby-sitter—when the girl had drowned. Havens's son had died in a general apartment fire caused by faulty wiring. In addition to that, Havens's whole history after Ricky's death, especially his book, would have made no sense if Havens had killed his son.

Did the verse mean, instead, that in some sense the murdered children were being offered up to something?

I picked up the phone by my bed and called the hospital, wanting to talk to Witmer; she was asleep and the nurse was adamant that she needed her rest. I thought of calling someone at GVPD, but Witmer and I had tried hard to make this case ours, and I didn't want to be handing it away. Anyway, this thing with the Bible verses was ambiguous and was going to take some thinking through. Tomorrow would be soon enough.

A pain shot through my skull and seemed to spread weakness through my entire body. I was in no position to think all this through tonight. Tomorrow—after I'd gotten some sleep.

24

My dreams and half-asleep images are feverish and unpleasant, but I'm so tired, I can't imagine making the effort to wake; anyway, with waking would come more physical pain.

I hear Bouffi barking, then other dogs farther away, their nightly ritual, especially in warm weather—some dog going by on the road, someone driving home late, or simply a mood—it doesn't take much to set them off. *I bark for unicorns,* I think, parodying the bumper sticker, and laugh—that would be perfect for the Bouffer. But the laugh hurts my head, so I stop and press my eyelids closed. *Shut up, Bouffer,* I think. *Shut up and let me sleep.*

It's so hot. In the dream I see flames, and children burning, and that face above me in the darkness. I cry out for help, and a voice says, *Don't be afraid,* and the face comes closer, but suddenly there's a huge weight on my chest, and I can't breathe, and when I try to breathe, there's a sickening smell. I'm afraid, and I try to fight, but I'm not strong enough.

Then . . . all at once . . . there's a feeling of peace. The fires are gone. And the heat. And the pain. And I'm drifting off—slowly, gently—into darkness.

David, I know you can't hear me, but I still want to tell you I'm sorry. When I saw you at the Bible and saw how you'd turned the page, I knew that you knew. So I have no choice. But I like you, and I wish it didn't have to be this way.

Words. They're there—I hear them—but they have no meaning for me. I float in darkness, and I am only that floating.

I WANT SO TO TELL someone the truth. But I can't—this is the closest I'll ever come to telling.

It's ironic that I feel so cut off from others when my book seems to put my self and my thoughts out there for everyone to see. It's not that the book isn't true; it's just not all of the truth.

I thought it was the truth. By the time the book came out, I thought I had found my peace—that I'd hit bottom and finally found a safe place to stand. But then the ground started crumbling, and all that awfulness started again.

The dreams of that hallway came back just when I thought I was done with them. I'd be crawling through the flames like before, unable to save Ricky, but in these new dreams I'd get just close enough to watch him burn. My son it was horrible. I'd wake up shaking and covered with sweat, and if I tried to sleep again, the dream would be there. The dreams went on every night, and I hardly slept, and without sleep, everything else started turning bad. I'd feel sick during the day. There'd be moments when I'd feel suddenly terrified. And even during the day, I'd get glimpses of flames in the back of my mind.

I didn't understand what was happening to me. I'd come through my troubles, I'd seen a therapist, I'd stopped drinking, I'd remade my life. I should have been okay, instead of being so confused and frightened. I thought, maybe I'd been through too much. Maybe all that alcohol had done some permanent damage to my brain. I didn't know. But I felt like I was going insane.

There's a lessening of darkness. I have a sense of lying down as if I am in my bed, and yet I feel vibrations, a jostling. I can see dark forms moving by as if at great speed, and beyond them tiny pinpricks of light. And there's that voice, so close. But none of it seems to connect, not the images, not the words.

I threw myself into my work, wanting to be that work and not the quivering thing inside me. I put up a front, not wanting anything I was feeling to show through. I was afraid that if people really saw what was going on inside me, they'd want to put me away somewhere. And I didn't want them to think my work was all a lie. It was so ironic that while I was falling apart, I was helping others become strong.

The Sullivans were nice people, but I could tell, when I started working with them, how limited and self-absorbed their lives had been before the death of their child. But through their suffering and our work together, they changed so much. They began to care, and to commit themselves to helping people in trouble. It was a beautiful thing to see. I guess Sylvia wasn't capable of anything so dramatic, but in many small ways, she's grown a lot. Karen was already a caring person, but she became more caring—and stronger—as she struggled with Ken's pain. As the weeks went by, when she spoke of her work, I could tell she was becoming a more patient and sensitive nurse. And the relationships all of them developed with each other in the group were so deep and good.

It hurt me when Ken fell away. I felt so bad for him. In my head I understood. In a world of suffering and death, it's inevitable that many people will be destroyed. But my heart wouldn't go along with my head. That day he screamed at me and blamed me for making light of the death of our children, some part of me agreed with everything he said. I knew that suffering was necessary—I really did believe it, I had to believe it—but something inside me seemed to have remained what it was before, wanting to curse the suffering and hate the world. I'd thought I was done with those feelings, but here they were again, back again, tearing me apart.

After that confrontation with Ken, everything got worse for me—the dreams, the panic, the flashbacks. My mind seemed to be breaking apart. I thought I was finally going crazy.

The voice goes on in my head as I lie back in semi–darkness, watching the dark forms speed by. I sense that somewhere not far from where I lie is a world of fever and pain, but I don't want to go there, I want to stay here where there is peace.

One day, in Chicago, I had to cancel a lecture at the last minute because I knew I couldn't handle it. I tried to escape from the noise and crowds and my own panic into a small, quiet museum. As I wandered through the museum, I came across a room full of medieval paintings portraying the suffering Christ. As I looked at the paintings, I thought about the story of a God who had given up His son to die, and I thought how much more that would cost—to sacrifice a child, rather than simply to mourn one. And I thought, if suffering is necessary to create good, then someone has to create that suffering. That would be the ultimate burden of God, not just to sacrifice His son, but to sacrifice half of humanity—a humanity he loves—on the altar of suffering. I thought, how it must hurt God to send His fire and His floods and His cancers to make the world a battleground where courage and loyalty and pity and so many good things can emerge. And I saw how the deepest love would not be the love that brought comfort and joy, but the love that brought suffering and death.

That night I had that dream of the hallway and of the fire and of Ricky for the last time. I was watching Ricky burn, and crying, and then suddenly the terror and the pain were gone, and I felt peaceful. In the dream I realized that God was there, at my side, and I told him that I'd try, somehow, to be as He was, to do His work.

You can see what is coming of it: Jack, moving from those inconsequential garden pieces to an art of depth and power; the Caldwells, moving away from their old, trivial lives—Craig toward the work of helping children to learn, Lisa to a religious searching. The Kiedriches will probably never ask to be in the group, and I'd have to turn them down if they did—having all the parents there would look suspicious. But I have been observing the Kiedriches from a distance, seeing how their bland faith is being tested, waiting to see what comes out of that fire.

I hurt, and I keep trying to cry out, and finally there's a sound like a small moan. There's a sudden change in the world, and a shaking, and I'm jerked forward, and then all motion stops. After a moment, I feel a weight pushing against me, and there is that sickening smell, but I don't fight it this time because I know in a moment it will bring an end to my pain. As I drift off into the darkness, the voice is saying, *I'm sorry, David, I truly am. But you, in your way, will be helping me continue the work.*

THE DARKNESS RECEDES. There's no motion now. Above me, there are dark, stationary forms and tiny spots of light. Then the pain comes, but it's confusing—it's as if the outside of me is wet and cold, and the inside is burning up. I try to burrow back into the blackness, but I can't find it anymore. I try to move, but it's hard because my hands and feet don't seem to work right. I lift my head, and I see, off in the distance, a light—not like those dots of light, they must have been stars—but flickering—a small fire. I stare at the fire, and then I see that it's moving toward me, and suddenly it doesn't seem so far away. I kick out with my feet—together, that's the only way they seem to work. I don't want this fire, I've had enough of fire, part of me is already burning

227

up. I kick all around it—it's hard to place it. Clouds of something begin to obscure the flame, and then I see with relief that the fire is gone.

I lie back, and as my arms fall toward my chest—together, they only seem to work together—there is a dull clanging sound as my elbow hits something hard. Then there is quiet, and I try to concentrate on what is happening—to pull my mind from sleep and figure out what's been happening to me—when suddenly fire comes at me through the air, a larger fire, and I sense something moving behind it, but all my focus is on that fire—I can't take any more fire. It's coming so fast, and I have to do something, and I try to roll away, but I hit that metal thing, and I grab it with both my hands, and turn, and hurl it toward the fire, and then I roll away—again and again—and suddenly there's an awful sound—a scream.

I look, and there's a face, and it's lit up by a fire that seems as bright as the sun. The face is all twisted up, as if in pain, but there's something else there, a look that seems almost triumphant. I see a flaming hand, and it seems to be gesturing to me, telling me to come, but I'm afraid, and I don't want to go, and so I struggle to get farther away, but then it gets hard to move, and I find myself falling down into darkness—blessed darkness.

25

I JERK UPRIGHT to a sitting position, panicked by images of fire and by the feeling that my hands won't move. Then, in the semi-darkness, I see the body on the ground and understand that the danger is over, even before I can remember exactly what the danger was. I feel suddenly nauseous—I turn on my side and vomit. When I am through, I feel better.

It's night, and I'm in the woods. Above me I see the forms of trees, and beyond them a night sky, a gray blackness with stars overhead and a full moon low down in the sky. I look down at my hands, and see that they're bound with rope. I work the rope off my hands, then untie my feet, which were also bound.

I try to stand, but the effort's so painful that I crawl instead, making my way over to the body. The body is on its back. The face is disfigured but I can see it is Havens's face.

I look around, trying to match what's here with my dreamy fragments of memory. Near Havens's body is a charred gas can and a stick that's draped with strips of charred cloth. Looking back at the spot where I was lying, I see a trail of ash connected to some unburned rope. The connecting point between the ash and unburned rope is covered with an uneven smattering of dirt.

Havens was about to do to me what he'd done to those children—that much is clear. He must have gotten into my house and taken me from my bed. That first remembered smell—different from the smell of fuel oil and charred flesh I'm getting now—must have been from the inhalant. He bound my hands and feet, drove me here, and laid me out on the ground, face up. He poured his combination of gas and fuel oil over my body—I can smell it now on my clothes—and lit his crude rope fuse. My kicking at it must have put out the fuse, that would account for the dirt over the rope. But what happened after that?

Witmer had indicated that the police knew the murderer hadn't left the murder scenes because, in at least one case, the rope fuse had gone out, and the killer had either relit the fuse or ignited the body by some other means. That's what must have happened here. The stick and strips of charred cloth must have been a torch—the torch I'd seen as the fire coming toward me through the air. The gasoline can, which normally lay by the victim and now lies by Havens's body, must have been the thing I rolled against, then threw.

I close my eyes and let Havens's words drift back to me, trying to understand. Havens worked his way through his suffering to a philosophy that helped others, but wouldn't quiet his recurring torments, whatever their source. His intellect was saying yes to suffering, while his deepest feelings were screaming no. He clung to the yes—to the acceptance of suffering—willing to go wherever it would take him. He followed it to some ultimate conclusion—or delusion—and it finally destroyed him.

I think about the numbers left next to the children's bodies, numbers that turned out to refer to Bible verses related to sacrifice and suffering. I still believe of them what I believed before—that they were a way of objectifying the fantasies in the killer's head without actually giving those fantasies away. Ritchie, who couldn't have known what the original numbers meant, but needed some numbers for his copycat killing, came up with his own one-time code that expressed his revenge. In Havens's case, the numbers expressed a cosmic system, making what he did meaningful in terms of that system.

Well, if he wanted to be part of that system, let him be—to the end. I think for a moment, then pick up a charred stick and scratch into the soil the numbers 1930. It's the verse that Havens mentioned in his book, from John 19:30, when the dying Jesus says, "It is finished."

I struggle to my feet and make it this time. I'm sick and sore and unsteady, but I think I can walk. Above me, the stars are spread across the sky like the embers of a great fire from long ago that is finally dying out. The embers don't give much light, but enough, I think, so I can make my way.

Acknowledgments

Thanks to the following people:

Joshua Bilmes of the Jabberwocky Agency and Keith Kahla of St. Martin's Press for their skillful help in bringing this novel to press.

John Murdoch and Barbara Yaley of Forensic Ink, Bill Mallett, Loren Reynolds, Jan Tepper, and Margo Trombetta for technical assistance.

Paul and Virginia for their great success with the Mitchell project. And hi to Liza.